Love Remains

Zrinka Jelic

F+W Media, Inc.

This edition published by
Crimson Romance
an imprint of F+W Media, Inc.
10151 Carver Road, Suite 200
Blue Ash, Ohio 45242
www.crimsonromance.com

ISBN 10: 1-4405-7046-9
ISBN 13: 978-1-4405-7046-9
eISBN 10: 1-4405-7047-7
eISBN 13: 978-1-4405-7047-6

"In *Love Remains*, Ms. Jelic has once again written a highly imaginative paranormal romance with believable characters that are both flawed and compassionate with a plot that will keep you guessing until the end."

Debbie Christiana, author of *Twin Flames and Solstice*.

"Zrinka Jelic has achieved a higher level of success with her time-travel story, *Love Remains*. Olivia had a difficult job, chopping employees' heads, and then to travel to another dimension where she had a husband and children was felling. However, as with any Jelic story, the romance is strong and I was happy to travel with Tom and Olivia. At the end of life isn't that what we seek—the warmth of love?"

jj Keller, Trade Agreement, LASR Best Book

*Dedicated to all women, juggling families and
careers, your love lives on in the lives of your children,
and that's something worth living behind.*

Acknowledgments

I'd like to thank my wonderful critique partners from Fantasy,
Futuristic and Paranormal critique loop, editors from Crimson
Romance, and all others who contributed and helped me shape
my novel to this final project.

CHAPTER 1

Poor fools, they made her laugh. Like squirrels busy digging for nuts, the Intelcorp's employees turned to work in hopes their name wouldn't get called. They knew their numbers would reduce when Olivia Owen from headquarters made her appearance, and so far she glided through her job of weeding out the slackers. The management preferred to call it a downsizing maneuvers—good for the investors and hell for the workers. Her gaze trailed a slouched man on his way out of her office. Bet now he wouldn't scoff at the early retirement package he'd refused two years ago.

The hot security guard shut the door after the man. The watchman assigned to her to protect her from possible verbal or physical abuse of disgruntled employees assumed his usual pose, straight back, wrists crossed in front. Since this morning, Olivia eyed the young guy every chance she got. He exchanged a few flirtatious glances with her, and the thought of what lay hidden under his navy blue uniform sent heat to her core.

His shirt stretched over his chest and shoulders and bunched around his biceps. He had everything she'd want in a causal sexual partner. She crossed her legs tighter, sending pleasant vibrations between her thighs. Both hands on her wristwatch pointed at three. If the last of the employees didn't give her any grief over getting laid off, she might squeeze in a hurried encounter with her personal guard. It always helped loosen her tension and clear her mind. With a head shake, she dismissed the notion and returned her attention to the task at hand. These employees weren't going to lay themselves off. She performed her duty with utmost professionalism and candor. That was why management sent her to their office in British Colombia.

But her best was never good enough. Not to the kind of mother she'd been dealt.

The elastic holding her hair in a ponytail left a sore spot at the back of her head. Loosening the band, stray locks of hair slid over her face. She gathered them in one hand and flipped them over her shoulder. A click of the mouse and the screen displayed the profile of the last unfortunate soul. This employee took too many sick days during the past year.

A seductive smile crept onto her lips and she nodded to the security guard. He replied with a smirk and a flick of his eyebrows. Yeah, she'd regret not getting him in the sack, damn her tight schedule. His trousers stretched over his taut butt as he bent to open the door and usher in the next employee to be chopped off, a thin woman named Nela Larin.

Olivia pointed at the chair in front of her desk. "Have a seat."

Nela plopped down, exhaling a heavy sigh. Olivia shuddered when Nela's tired eyes settled on her. Odd. She'd done this job for the past five years without so much as flinching, but this exhausted woman made her tremble with only one look. Of course, the employee knew why she was summoned.

From across her desk, she scanned the woman. Stringy hair tucked behind her ears, ordinary office attire, a grayish shirt and a pair of black slacks. Besides her plastic wristwatch, the girl wore no jewelry. Olivia's routine was proven: Thank the employees for their contribution, slide the envelope to them and wish them all the best in their future endeavors. Never get on the pity wagon with them. It was what management required of her. She didn't always agree with the big boss, but she kept her tongue in check.

"I believe you'll find everything you are entitled to in here." Olivia slid the brown envelope toward Nela. "On behalf of Intelcorp I wish to thank—"

"I'm a single mother." Nela's stern voice made Olivia flinch. Or could it be her thick accent, the way she stressed her r's hard. "If you fire me you'll be taking food and shelter away from an innocent child." Her mousy appearance fooled Olivia. The woman had some guts after all.

Olivia nodded to the security guard. When he straightened from the wall he'd leaned on, she returned her stern gaze to Nela. "I am sorry about your—"

"The hell you are!" Snatching the dismissal package from the desk, Nela sprang to her feet. "It's a cold day in this province when a woman gets fired because she stayed home with a sick child one too many days. What was I to do? Hmm?"

The security guard stepped to Nela and grabbed her elbow. "Ma'am, please leave the office," he said.

"Don't worry," Nela retorted with a trembling chin, pronouncing w's as v's. She freed her arm of the man's hold. "I powered my computer down and emptied my desk as instructed. There's no need to escort me out. I can find the door by myself, thank you very much."

A long breath failed to loosen Olivia's tight chest at Nela's stormy exit. Eyes fixed on the computer screen, she addressed the security guard. "She was the last one. Your duty is over."

He stepped to her desk, cocked his head and gave her a suggestive wink. "You dismissed a lot of employees today. Maybe I should escort you on your way out?"

A minute ago, she might have said yes. But now, she regarded him with a cold stare while she scrambled into her jacket. After the exchange with Nela, the atmosphere in this room had changed. All Olivia wanted was to get out and home as fast as possible "It won't be necessary."

The tall man nodded once and left the spacious office.

The familiar log out tune chimed on her laptop. She lowered the lid and stored the Dell in its suitcase. On her way out, she stopped by the manager's office. "If there is nothing else on the agenda, I'm off to the airport. My flight leaves in three hours and I want to avoid the afternoon rush-hour traffic."

The man stood, unbuttoning the suit jacket over his round stomach. "That is all, Miss Owen. Unless—"

Need sparked his brazen gaze, while disgust churned her stomach. A little drunk and very lonely at a last year's Christmas office party, he turned out to be a mistake that would never leave her. "No, Charles, and you should think of your wife."

"Have a pleasant flight." Frost laced his voice. He took a long step back and returned to his desk.

Without thanking the manager, she continued down the office. The whispers behind her back followed the glares of the remaining employees as she strutted past their cubicles. She was the bitch from headquarters who made her appearance once every year only to throw more work on those fortunate enough to keep their jobs.

Sticks and stones. She didn't allow a hint of regret. Though she lost all her friends along the way, her hard work never let her down. It got her where she was today—two notches below the top of the corporate ladder. At thirty-five, she was the youngest in the history of Intelcorp to get to such high position. And if she pushed hard enough, in another year, two at the most, she'd get on top. Yes, her biological clock was ticking, but this was her choice.

Yeah, she could keep saying it, but she wasn't fooling anyone. She'd never had a choice in her career. *Listen to your mother, Olivia. In this world, nothing's free. You have to learn a business that will put food on your table. Then you can peck at piano keys if that's your fancy.* Mother knew the best, of course.

The pouring rain washed the city, making the streetlights lining the parking lot glisten on the pavement. Clutching tighter to her jacket, she closed the distance from the building entrance to the limo in a few long strides. The heated leather seat inside the luxury vehicle soothed her backside. She pulled her raincoat tightly around her as a chill settled in her chest. Dark gray clouds hung low above the city, as if striving to touch the roofs of the skyscrapers and hide the mountains in the distance. November in Vancouver was too depressing. Not that it was any better in Toronto, but she longed to return to her house, order her favorite chop suey and soak in the tub.

She tilted her head to the side, counted the raindrops sliding down the glass. Nela Larin would have plenty of time to do the same now that she was unemployed.

A yawn broke Olivia's thought and she pressed her hand to her mouth. Why should she care about that woman? She'd accomplish a lot today and tomorrow was another day.

Arriving at the airport, she queued up in the excruciatingly long line at the luggage check-in then headed to the boarding gate. The same routine played out every few months in her life. Seatbelts snapped in the plane's cabin. The flight attendants in navy blue uniforms closed the overhead compartments. She gave a polite smile to her seatmate, a large woman in a sari, then changed her focus to stare out of the window as the city disappeared under the gray blanket.

The seatbelt light went off, and she reclined her backrest. The captain's voice came through the speakers, welcoming them aboard the Air Canada non-stop flight from Vancouver to Toronto. A few rows back, in coach, a baby cried with all his might while its mother pushed the bottle in his mouth. Honestly, people with small children should stay at home and not subject others to their kids' cranky behavior. Reaching into her purse, she pulled out noise cancelling headphones and plugged them in her iPod.

Getting comfortable in the business class shouldn't have presented a challenge, but shivers raked through her body. Again, she thought of the last employee she'd dismissed today. Damn woman wouldn't leave her. Olivia tucked the blanket under her chin and nestled her head into the sterile aircraft pillow.

Fuzziness surrounded her. The relaxing music coming through the headphones finally calmed her down. She yawned. Normally she wasn't an afternoon nap-taker but it had been a long and tiring day. Her heavy eyelids fluttered as she struggled to keep them opened, but she lost the fight within minutes and drifted off.

• • •

"Miss?"

Olivia opened her eyes to find a thick hand grabbing her shoulder. She turned to the flight attendant in a white shirt and red bow tie. "We're on our final approach, I need you to return your seat to upright position and fasten your seatbelt."

Dazed, she nodded.

God, she had barely slept. She must have fallen into a sleep coma. Her seatmate was gone. Maybe the woman joined someone in coach. Olivia scanned the business class. She hadn't paid too much attention to any of the passengers upon boarding, but she could have sworn she never saw these people. Even the flight attendants were dressed differently. Their uniforms and round caps now flashed in a bright red, not blue as when she boarded. Sitting up straight, she moaned as her knees bounced into the seat in front of her. What the hell? How could the space have shrunk while she slept? She scanned the rows of seats behind her. The sight reminded her of the movie scene of an overfilled bus on the muddy roads in Columbia, not a first class cabin. A few rows down, there was no mother holding a baby. Instead, a man with a cowboy hat gave her an acknowledging smile. What on earth was going on?

After a smooth landing, she grabbed her carry-on and staggered out of the plane. She'd get a coffee at the first stand to chase this sluggishness away.

In the baggage claim, limo drivers held up signs with names of their passengers, but none carried hers. Her ditz of a secretary had forgotten to arrange an airport pick up, again. She dumped the half empty coffee cup in the bin, reached inside her purse and pulled out her cell. She highlighted the number from the list then pressed the call button. Three rings later, her assistant's voice sounded through the phone.

Hi, you've got Jess. Leave me a message!

"What?" Olivia shrieked into the mobile as anger flared in her. "This phone is never to be left on voice mail. Where is my limo? This is inexcusable. Do you expect me to grab a cab? Consider yourself fired!"

She snapped the phone shut. Her outburst should have made her feel better, but a long line at the taxi stop caused her to grind her molars with anger.

An hour of waiting got her into a cab that smelled of stale coffee and god knew what else. The driver's name displayed on the license was unpronounceable.

"Where to?" he asked with a thick Indian accent.

"Turn this music down," she yelled over the Bollywood tune coming through the speakers.

The man's dark eyes widened. "You don't like Chack De India? Very, very popular."

"I'm sure it must be, but my head is just short of exploding." She pressed her fingertips to her temples, holding the pressure until the throbbing eased.

Shaking his head, the cabby lowered the sound to bearable decibels. "So where to?"

With a loud sigh, she sunk into her seat at the back. "Ninety-seven Rosedale Avenue."

"That's downtown." The driver threw his remark over his shoulder. "It'll be twenty dollars extra. Cash only."

"Of course." No doubt the man smelled money on her as soon as he figured she lived in one of the posh parts of the city.

The first drops of rain left streaks on the dirty windows as the cab rolled away from the airport. Olivia tapped her fingers, pondering whether to fire her secretary. This miserable, smelly taxi ride certainly could have been avoided. A smile crept to her lips, despite the worse than bad situation. She'd make the airhead walk on eggshells for the rest of her pathetic life.

The traffic on eight-lane 401 highway thinned out across the core of the city. The cabby swirled in and out of the lines, and from his snippy tone, Olivia concluded he was cursing in his native language while passing trucks. One hand on the door handle, she clutched her purse to her chest with the other.

Forty minutes later, the cabby parked in front of her house. "That'll be sixty three dollars."

She pulled four twenty dollar bills from her wallet and handed the money to the driver.

"I don't have any small change," he said, pocketing the cash.

The door opened with a clatter and she placed one foot on the interlock driveway. "In that case, you'll have to stick with sixty dollars."

He threw a look of disgust her way. "The meter says forty three plus twenty for downtown drop off."

"Seventeen dollars is a hefty tip for your service." The cabby appeared to have no intention of hauling her luggage out of the trunk.

He released his breath through his nose and handed her the money. "I always help those in need."

She stepped out of the car, dragged her suitcases out of the trunk and slammed the lid down. The cab reversed from her driveway onto the street and drove away, tires smoking and screeching.

Keys in her hand, she took the two steps to the front door. She had left a few lights on, but the smell of home cooking wafting in the air stood her hair on end. Who the hell was in her house? Heart drumming, she gripped her cell just in case she needed to make a fast call for the police, then she crept through the foyer toward the kitchen. The candlelit table set for two in the dining room indicated whoever was here expected a romantic evening.

His back to her, a man stirred a pot on the stove. His tight butt swayed to an Elvis classic coming from the stereo. Had she made a date prior to her trip but forgot to cancel it? Impossible, she wouldn't pass up on such a handsome man. Despite her dry mouth, Olivia swallowed. Whatever food the hunk was preparing on the stove smelled delicious.

The frills on his apron swirled around him as he turned to her with a smile that would have melted ice caps. Light from the ceiling reflected on his wavy brown hair. "Hi, honey. I was beginning to worry."

He stepped to her, leaned down and pecked her cheek with an odd familiarity. "Your trip must've been exhausting. I'm sorry the flight was overbooked, but at least the airline found you a seat in coach."

She wiped her cheek where his kiss still simmered on her skin. Rubbing his palms together, he turned to the stove. "Hope you're hungry. I made your favorite, ravioli á la moi. I just have to pop garlic bread in, but that won't take too long. So go get comfortable."

Frozen, she stared. His eyebrows furrowed. "I should have picked you up from the airport. Next time, I won't let you talk me out of it."

Her legs refused to co-operate. She couldn't get them to move, but she managed a sharp breath. "Who are you?"

The hunk's thick eyebrows drew closer and he cast her a puzzled glance. "Are you all right?"

She flipped the phone clutched in her hand and dialed. "I'm calling the police."

"Olivia?" He straightened. An insecure laugh crossed his lips. "What's wrong with you?"

"Nine-one-one, what is your emergency?" The voice came through the cell.

Her dry lips scraped her tongue like sandpaper across weather-beaten wood. "There's an intruder in my home."

"Ma'am, is the intruder aware of your presence?"

She leveled her gaze with the man's face and met his warm honey eyes. "Yes."

CHAPTER 2

Concern flashed in the eyes of the handsome man wearing an apron. The tight bend in Olivia's chest loosened a notch. Maybe the idiot cabby had dropped her off at the wrong place. No, her house key would not have worked nor would this man address her by name. She cast a long gaze over the room. Granite kitchen counters, brushed chrome appliances and double French doors drew her eyes to the maple rectangle dining room table. Her table. This was her home. Except for the man in front of her, whose warm and steady look once again held her captive. The sharp, deep voice of the 911 operator brought her back to the problem at hand. She broke eye contact with him and pressed the phone tight to her ear.

"Ma'am," the operator demanded. "Is the intruder threatening you in any way?"

The pot on the stove boiled over and the stranger whirled back as the liquid hissed. "Damnation." In two long steps, he closed the distance to the appliance.

"Ma'am, are you still there?" The operator's voice grew more demanding.

She clutched the phone to her ear. "No, he's…um…"

Despite the strange situation, she had to admire how smoothly the intruder moved around the kitchen.

"Do you need help?" The operator's voice snapped her from ogling.

"No, he's cooking." She sounded ridiculous to herself let alone to the emergency person.

"I see." The operator's voice fell flat. "He is *cooking*." No doubt he believed she was trying to pull a prank. After a short silence, he continued with the same tone. "According to your phone record, you are at ninety seven Rosedale Avenue, correct?"

"Yes, that's the address."

"The house belongs to Mr. and Mrs. Tomislav Medar."

"No," she shouted, not believing the operator's words. "The house is mine and my name is Olivia Owen. Single home owner."

"According to the records, you are Olivia Medar, nee Owen."

Her mind spun. The attractive stranger was her husband? "Impossible. That's not true."

"Ma'am, it's a serious offense to waste the time of the emergency service personnel."

"Please believe me. This is not a prank call. At least dispatch a patrol car." Olivia pushed the words out. This was demeaning and beneath her. However, years ago she'd learned begging never worked. At least not on Mother. The situation left her no other choice.

"I'll see what I can do." A click and the connection went dead.

She darted for the garage. Her BMW and Mercedes better not be damaged. In the foyer she opened the side door leading to the garage. A black Lexus sat in the spot designated for her vintage Mercedes, right next to…a minivan? Her eyes zeroed on the stroller in the corner and a small bicycle with training wheels. The sight caused her legs to give way, but strong arms caught her before she crumpled to the tiled floor.

• • •

A dark triangle shape floated in front of Olivia's eyes and took form as she came to consciousness. The man—Tomislav—sat on the edge of the couch where she lay. He pressed a cold compress on her forehead.

"You're scaring me, Olivia." He rubbed her arm. "You're acting as if you don't know me. What happened to you?"

At the sound of his deep yet concerned voice, her heart sped up. She pulled the soft cloth pad off her forehead. "Look…"

Her attempt to sit up was met by his hands on her shoulders. "Stay lying down until your head clears."

The coldness seeping into her forehead from the compress brought a breath of relief to her. "Tomislav, was it?"

"You always call me Tom."

Presumptuous jerk. She yanked the ice pack off her forehead and sat up. "I don't know you."

"Olivia, do you remember hitting your head, hard?"

"No." She blew an exasperated breath. If he tried to convince her he was her husband, she'd explode. "I don't know how you got in my house, but I'm willing to let it go *if* you leave immediately."

His brow furrowed. "I think we need to get you to the hospital. You're acting strange. Are you experiencing any pain? If you hit your head and can't remember it—"

She sprang to her feet, anger flaring in her. "I did not bang my head, I remember everything perfectly." Finger pointing at him, she shouted, "You don't belong here. Leave."

He stood and placed his hand on her shoulder. "Let me take you to the hospital." Lines deepened around his concern filled eyes. "Please. If you didn't hit your head, your confusion could be the first sign of brain aneurysm."

Her lips pressed tight, she yanked his hand off her shoulder. Dread stirred in her stomach with his words, but she dismissed the notion. She lacked any other accompanying symptoms of aneurysm. "I don't need a hospital. Now leave."

"Leave? This is my home as much as yours and I can prove it. Do you want to see the purchase agreement? Both of our signatures are on it." With hands propped on his narrow hips, he appeared quite sexy. Under different circumstances, she'd be ushering him to her bedroom. "Promise me tomorrow you'll see the doctor"

She pressed a hand to her forehead to stop her head from spinning. "Fine, I promise." It was more to get him off her case than the solemn pledge, but his shoulders relaxed. "Documents can be forged. How do I know you're showing me the original?"

"Show me your purchase agreement. If it states differently, I'll leave."

Her desk appeared miles away, but she staggered on wobbly legs and opened the bottom drawer. The file folder she pulled out contained clippings of food recipes from baby magazines.

"What is happening?" Her words came out in gasps while she tossed through the papers. Maybe she'd moved it. Every place she searched, she found fashion and parenting magazines, not her house purchase agreement. "Not possible."

Tom slipped some papers under her nose, flipped to the page showing her signature.

"See." He pointed to the bottom. "We bought it together after a long and, if I may say, exhausting house hunt. I'd do it all over again to see your eyes light up as they did when I brought you to see this house. It was way over our budget, but we got the price knocked down because the roof needed replacing."

Ice cold sweat spread down her back. Deep inside she sensed his story was true, except she remembered she'd bought her house through a short, balding real-estate agent. She took the papers in her hands. "What did you do with my document?"

"Listen to you, your document." He flicked his hand, his tone mocking. "This is our copy. The original is in the bank."

She tapped her finger next to her name. "This is not my signature. I wouldn't sign it as Olivia Medar."

"But you can recognize your handwriting?"

Examining the document under the light of the lamp on the desk, she nodded. "Looks every bit like mine, but how do I know it wasn't forged?"

Tom left the room and a few moments later returned with her purse. He handed it to her. "Try to check your driver's license."

Of course her documents would prove him wrong. Why hadn't she thought of it before? She drew her valet out and snapped it open. Her enthusiasm burst at the sight of her signature on the license, identical to the one on the house papers. Her bank and health cards and other documents bore the same name, but it was the spousal credit card that knotted her stomach. She was at this man's mercy and he knew of her every purchase. In fact nothing was solely hers anymore.

A panic tingled deep in her guts, but she swallowed it down. Losing her control wouldn't help her out of the situation. Time to put her big girl's panties on and show him who cracked the whip around here.

"This is unacceptable." She waved the card in his face.

He opened his mouth as to say something, but the doorbell rang. He turned his head toward the front hall. "Hold that thought."

She followed him to the entrance. Red and blue flashing lights of the police car blended through the frosted glass, but brought her some ease. Tom pulled the door open. On other side stood a young constable, his thumbs tucked in the loops of his belt near the hilt of his gun.

His eyes widened at the sight of Tom. "Mr. Medar? I was dispatched to this address for possible intrusion."

"It's quite all right, Constable Sealy." Tom put his hands up. "The Mrs. seems a bit confused after her long trip, that's all."

The young constable touched the rim of his hat. "In that case, I'll be off."

"Can I count on your court appearance?"

"Of course, Mr. Medar, it's my duty as an arresting officer." The cop nodded to her. "Ma'am, you have yourself a good night." He then turned to his car.

Tom locked the door. "Convinced now?"

Perplexed, Olivia stood in the hallway, staring at him. "I don't believe this."

Finger pointed at the door, Tom shook his head. "The constable can't have any contact with me before the court trial. He was the first at the crime scene and arrested my client."

"You're an attorney?"

"Olivia," Tom huffed. "Please try to remember. Have you suffered a head injury?"

There he went again about her possible memory loss. But his persistence sent her mind racing. She would remember if she'd bumped her head. Things started to go strange when she woke up on the plane. "I said I'll go see the doctor in the morning."

Tom caressed her elbow. "It's getting late and you've had a tiring couple of weeks." Pinching the bridge of his nose, he shook his head. "Why don't you take the master bedroom and I'll sleep in the guest room. You'll feel better in the morning."

Still struggling to process the events, she nodded absentmindedly. A lonely feeling swept over her. If he left now, she'd be all alone in this big house, and what if she really needed medical attention sometime during the night? Tom's concern about her well-being seemed genuine enough to help her if it came to that. His suggestion was acceptable.

The sound of utensils clanking brought her back to the kitchen. He dumped the entire dinner in the garbage and scrubbed the pots in the sink. A hint of guilt spread through her. Her husband, as strange as it sounded, had prepared her a nice meal and actually looked forward to a romantic evening. He must think of her as some spoiled kid. A strange urge to apologize pressed on her, but the words wouldn't form in her mouth. Instead, she removed her boots and coat. She had to get to her room, get out of her tight trousers and sort out this confusion.

Her heavy feet treaded on the hardwood floor as she climbed the stairs to her bedroom. At the first landing, she paused in front of a large wedding portrait. Her framed university degree had been in that location when she'd left for her business trip. Her breath caught. She certainly never appeared this happy in any of her pictures nor had she ever visited any place with all that greenery around her. The picture could have been Photoshopped, not impossible with today's technology. To add to her confusion, Tom seemed to stir emotions in her she didn't know she possessed. Deeper than plain lust, love maybe. She sneered. What had she known of love?

Rubbing her neck to stop the urge to be in his embrace, she continued up the stairs, but her gaze remained on the portrait. If Tom had forged this photo, at least he picked a perfect wedding dress for her. Cinderella style suited her.

She entered the master suite. Tom's neatly folded business attire hung over a wicker chair. His sea breeze scent lingered in the air and stirred butterflies in her stomach. She picked up the clothes, pressed them to her nose and drew in a long breath before moving them to the bed. The man smelled fantastic. She propped the chair under the doorknob. Reminded that she may need to rely on his help, she returned the seat to its original place.

A picture on the nightstand came into focus. She picked it up and almost dropped it. It was her in the photograph, with a huge belly. No, this was definitely Photoshopped. Something about the photo of herself pregnant shook her doubts. It felt familiar, yet she had no memory of having a baby. When she recalled the stroller in the garage, her arms longed to hold the baby she couldn't even imagine. The picture frame thudded as she put the photo back on the nightstand. Still, one could never be too cautious. Inside her closet, under the folded pile of shirts, she reached for the box storing her gun and gasped when her hand grabbed empty air. No one in the world knew she possessed a weapon. Except her boss.

• • •

Tom had anticipated a romantic dinner followed by hours of slowly pleasing Olivia, but now all excitement abandoned him. He shoved the last of the dishes inside the machine and slammed the dishwasher's door shut. Worry replaced his initial anger. Olivia had never acted so strange, not even after the many nights she'd paced across the nursery rocking their colicky son in her arms. To her credit, for weeks she'd been quite concerned about her sister's surgery. But even that couldn't explain why his wife stared at him as if he was a total stranger. If it wasn't a head injury that caused her to lose her memory, could it be some kind of delayed postpartum depression? Whatever it was, he should call her doctor despite her protests.

He hung the wet dishcloth over the stove handle and headed upstairs. The light under the door of master suite drew his attention.

"Olivia." He knocked on the door. "I need to get my toothbrush out of the bathroom."

The door flung open and she held a flannel plaid cloth in his face. "What is this?"

"Your pajama bottoms."

"This can't be mine. It's huge and ugly."

"You love sleeping in it." He smiled, balling his hands into fists to stop from wrapping her in his arms. She appeared in need of reassuring and at the same time stared at him with that same blank expression. He'd never seen her grey eyes this cold.

The overhead light shone on her long, raven hair as she threw the pants on the bed behind her, where he'd planned to make wild love to her. It had been a while. "Where's my black, silk nightie with thin straps?"

"Oh, that little number?" He couldn't stop from grinning. "Well, let's just say, the last time you put it on, nine months later, we had Rosie."

She shot him a sharp look. "Don't try to slip your kid as mine. Not going to work."

He shrugged one shoulder. She was starting again. "I'm not trying anything. And it's kids. More than one."

Her eyes narrowed and her look turned dubious. "How many kids do you have?"

"We," he said, pointing a finger from her to himself, but his annoyance with her mellowed. She gave him his kids after all. "You and I have two kids. A boy and a girl."

With her finger straight up, she stepped closer to him. "You and I have nothing together. Understand?"

"Honey, don't start aga—"

"I'm not your honey," she shouted, and her face turned red.

Tom nodded at the door to his left. "Keep your voice down. Rosie's nursery is right there."

A baby's cry pierced the air. He exhaled in exasperation. "Great. It took me hours to put her down."

Olivia slouched, wrapped her arms around her chest and cried out as if she was in pain. She pulled her hands away and stared at them in bewilderment while wet spots formed on her shirt.

"I'll get a bottle." He turned toward the stairs, hoping she had not noticed his bulging pants. The mere thought of her breasts swelling up and bursting with milk tightened his crotch to painful levels.

"I'm lactating?"

"You barely stopped nursing two weeks ago. With Milo, you got engorged when you weaned." He grabbed her shoulders, pushed her toward the suite bathroom. "If Rosie smells breast milk, she'll scream like a banshee. Go shower."

He yanked on his pants to loosen the pressure on his groin. The running water in the shower stirred his imagination again. He pushed on the bathroom door. To his delight, Olivia had not locked it. She never did. He peeked inside. Her gorgeous figure showed through the frosted glass of the cubicle door. Shower foam hugged her curves. Another wave of desire slammed into his pelvis. Damn, he should be kissing every inch of her.

The wailing baby snapped him back to reality. He retreated to the kitchen and pulled out a bottle from the fridge, then shoved it into microwave. Twenty seconds later he retrieved the warmed bottle, tested the temperature on the inside of his wrist and headed back to the nursery. He set the bottle on the dresser and leaned over the crib. "It's all right baby girl. Daddy's here."

He picked up Rosie in his arms and snuggled her to his chest.

"Shhhh, there now," he whispered as he pressed the button on her toy aquarium hanging from the crib railing. The soft and monotonous sound of waves hitting the shore filled the room. He lowered himself into the rocking chair. Rosie latched onto the artificial nipple and sucked with all her might. The bottle in his hand shook.

A smile crept to his face while he waited for Rosie's dark eyes to close. With every passing day, she resembled her mamma more and more. How could Olivia not remember any of them? Her belly full of warm liquid and the room softly lit, the gentle rocking lulled the baby back to sleep. Tom's head dropped a couple of times, too. He stood up, kissed her soft forehead, then put the sleeping cherub in her crib and left the nursery on his toes.

No light under the master suite door worried him. Either Olivia had fallen asleep or she'd left the house. A quick check would set his mind at ease. The door opened at his push. He poked his head through. Olivia's even breathing through the darkness calmed his nerves. With some luck the attempted murder trial currently on his plate wouldn't take months or worse, years, to wrap up so he could pay all his attention to his wife and family. Of course, he'd give the best legal counsel. The fact the client had come through the legal aid clinic would not tamper with his ability to be the perfect lawyer for this job. Not even the flashing cameras or questions shouted from journalists churned his stomach, though, like having to leave Olivia alone with kids for an entire day in the weird state she was. Maybe by Monday she'd snap out of whatever gripped her.

CHAPTER 3

Olivia stretched under the covers and flipped to her side. A few more minutes in the warm bed suited her still tired body. God in Heaven, what a vivid nightmare had pinned her to the sheets. Had she actually lactated in her dream? An involuntary shudder passed through her, but she patted her breasts all the same. Her shirt was dry.

A couple of kids and a husband? This had to be the first time her biological clock projected her fears into her dreams. So what if she was getting older? She wasn't afraid to die a spinster. Her goals had been set and marriage wasn't in the scheme.

She didn't need to end her career by tying herself to a husband and a couple of snotty kids. She blew a strand of hair off her face. Christ, she grew up listening to her mother's incessant, bitter complaints. Sure, nowadays women juggled employment and families, but her work demanded a lot of her time. The corporate world had not changed much since mother's days. Olivia had seen many women lose their jobs the moment management suspected their delicate conditions. Hell, she had even fired a few on the directive of upper management. Then had filled those vacancies with middle-aged women with fewer qualifications and experience, and no possibility they'd take off on maternity leave. Sad, but she didn't set the rules.

She drew in a long breath, and the smell of freshly brewed coffee mixed with sea-breeze male scent jolted her to a sitting position. Pinstriped pants hung from the back of the wicker chair. Her mouth tightened. A few of her one-night stands had tried to get a second date by "forgetting" something, but none had left pants behind. Her gut twisted. That man—Tomislav Medar—was still in her house. Dare she call the police again? Not after last night's fiasco. The dispatcher and the constable had seemed to think she was his wife. Though he spoke without an accent, his name indicated he may be a foreigner. Was he some kind of a poor immigrant that had stalked her, discovered she lived alone and devised this diabolic plan to get her house and possessions? Whatever and however gorgeous he was, it was time for him to gather his brats and go. Throwing the covers off, she jumped out of bed.

"I'll be damned." She stared down her legs. The ugly, huge and plaid flannel bottoms fit her fine. In fact, they were far more comfortable than her sexy lingerie.

She glanced at the clock on the nightstand and winced. Seven forty flashed on the screen. That couldn't be right. She had less than an hour to get ready and arrive to work on time. Damn, she'd just have to enjoy kicking her guests out later. Her gaze darted to the scale on the tiled bathroom floor. No matter how pressed for time she was, the curiosity forced her to step on. The numbers on the digital display kept going up and up and finally flashed three times. *One hundred and eighty? Christ! I couldn't have gained twenty pounds overnight.* Hopefully she'd finish her duties early enough to stop by her gym.

After a refreshing shower, she wrapped a towel around her body and scurried to the walk-in closet. Hangers scraped the rod as she shoved them to one end. Feminine and colorful items with frills and lace had replaced her stiff, dark designer power suits. She pushed down the panic rising up in her throat and told herself she had simply forgotten a recent shopping spree. What had she been thinking buying such garish prints?

She managed to piece together a semi-decent outfit of navy blue slacks and burgundy jacket then rushed down the stairs.

Tom waited at the foot of the staircase. Her favorite cup depicting two cats in sneakers rested in his hand. Steam curled from the mug in tantalizing ribbons.

"Your fresh look tells me you're feeling better." He offered the cup to her. His sensual lips stretched in a seductive smile.

She accepted the mug. His thumb brushed her hand and sent tingles racing up her arm. She sipped as if she'd done this for years. The smooth blend of vanilla and coffee filled her mouth and pleased her palette. He sure knew how to fix her morning brew. "Please, Tom. Don't start your argument now. I'm going to be late for work."

The smile faded from his handsome face. "You still can't remember."

Blowing the steam off her beverage, she studied him. He stood with his arms crossed over his broad chest. The narrow foyer appeared smaller with his impressive size. Between the walls were framed family pictures. Olivia focused on the face of a baby girl. No, it couldn't be. The face before her was strikingly familiar. If Tom Photoshopped this image, he'd have to know her mother, since she'd kept all of the pictures from her childhood. Perhaps she should hear Tom's version of her life, so she'd be able to discover some clues and valid reasons to have him thrown out of her house.

"No, I can't. Why don't you fill me in? And fast. I'm running late." She took another sip and glanced at her watch. Less than half an hour to arrive at work and he was in her way.

He exhaled, long and slow. "First, you're on maternity leave. And second, after it runs out, we agreed you'd stay home with kids for another year or two."

She gulped a mouthful of scalding coffee, sputtering when it burned her throat. She coughed and patted her chest. "Me? On maternity leave? Mr. Hiltorn would have me fired. Or he'd make me fire myself, since I'm good at doing his dirty work."

Tom frowned, but she continued, "You must be crazy if you think I'd sit at home for a couple of years and watch my ass get any bigger than it is."

Another exasperated sigh came from Tom. "I was afraid you'd change your mind. Need I remind you of the troubles we've had with daycares and babysitters? We've picked up Milo with a diaper so wet it had soaked through his clothes. Sometimes he had scrapes and bruises and no one knew how he got them. I'll never forget the day you came home so irate when the staff couldn't be bothered to administer his prescription."

She frowned. Hadn't she just fired a woman who'd taken too many days off to stay at home with her sick brat? It was possible parents really didn't use their kids as an excuse to get a day off here and there. Had she fired that woman without just cause? "Why did your kid need medication?"

He scrutinized her. Her question must've angered him, or maybe it was her tone. "Our son had strep throat. Obviously, you don't remember rushing him to the emergency with a high fever. Daycares are full of germs."

"Mommy, you're back," squealed the shrill voice of a child. A little boy ran down the stairs, grinning.

Olivia stared at the front of the boy's pajamas, a picture of a rusty tow truck with perturbing front teeth. *Hey there Mater* was written across the bottom right next to a Disney-Pixar logo. The boy wrapped his short arms around her legs and tilted his chin up. "Was Auntie Tadem sorry you couldn't bring me?"

"Auntie Tadem?" She gasped. Her sister born with Down's syndrome, institutionalized by mother and forgotten by the world, was this kid's aunt? Since when? No, Tadem was no more his aunt than she was his mother. Petrified, Olivia stared at Tom, who stood with his back leaning against the wall. From the funny expression on his face, he found the whole situation quite amusing.

"I miss Auntie," the kid chatted on, breaking into some kind of bouncing dance. "But guess what? Andy invited me to his birthday and it's at Chucky E Cheese's and Daddy will take me to the store to pick a present for Andy and then we'll go and play the games and have cake."

The kid's fast, high-pitched voice pierced Olivia's brain. She couldn't stand another second of this chatter. Tom's widening smile sent her over the edge. "Does he ever shut up? What's wrong with your kid?"

She regretted the words as soon as they left her mouth. The boy's lip trembled and tears welled in his brown eyes, the same rich honey shade as his father's. Tom pushed from the wall and pulled the boy into his arms, giving her a scowl that curdled her blood.

"Milo," he said, cradling the boy against his chest. "Mommy's not feeling well. Why don't you go back to your room and get ready for school."

Milo nodded and wiped his tears. Tom's eyes blazed while the boy climbed the stairs. He waited until the upstairs door closed with a soft snick before breaking the tenuous silence. "If for some reason you want to hurt me, that's fine. I can take it, but Milo is just a five-year-old boy for Christ's sake. He doesn't understand your sudden coldness."

His harsh tone and stern face caused her stomach to turn and knot. Excruciating silence prevailed. She didn't know what to say other than clear her throat and stare at her feet.

Tom spoke again, his voice soft. "You promised to see the doctor today. I'll drive you over to the office as soon as I put Milo on the school bus and get Rosie ready. She should be up soon."

She met his gaze, stunned by his abrupt mood swing. Warmth shone in his eyes again, a soft smile lit his face and tingled her spine. His quick mellowing suggested he couldn't stay angry at her. If she had to put a word to it, she'd say he loved her. *Right, Olivia. Now you're getting delusional.* Still she owed him an apology.

"I'm sorry for hurting Milo. I'm not used to having kids around." She licked her lips and drew a long breath as she put the mug on the corner stand. "I'm confused. You think I don't remember, but I do. It's just what I remember is different."

"Honey," Tom pulled her close, his rich, male scent filling her with an instant calm. "We'll get to the bottom of this, I promise." He released her from his bear hug, though she wished he hadn't. "You weren't comfortable with kids the first time I brought you to meet my family. My cousin's wife handed you her baby and you didn't know what to do." He grinned. "To save you, I took the baby, but you've come a long way since then."

Despite her effort to suppress her smile, her lips curled. His story, however sweet, sounded farfetched. "Look, Tom, I'm afraid your story doesn't fit with mine. I have to figure this out for myself." She wrung her fingers while her mind raced. How could she leave her house with him and his kids inside? She had no choice. If she didn't hurry she'd be the one standing in the unemployment line. "I'm late for work for the first time in my life. If your story proves true, I'll stop by the doctor's office and see if there's something wrong with my head." The familiar scent of rosemary surrounded her as she opened the coat closet. The smell must have lingered from Tom's cooking. Her mouth watered at the thought while she pulled her boots on and scrambled into her parka. "Where's my briefcase?"

Tom picked up a pink bag patterned with white blossoms. "I just wish you weren't stubborn about getting medical help, but that is so you." He handed the flowered bag to her, concern dissipating from his eyes. "Your briefcase has been replaced by the diaper bag."

The absurdity made her smirk. Even if she used such an item, it would be plain and all-business, not girly and feminine. She grabbed her purse from the corner stand and surprised herself by flashing Tom a warm smile. It would be nice to stay home with him. A thought stopped her mid-stride. Where did that come from? She'd always been a career woman at heart. Odd. Better leave now before things got any crazier.

"I really should be going."

"Are you sure you're in a condition to drive?" He lowered the arm holding the diaper bag in an "I give up" gesture.

"I'm fine."

"Make sure your cell's on and call me." His fingers brushing her cheek and his irresistible smile sent prickles to her neck.

One hand on the knob of the garage door, she paused and arched a mocking brow. He thought she was an invalid, incapable of taking care of herself. "I promise to see the doctor as soon as I can."

He kissed her cheek with the same familiarity as last night. Then he slid a set of keys in her hand. "Don't forget to tell your prick of a boss you're not coming back to work. And by the way, you're driving the van. The tank is full and snow tires are on. You're all set for winter."

At least he got one thing right—Mr. Hiltorn was a prick. On the other hand, he knew the business inside out. There was much to be learned from him. She glanced at the keys in her hand, then back at Tom. "Maybe you can tell me what happened to my vintage Mercedes."

A nostalgic smile crossed his face. "I loved that car, too. But with two kids, we needed something much bigger than a two-seater and it eventually became a money pit, so we sold it."

She nodded. The car was getting old and had needed a new engine. And yes, she'd been thinking of selling it. "Hope we got good money for it."

"Oh we did." Tom chuckled as if in memory. "I think the collector who bought it would've paid any price. And we traded your BMW in for the van."

She studied his aquiline profile. *He's a sweet man.* A strange impulse came over her. Before opening the garage side door, she leaned to kiss him on the cheek.

Happiness replaced concern in his eyes and washed away his initial astonishment at her unexpected action. She longed to kiss him again, on his lips. Why not? In this surreal time, she was his wife.

"Call me if you need anything. In the meantime, our son is taking his time getting dressed for school. I should see to him." He patted her shoulder and she stood rooted, staring as he ran up the stairs to get Milo. Their son.

With a sigh, she crossed the garage floor to her vehicle. Seated in the van, she scanned the dashboard, noting every detail. Well, this Nissan Quest had everything her gas guzzling Mercedes did not. She turned on the engine then shifted in reverse when the garage door glided up. As she twisted to back out, she winced at the two child car seats in the middle. She imagined fighting traffic with two screaming kids strapped in there. It would probably add to her pedal to the metal driving.

The cluster of downtown skyscrapers loomed in the distance while the Don Valley Parkway, long after rush hour, still resembled a parking lot. She tapped her fingers on the steering wheel and turned on the radio, hoping to find a traffic report. The speaker's smooth voice muffled the drone of the engine. The talk about alternate lives grabbed her attention.

Did he say "alternate life?" Oh, he meant alternative lifestyles. Still years ago she'd read countless books on the subject because she found it fascinating. Of course that was before she cast the fiction for reality. If her memory served her right, everything she'd learned then indicated she was in some kind of alternate life now. Maybe Olivia from this world was lost and helpless in hers. She exhaled and eased her foot off the brake. Though nothing had changed in her physical world—even the road construction in center lanes continued to cause delays. The taillights of the cars ahead flashed red again and she stopped. A hint of relief flooded her. In every story, the characters got returned to their lives after they fulfilled some quest.

Her cell clipped to the console, chimed. She read a text message on the screen. *Hope you're having a smooth drive, love Tom.*

Little buttons on the dial pad of her mobile clicked as she replied. *Getting there.* She hesitated for a moment, thinking whether to add "love, Olivia," but decided against the endearment and pressed the send button.

Twenty minutes later, she pulled into the Intelcorp parking lot and took the employee card from her purse. A hint of hope kindled in her at the sight of her real last name, but it was quickly extinguished when the arm barring parking lot entrance remained lowered. Neither did the red light change to green.

Two more trials of scanning her card produced the same result. She reversed from the entrance and parked in the visitors' spot. If she weren't late already, she'd march straight into the security office and give them a piece of her mind for deactivating her card again. As it was, she'd just have to fire off an angry email to their supervisor.

Gray clouds raced over Toronto's downtown skyscrapers. She pulled the zipper of her coat all the way to her chin as cold winds whipped around her. In a few long strides, she crossed to the revolving glass entrance.

The receptionist's face lit up when Olivia stepped in the lobby. "Good morning, Olivia." The middle-aged woman leaned to the side and peered behind her. "Did you bring Rosie? She's such a cutie-patootie. The whole office is crazy about her."

Olivia halted in her tracks. It wasn't the woman's inquires about Tom's kid that stunned her. Since when was she on a first name basis with a receptionist?

"Olivia." She spun on her heels at the shriek. Airhead Jess came running down the stairs, her blonde curls bouncing on her shoulders. She too leaned to the side, expecting to see someone behind Olivia. "Is Tom with you? The girls from accounting and I haven't drooled over him in a while." Jess waved her hand. "Oh I got your message from last night. I'm fired?" She broke into a giggle. "Hilarious."

Her mouth dropped open and dried, yet her palms turned sweaty. Olivia stared at her workers. Things were happening too fast for her to process. This was her place of employment, her sanctuary. The people here always treated her with respect, addressed her by her last name, averted their glances from her and whispered behind her back as she made her way to the corner office.

"Medar." Mr. Hiltorn's stern, rasp called from the front door. Even in this alternate world, some things never changed. He still treated the employees as if they were part of a football team, and he was the head coach.

"Mr. Hiltorn," she gasped, whirling to face him. He'd be livid with her coming in so late. "I'll stay after hours as needed."

"What are you talking about?"

CHAPTER 4

The gray walls of Intelcorp's lobby closed in on Olivia. The muffled voices of the employees addressing her by first name, as if she were their equal, mingled with the sound of her pounding heart. Cold sweat glued her blouse to her back, and her chest tightened. The chime of the elevator reaching the main floor snapped her attention to the sound.

Mr. Hiltorn shifted his briefcase to his other hand. "Have you come to your senses and decided to cut your leave short?"

"No, Mr. Hiltorn, I'm not on the—"

The elevator's door slid open. He stepped in and slammed his hand on the pane to stop it from closing. "If you're not here to work, get lost. These employees are on the clock and wasting time fraternizing with you."

The brass door closed. Olivia stared at the numbers above the frame lit up one by one. She drew in a long breath when the light stayed on number eight. Someone else sat in her office across the floor from Mr. Hiltorn.

Jess took the mail from the receptionist and turned around. Her fake smile dropped. "Olivia, you're so pale. Are you all right?" She pressed her hand on Olivia's arm. Her shoulders tensed and Olivia took a long step back.

"I…" Olivia glanced from person to person. Even the delivery guy doffed his brown baseball cap and addressed her by her first name, as if he'd known her since kindergarten. Suddenly, there wasn't enough air in the spacious lobby. She scrambled toward the exit. "I have to get out of here."

"Olivia! Where are you going? Wait." Jess's calls grew fainter as she rushed away. Her insides twisted and tears burned her eyes, obstructing her vision. Out through the revolving glass entrance, she stepped onto the sidewalk.

She stormed to her car and sat with her forehead on the steering wheel. Where should she go from here? Again, her mother's voice whispered to her. *Don't let this hurt you. You'll figure it out. You must.* Olivia wiped her tears away. Damn it, she built herself into a tough person and was beyond these messy emotions. This crazy-scary life-hopping should not get the best of her. She'd been through worse and got out without anyone's help.

When her breathing calmed and her throat loosened, she sat up straight. This whole world-shifting might drive a person straight to the nearest bar, but not her. She placed the key into the ignition, started the engine and rolled out of the parking lot. Gathering her thoughts, she drove aimlessly through the streets. If her theory were right, she was in some alternate life, married to a hunk who appeared to love her while every woman nearby drooled over him. Not the worst that could happen.

Storefronts on the Yonge Street with Christmas decorations drew her attention. A few parents dragging their children away from plastic Santas and reindeer coaxed a smile from her. Would having two children in this life really be so bad?

Until today, she'd practically run Intelcorp. She could handle a husband and a couple of kids, right?

She slammed on the brakes and leaned on the horn when a bicycle delivery guy dashed in front of her. "Dammit!"

But it was her thoughts that infuriated her. She wasn't fooling anyone, least of all herself. How could she compare running a company to raising kids and having a husband? Not in her life. The corporate world was where she thrived. If she had to sit at home day after day, watching soaps and eating ice-cream or whatever stay-at-home moms did, she'd go insane. And if Mr. Hiltorn replaced her with someone he liked better, he'd find a way to get rid of her.

A hollow realization grew in her stomach. While she was on maternity leave he couldn't fire her, but the minute she returned she'd find her name tag removed from the office door. *You're not meeting the company's needs.* Hiltorn's standard termination lingo. In fact, he'd have his new human resources person say it, just as she'd said those exact words to many.

Drops of rain streaked her windshield as the tall buildings of downtown grew smaller in her rear-view mirror. Soon, the droplets changed to frozen pellets that clonked against her car. She turned the wipers and the defroster to the max, and shivered as the cold infiltrated the interior of the car.

What would her mother do in her situation? Get her normal life back, of course. Meaning, Olivia must discover her purpose in this life, fulfill it and she'd return to her world. At least that was how it always worked in those books she'd devoured.

The frozen pellets changed to thick snowflakes. The wiper blades swished across the windshield at full speed, clearing her view of the road. The brass sign of a tall building she pulled in front of read *Dr. M. K. Law, MD.* She *had* promised Tom she'd see a doctor.

Would the old doctor see her? Of course. He wasn't only their family physician but an old friend and distant relation to her mother. Last time she'd seen him, she was twelve and Mother had finally brought her in when "a touch of flu" turned into a bad case of pneumonia. Maybe this other Olivia had been blessed with a better mother. Hopefully they wouldn't meet. If she were a nurturing mother, she'd expect a hug and maybe a kiss on the cheek. Olivia would freeze not knowing what to do. Though she gave up hope for a loving mother years ago, a hint of jealousy squeezed her heart. It must be nice to have someone in life who would care.

She got out of the car and stepped to the front door. In the building's dark glass, her tense expression reflected back on her, all the panic she was barely repressing showed in the set of her mouth and tension around her eyes.

The thick glass door opened at her push. She proceeded to the reception desk.

The receptionist's gray hair came loose from her clip when she snapped her head toward Olivia then tilted her chin at the phone receiver pressed to her ear. "I'll have to call you back." She lowered her glance at the stack of mail on the desk. "Can I help you?"

"I need to see Dr. Law." Olivia tapped the reception desk. A thought crossed her mind—what if the doctor had retired? But if he had, his name wouldn't be on the door. No. This secretary must have replaced his ancient one. Or she was a temp. "Do you have an appointment?"

Olivia's fingers ceased and she faced the woman. Her name tag read Doris. "No, I don't."

Doris pulled her glasses off, letting them dangle on the chain around her neck. She puffed. "Well, he's busy and won't see you without an appointment."

"Tell him Olivia…" What last name should she use? Since everyone seemed to call her Medar, she opted for Tom's last name. "Olivia Medar is here and it's urgent."

The receptionist swiveled her chair and typed on the keyboard. She tapped her chest, feeling for her glasses, put them on and peered at the screen. "Medar, Olivia, nee Owen." With a sharp twist of her chair, she faced Olivia, a questioning frown on her face. At Olivia's nod, the receptionist lowered her glasses again. "I doubt he'll see you. We're booking for February, Mrs. Medar. If you'd kindly make an appointment, he'll—"

"It's only November, Doris, and your waiting room is empty." Olivia stepped to the nearest seat in the waiting room. With narrowed eyes, she lowered into the first leather chair and scrutinized the secretary.

Her practiced stare worked, because the woman averted her gaze and rummaged through the papers on her desk. "He's with a patient now. I'll see what I can do."

Releasing a breath, Olivia glanced at a stack of folded morning papers on the low table. She picked up the section with the headline: *Medar Maintains the Innocence of his Client.* Tom's picture and an article filled the front page. She glanced down to read the bulk of the story.

"Evidence is mounting against Mr. Medar's client, Maria Stokić. She has no solid alibi or a witness. Yet her attorney maintains the woman's involvement in the shooting is purely circumstantial. As previously reported, on October 20, a domestic employee of Baldwin estates was found slouched over Mr. Erich Baldwin. CEO and founder of C-Two Media, the filming industry giant is in a coma with a shotgun wound to his chest."

Olivia's hands shook and she tried to swallow the lump of fear in her throat. Her missing gun filled her mind. The weapon was to scare her dates who might get any wrong ideas. Thank God she'd never had to use it. It had to be at least a year since she'd checked on it and last night the gun was gone from its hidey hole. But she was in a different life. Olivia from this world might not possess a weapon. She bit her lip to stop from yelping. Maybe her alternate wasn't strong enough to help Tom defend his client and win the case, and some unknown entity switched their places. This could be Olivia's purpose here.

"Dr. Law will see you. Please, come this way." The receptionist's stern voice jolted her back to the moment.

"I knew he would." She tossed the paper onto the table and followed the thin woman down the hallway.

Doris ushered her into a small examination room. "He'll be right with you."

Olivia sat on a chair and tucked her still shaky hands between her thighs. Two knocks sounded on the door.

She assumed a casual pose. Her foot tapped nervously of its own accord. "Come in."

The door swung open and Dr. Law entered. His graying hair confirmed she hadn't seen him in quite a long time, but maybe the other Olivia had.

"Olivia," he said, taking the seat on a round stool. "What's wrong? It's not like you to come in without an appointment."

"You've known me since I was a child." She sniffed, hoping the good old doctor would see how disturbed she was.

His thick moustache twitched with his frown. "Yes, I have."

"Have I ever behaved irrationally?"

"Many times, in fact, but you were set in your ways." His keen gaze settled on her. "Is this about Tadem's surgery? It will be a long road to recovery and she's lucky to have the best sister in the world."

The best sister? She turned to look behind her, only to see the wall. *He means me.*

Her hopes died with his words. Every person she came in contact with knew Olivia from this world, not her. On this rare occasion, she was at a loss for words.

"With a mother like yours, it is no wonder you two are so close. Tadem hasn't been my patient since she was a year old, so I can ask. Does your mother even know her daughter had a surgery?" When Olivia didn't respond, the doctor shifted in his seat and quickly changed the subject. "Is your mother on a Caribbean cruise?"

Well, alternate life or not, Mother stayed the same. Olivia of this world had not been lucky either. She mustered the courage to speak, but dared not disclose her theory. "I don't know. That's why I'm here. I seem to have amnesia, or something. You see, I don't have any memory of visiting my sister nor of Tom or the kids. What I remember is a different life."

Dr. Law leaned backward, his bushy eyebrows furrowed. "Did you suffer a head trauma?"

Him too! She shook her head. "I'm positive I didn't lose my memory, as I'm positive I never visited my sister, or married Tom or even had his kids. None of this is my life. The life I know and remember is different."

A solitary life, devoted to a corporation. In which she'd watched in disgust when people rushed from work to see their families while she'd gone home at the end of every long day to an empty house.

Dr. Law's silent stare raised the hairs on her nape. He straightened, rolled his stool closer to her and cupped her chin. Pulling down her lower lid of one eye he pointed at the ceiling. "Look up."

The low ceiling revealed the brush strokes of recent painting. He flashed a light in her eye. "Looks good. Now the other," he said and repeated the action.

Grimacing, she rubbed her eyes while he replaced the light in its spot on the wall rack. He reached for a blood pressure cuff. The sharp rip of Velcro release filled the silence. "Let's see how your pressure is."

He wrapped and secured the black strap around her bicep. Air hissed as he squeezed the pump, filling the band. "My wife and I attended your wedding. It was such a lovely event. You don't remember the Butchart Gardens?"

Tears stung her eyes and she blinked fast. Her dream was to have her wedding ceremony in the Butchart Gardens, if she ever did tie the knot. "Why would we hold our wedding all the way in Victoria?"

"You discovered the hard way how much Tadem is terrified of flying and isn't comfortable out of her surroundings. You didn't want to put any stress on her and opted for sunny British Columbia instead of rainy Ontario. I never saw her so happy. She beamed. So did you." After placing the stethoscope ends into his ears, he lowered his gaze to the dial. The tightness around her arm loosened and air seeped out. "You blood pressure is slightly elevated, but it's still within normal. This is nothing to worry about. Do you experience any dizziness?"

"Once, last night. I fainted when I saw the stroller in the garage." She averted her glance to her fumbling fingers. So powerful were the bonds of Tom's family that she hated letting them down, even if they weren't hers. The doctor knew more about her sister, the kids, and her husband than she did. She should call the facility where their mother had disposed of her "daughter who would never amount to anything" and inquire about her only sibling. Perhaps even visit before her quest in this life was fulfilled and she returned to her ordinary world. Remorse raked her. If Tandem had the surgery in this life, the poor thing must be scared and so alone.

Dr. Law brought a form up on the screen of his computer. "An MRI would tell us more. I should order one, to rule out any internal bleeding or tumor or damage to your brain." He glanced at her and stopped filling in the form, his finger poised over the mouse key. "I can see from your expression you don't think this is necessary."

He pulled the sheet from the printer tray and handed it to her. "Do it, Olivia. It's for your own good."

She nodded, taking the form. This world's Olivia seemed equally stubborn. "If everyone will stop pestering me about banging my head, I will."

Her vision went black. She slumped over the exam table, trying to grab onto the consciousness slipping from her, even as the room spun. Dr. Law's voice and his hand on her shoulder were the last things she remembered.

...

Tom stirred the mixture of cubed beef, potatoes, and mushrooms in the slow cooker. He closed his eyes, as he breathed in the spicy scent. His stomach rumbled, but he replaced the lid. The stew needed to simmer for a few more hours on low for the spices to blend. Last night's attempt at a romantic dinner had gone to waste, but tonight he would wow his wife with his savory creation.

Rosie kicked her feet and pounded the sippy cup on the tray. Her loud protests and wiggles meant she disapproved of sitting strapped in the highchair.

"Okay girl. Your turn." He put down the stirring spoon, crossed the kitchen, wiped biscuit crumbs of his daughter's face and fingers and took her out. Rocking her in his arms, he paced around the table. He should be preparing for court trial on Monday, but he couldn't concentrate. His law firm allowing him to work from home was his saving grace. Pausing next to Milo, he peered over his son's shoulder to check his homework.

"Son, try to write a bit neater. Your teacher needs to read this, you know." He remembered the long hours he'd spent as a child, writing letters neatly, line after line. Schools didn't practice letters anymore, but as a parent he wanted his child's penmanship be at least legible. Tom switched Rosie to his other arm. Her babbling made him chuckle.

His little cherub must've grown in the past week because his bicep ached under her weight.

"Try again, Milo." He ruffled his son's brown hair and went to his study to check the van's GPS on the computer. It had been parked at Dr. Law's building for the past hour. Maybe he should call the medical office, but he had to let Olivia find the answers on her own. She wouldn't accept his explanations. Not that he had any.

His phone rang and Dr. Law's number flashed on the call display. Tom's guts twisted. He wrapped one hand around Rosie perched on his knee and yanked the receiver to his ear. "Olivia?"

"Mr. Medar." Urgency edged the woman's voice. "I'm calling from Dr. Law's office. He needs you to come here right away. Olivia collapsed."

CHAPTER 5

Sharp beeps pierced the darkness, jolting Olivia awake. What had happened? The last thing she remembered was dimming vision, trembling legs, Dr. Law ordering her to lie down despite her protests, the black curtain closing in.

Thin paper crinkled under her as she wiggled to loosen her stiff back. The blaring noise that woke her had ceased. Good. Her mind and body wanted to go back to sleep.

Through her lashes, she caught Dr. Law's hand waving in front of her face. "Was I out for long?" Shivers set her spine on tingle with her barely audible whisper.

"A few minutes." He pressed a stethoscope to her chest. "Take a deep breath."

She obeyed. Her ribcage expanded with air intake and burning pain shot through her.

"Let it out slowly. Good." He glided the round disk on her skin. "Another deep breath in and slowly out. Good." He removed the stethoscope earpieces. "Are you experiencing any discomfort?"

Pain stabbed her neck when she shook her head. She winced and squeezed her eyes.

"If you are still lightheaded, don't make any fast moves."

She nodded, lifting her brows to force her eyes to open but they refused to cooperate. God, she was trapped in her own body, barely able to relay anything.

"I have to step out for a moment." Dr. Law's voice sounded far away, as if he were speaking in the other direction, then the click of the door handle confirmed he was gone.

"Olivia, honey, I'm here," Tom said, worry lacing his voice.

She pressed her hand to her aching head and moaned. Had that deep and throaty sound come from her?

With great effort she peeled her eyelids apart and blinked at the light on the ceiling. "Good," she whispered.

His fingers brushed her face. "Dr. Law's calling an ambulance. They'll be here any minute. A specialist will see you at the hospital."

Hospital? Her stomach knotted at the mere mention of the word. She certainly didn't need this. Tom's hand pressing on her shoulder stopped her attempt at getting up. "No need, really. I'll be fine. Just let me rest."

"Take it easy. It's is not like you to faint. You didn't pass out that time I cut my thumb and bled all over the kitchen, why now? It's better to find what is causing this." He smoothed a lose strand of hair from her forehead. "I notified Gregory and he'll see us right away."

Tom stroked her hair, and she tried to relax. She drew in another long breath. "Gregory?"

"Susan's husband, the neurologist." Tom cupped her cheek. His baritone calmed her frail nerves. It took a few seconds before his words sunk in.

Her eyes popped open. "Susan? My ex-best friend? She hates my guts because I—"

Surprise flashed in Tom's narrowed eyes. "No, she doesn't. Besides that quarrel is ancient history."

The questions on his scowling face squeezed her chest. The door opened and Tom turned his head. Her double had patched it up with her only friend. If only she could do the same in her old world.

"The ambulance is here," Dr. Law announced, closing the door while Tom helped her to a sitting position.

Two paramedics waited in the hallway next to the gurney. She shuddered and exhaled a shaky breath. "Is this really necessary? The fuzziness in my head is clearing. I'm fine."

Dr. Law's hard stare tied her stomach in knots. She'd remembered his stern look when she wouldn't cooperate as a child. "If you don't mind spending the night on a hard seat in the waiting room."

Tom wrapped his arm around her waist, his biceps bunched. "No more complaints. I'll help you to the gurney."

She leaned against him and inhaled the faint scent of his piney aftershave. *God, he smells good.* Butterflies fluttered in her stomach and replaced the initial tightness. With his arm holding tight and each slow step he took toward the stretcher, he created another wave of tingles in her core. The paramedic's hand around her arm shattered her short moment of euphoria, even if she had not showed it.

"We've got her from here." The man in the navy blue uniform held her by her shoulders while his partner brought the gurney closer.

"Easy." The man helped her up and proceeded to snap the straps. Pulling a rough woolen blanket over her after he strapped her down, he glanced at her as if reading her baffled expression. "It's a procedure, every patient must be strapped."

The paramedics rolled her through the waiting room, now filled with patients. Embarrassment seared her cheeks. She wanted to disappear under the covers, but the restraints kept her exposed.

The ambulance parked in front of the main entrance, lights flashing red, deepened her humiliation.

"Can we ride without the sirens? This is embarrassing enough." She clutched the gurney's railing while the two paramedics glided the stretcher into the back of the emergency vehicle.

"I'll meet you at the hospital. Don't give the paramedics a hard time." Tom leaned over her and placed a soft kiss on her lips, sending her heart racing all over again.

The woman paramedic leaped in the back with her while the man closed the rear door. Thank God, the ambulance took off without blaring sirens. Olivia's relief was short lived. A whining sound pierced the air. Damn. They must've simply been waiting until they turned onto a main road.

She swayed as the vehicle swirled through the traffic. The blasting siren stopped and the ambulance slowed down. The ride to the North York General had taken less than ten minutes.

"We're here." The woman paramedic stood up, but remained slouched. She released the brakes on the gurney's wheels.

The rear door popped open, cold air sliding into the heated interior. The gurney touched the pavement just in time for Olivia to see Tom running across the parking lot. His arrival meant he'd matched the ambulance's speed.

The earlier snow had stopped and Tom's steps crunched on the light blanket of powder. The paramedic turned her gurney toward the glass entrance of the hospital and the panels slid open. Warmth caressed Olivia cheeks as the EMT pushed her indoors. The stringent smell of bleach stung her nose and reminded her how much she disliked hospitals.

The paramedics stopped the gurney by the triage desk. "Mrs. Medar is here to see Dr. Mason."

The nurse in flowery scrubs seated behind the glass window spoke, but her voice came across muffled. She pointed to her left. Olivia's gurney moved again, leaving the waiting area filled with people. Dr. Law's words rang true—only the sickest people got the prime attention.

Olivia counted the rectangle lights on the ceiling of long corridors until her stretcher finally stopped in front of the door with a sign indicating Diagnostic Imaging.

"Gregory assured me this won't take long," Tom said, trailing alongside her. At the reception desk, the paramedics handed Olivia's paperwork to a nurse in bubble-gum pink scrubs. She led them to a tiny room where they transferred Olivia to another bed on wheels.

The nurse who took papers from the paramedic came to her bedside and flashed a big smile at Tom. "Hi, my name is Cindy, I'll be her nurse. Dr. Mason is ready. I'll help your wife change into these gowns. If she has any jewelry, please have her remove it. The changing room is behind those curtains."

Cindy barely glanced her way and continued to gawk at Tom, whose initial smile vanished, replaced by a frown. *Great! Another woman drooling over Tom.* Olivia yanked the washed-out, folded fabric from nurse's hands. "My husband is not your patient. I am. I'm right here and I can speak and change myself."

"Oh, in that case, I'll be back in a moment. Please make sure your wife is ready." Cindy coughed in her fist and her cheeks blushed. She left the room.

"Mrs. Medar, if I didn't know you better, I'd say you're jealous." Tom winked at Olivia. "Don't worry. I only have eyes for you."

"Me jealous?" Though she must admit, her lashing out at the nurse was an emotional display, but Tom didn't need to know this. "The nurse couldn't be less professional if she wanted."

"Could be worse, the hospital staff work long shifts. Cindy is trying hard to be pleasant." He stood when Olivia slid the curtain open. "Do you need help getting to the changing room?"

"I can manage." She stepped into the narrow bathroom. Hell, her broom closet was bigger than this. In haste, she unbuttoned her shirt. She removed her blouse and trousers then slipped on the hospital gown. Light blue was not her color. The two sets of strings on the back of the gown presented a challenge, but she managed to tie them with some elaborate twisting.

"Mr. Medar? Or can I call you Tom?" Cindy's sugar-laced voice drifted to Olivia through the closed curtain. "Your wife is not ready yet? Cold day today, isn't it? Getting ready for Christmas?"

Olivia snapped the curtain open. Tom turned to her. A smile lit his face, replacing his bored expression.

"If she's ready, we can proceed," the nurse said, twirling a few strands of her streaked blonde hair around her finger. When Olivia nodded, she pushed a wheelchair next to the bed. "Can she sit here?"

Olivia stared at her transportation. "I need a moment alone with my husband."

Cindy's eyebrows arched, her glance switched to Tom. "Of course. Let me know when you're ready."

Olivia drew in a long breath, keeping an eye on Cindy's slow retreat, then turned to Tom, unsure whether his concerned look or her dislike of medical buildings made her stomach flutter. "I don't like hospitals."

Tom shrugged. "Who does?"

"You don't understand. I spent countless hours in waiting areas doing my homework while my mother dragged Tadem from one specialist to the next in some hopeless attempt to make her normal. When she finally realized the impossibility, she ditched her in the home for the infirm."

"Honey, your mother did the best she could for Tadem. And you have nothing to be afraid of." He pulled her in his embrace and she took the opportunity to take in his scent again. His endearments grew on her. She loved it when he called her *his honey*. "I won't let go of you."

His words boosted her with a pinch of encouragement and a realization. Perhaps her mother chose the best option. She wouldn't be able to provide the kind of care Tadem required. Cindy approached. Tom wrapped one arm around Olivia's shoulders and nudged her toward the wheelchair.

"Must I sit in there?"

"It's just a procedure. I also need to ask if she has any implants, such as a pacemaker or cochlear implants." Cindy tucked the pen in her scrub's pocket.

"No she doesn't, but why do you keep asking me? My wife is right in front of you." Tom's sharp voice indicated he was getting annoyed at the nurse's flirting. He brushed Olivia's cheek. "I'm sure you can walk, honey. But please, sit in the chair so we can get this done."

Olivia snickered at Cindy's beet red flush before getting in the chair. Served her right. The nurse took her for some ditz who couldn't answer simple questions. "Let's go."

"The procedure doesn't hurt at all. In fact, some of our patients have said it's quite relaxing." Cindy pushed the wheelchair through the narrow corridor. "You may feel a bit warm. Oh, I hope you're not claustrophobic, because the chamber is rather small, like a tunnel."

Olivia wrapped her fingers around Tom's hand. The nurse must've finally understood his earlier scowl as a sign to change her tactics and address his wife. "If I were, I would have freaked out in the broom closet you call a changing room."

Cindy's giggle bounced off the long corridor walls before she stopped and turned the wheelchair around. Pushing her butt against another door, she slid Olivia through. "We're here."

An enormous metal machine occupied most of the space behind the glass wall. Its buzz filled the air. A tall man nodded to Tom then lowered his gaze to her. "Nice to see you again, Olivia."

She studied him. Dark hair touched by silver circled his handsome face. His gray eyes focused on her, but she was absolutely certain she had never seen him before.

He read her baffled expression and extended his hand to her. "I'm Dr. Gregory Mason. I'll examine your MRI."

Placing her hand in his, she licked her dry lips. "Nice to meet you, Dr. Mason. I understand you're Susan's husband."

"As I explained over the phone," Tom addressed the doctor, worry apparent in his voice. "She's been acting very strange since she'd got back from Vancouver."

"Yes, I'm Susan's husband and we've met before." Gregory pulled his hand away from Olivia, placing it on Tom's forearm. "We'll get to the bottom of this." He waved at the white table protruding out of the round scanner. "I need you to lie down here. If you'd like some music, there are headphones attached to the console and feel free to cover your eyes with the mask from this box before we start. The examination will take about forty minutes and then we'll go over the results."

"I'd like some music, thanks." Olivia took Tom's hand and pushed out of the wheelchair then climbed up onto the table. Holding the headphones above her head, she paused and looked at Dr. Mason. "You've been married to Susan for long?"

"Since I convinced her she should thank you for saving her from a lifetime of heartache."

Olivia swallowed a lump at the memories of losing her only friend. "Love blinded her." Afraid Tom would think she was a boyfriend snatcher, Olivia darted a glance at him. "I wanted her to see she was about to make the biggest mistake of her life, but she wouldn't listen. I knew she'd be back any moment so I invited her boyfriend to our dorm. He didn't need any encouragement. When she caught me with him, she stormed out and I never saw her again."

Tom's kiss on her temple instilled her with reassurance and eased her tight ribcage. This was the first time she'd confessed her guilt out loud and to another being. "You saw her two weekends ago."

No, it had been his wife who'd seen Susan. Olivia pressed her lips tight and fought the urge to blurt her theory. He thought she was going crazy already.

A smile softened his eyes. "That's in the past now, honey. Try to calm down and let Gregory proceed."

Soft music surrounded her ears as she placed the headphones on. She pulled the black eye patch on and lay back, willing her body to settle. Cindy had been right about one thing. The warmth in the tunnel, the new age music and cushy bed relaxed Olivia. By the third song she pictured green pastures sprinkled with yellow flowers. A little girl—one that looked like her at six years old—spun with her arms spread wide, the sun warming her face.

Olivia couldn't remember seeing the place before, but perhaps this meant her memories and those of Tom's Olivia were beginning to blend. She gave in to the fuzziness in her head and floated as if on gentle waves for another song or maybe three. The same beeps she'd heard in Dr. Law's office pierced through her haze.

The music in the earphones ceased and Dr. Mason's voice came through. "We're done." The table slid out of the tunnel and the low buzzing coming from the MRI machine stilled. "Remove the eye mask slowly to allow your vision to adjust to the bright lights in here."

"Come with me, Olivia." Tom extended his hand to her. "It's time to find out what's wrong with you."

Olivia hesitated. Did she want to know? Not if she had a tumor or a brain injury.

"Come on." Tom's gentle nudge melted away her doubts. "Whatever it is, it's better than not knowing."

With her hand in his, she got on her feet and followed him to the desk where Dr. Mason sat viewing her MRI images.

"This is quite perplexing," he said, glancing at her then back at the computer screen where he pointed at the middle of the scan. "There are no signs of brain damage or any unusual growth. There is a slight elevation of the brainstem activity in your sleep promoting area. That is where REM sleep originates."

She leaned closer when Dr. Mason pointed to gray and black picture on the computer screen. "Are you saying I'm dreaming all of this?"

The doctor slid his hands into the pockets of his white coat. "No, you're awake and aware. I'm not certain why your brain is firing these neurons. Perhaps more observation is needed."

On the verge of disclosing her theory, she clamped her teeth and forced her thoughts to Tom. His wife would return someday soon, and she'd find herself once again in her empty house with not a soul for a friend. "So, what do I do now?"

"You're feeling fine, so I'll discharge you. I hope Tom is satisfied with my decision." Dr. Mason arched one eyebrow at Tom.

Tom's long, loud sigh confirmed her suspicion: Dr. Mason's diagnosis, or lack of it, was not satisfactory. "At least promise me you'll re-examine her scans and make certain you didn't overlook something."

"I promise. And if her condition doesn't improve or worsens with time, I'll conduct another scan." Dr. Mason extended his hand to Tom.

Tom shook the doctor's hand. "Thanks, Gregory. I appreciate this."

"Don't mention it." Dr. Mason extended his hand to Olivia. "Don't beat yourself over this. Take it easy. Even the smallest thing can trigger your memory to return and I hope it does."

If he only knew that her memory never left her. She took his hand and shook it. "I do hope so too, Dr. Mason. Thank you for all your help."

Olivia met Tom in the hallway. Frigid air wrapped around her as soon as she stepped onto the sidewalk. She welcomed the coldness, hoping it would help clear her head.

"I'm parked just over there." Tom pointed to a row of cars in the emergency parking lot.

The sight of her Nissan Quest brought her a sense of home. "Where's your car?"

"I cabbed to Dr. Law's office and drove your van." He took her hand. "You must be hungry. Have you eaten at all today?"

She pressed her hand on her growling stomach. "Now that you mention it, I'm starving."

"I've a nice stew simmering in the slow cooker." He opened the door for her then shut it after she took her seat.

When he slid behind the wheel, his nubuck coat creaked. "Let's go home. The babysitter has an early class tomorrow."

Wow! He'd thought of everything. In all this craziness, she'd forgotten about the kids. She studied his aquiline profile in the fading light of the short wintry day. She was getting used to him looking after her. When his real wife returned and she got pulled back to her ordinary world, it would be so hard to go on day after day without him.

Perhaps it would be better if she never disclosed her theory to him, or helped him solve the attempted murder case. She could stay in his world forever.

No, it wouldn't be fair. This sweet man deserved to have his wife back and his children needed their mother. That was something she could never be.

With a hard swallow, she clamped down a sudden desire to play his wife. "Tom, I think I know the source of this confusion."

CHAPTER 6

The crawl of evening rush hour traffic along Young Street put Tom's patience to a severe test, but getting angry at the gridlock wouldn't open the road ahead of him. Fresh snow crunched beneath the tires while his foot pressed down on the brake pedal. His Nissan Quest stopped behind a long line of red taillights at the intersection illuminated by street lights and shop windows. Heat poured from the car's vents, his hands warmed up enough to remove his gloves.

Dancing snowflakes flickered in the headlights, reminding him of gold dust in a fairy tale he read to Milo every night before bed. The memory calmed his thumping fingers on the steering wheel.

He turned to Olivia and his chest clenched. Her reflection on the tinted passenger's window showed she raked her fingers through her hair. She sat stiff spined, her brow furrowed. He gave her shoulder a gentle squeeze and gained her attention. "Don't be afraid to say what's on your mind. Gregory said the smallest thing can be important. If you have any theory about your memory loss, please tell me."

She licked her lips, leaving behind a trail of glistening moisture. "I may sound crazy. I haven't thought this through. But let me wing it, no matter how farfetched, okay?"

Tom cupped her chin. She closed her eyes at his finger stroking her cheek. "You won't sound crazy."

Her grey eyes shone like the slivers of moon when she opened them again. "Do you believe in the alternate life theory?"

His grip on her chin tightened. This was the last thing he expected. "You're not talking about the website where one can create some virtual life?"

"No." She lowered his hand, but kept a hold on him. "What I mean is…your wife and I somehow switched places. She lives my life while I'm here in hers."

Tom's stomach flipped and he stared at her. Then he burst into laughter. His first guess about the website seemed less threatening. "You're right. That is farfetched. You can't really believe that."

"I don't know what to believe anymore, but this is all I've got." Her tone turned icy and stern, and she shoved his hand from her lap. He curbed his laughter and reconsidered. Unbelievable as it sounded, her theory somehow made sense.

"I'm sorry, I shouldn't have laughed," he said, straightening and pushing the gas pedal to follow the slow moving traffic ahead before braking again. "But how could an alternate life be possible?"

"I've read many books on the topic and in every single one, there's a higher power moving us helpless humans like chess pieces."

"Honey, I believe the term for those books is fiction." Olivia scowled and looked away, but not before he'd seen the hurt in her eyes. He regretted his words and took her hand. Perhaps he shouldn't have been sarcastic, but he knew his wife and never before had she babbled such nonsense.

"Don't mock me. I'm aware of the fact this may be a crazy talk. What I'm saying is your real wife will return after I fulfill some task or quest I've been sent to do here."

"I'm sorry, but this is hard for me to comprehend. If I've got this right, you're on a quest." The wheels locked as he turned onto their unplowed street. He slammed on the brakes before putting the car right into a snow drift. "Ugh! First snowstorm always catches the city by surprise. They are unprepared and everyone forgets how to drive in these conditions as if winter never happened before." He turned to Olivia, her white knuckles clutching to the seatbelt. "My apology—I wasn't prepared for the hard braking. Go on."

"All I know is some games are meant to be played until the end and I've yet to discover my purpose." She paused, averted her glance to her lap. He placed his hand over hers, stopping her twiddling thumbs. Her nervous gesture was a signal she had more to say. After years of marriage, her gestures were as familiar to him as his own face. He decided patience was his best bet. She needed time to open up to him on her own.

Reluctantly he let go of her hand, pushed the button on the garage clicker and turned the car onto their driveway. Thank God for SUVs. Plows would not clear their side street until the morning and, as usual, block the foot of the driveway. He would shovel it then. "All right, honey. What can I do to help?"

She stared at the garage door gliding up then turned to him. "Since you know everything about me, I think it would be only fair of you to tell me things about yourself."

He parked inside the two-car garage and turned off the engine. The seat leather squeaked beneath him when he leaned back. "Yes, it's only fair. What would you like to know?"

She blinked, meeting his gaze then a soft smile crept to her lips. "At first I thought you may be an immigrant, was I right?"

"Why would you assume that?" He returned her smile.

"Your name, Tomislav Medar. It's unusual, not something I've heard before."

"You're half right. Both my parents are from Croatia and so is my name. My father came here in the early seventies. My mother followed him two years later, with my sister and brother who were six and four years old at the time. I arrived about nine months later."

Olivia's eyes widened as his words sunk in. "You were born nine months after your mom came here."

"Yes. Like our Milo, I was a 'surprise' baby." He rolled a low chuckle. "They didn't plan to have more children, but they hadn't seen each other in over two years. Can you blame them?"

Olivia turned away from him and played with the buttons on the passenger door. "They must love each other very much."

Sadness washed over Tom, making him sigh heavily. "My father passed away eight years ago, on Mother's Day. My family is still healing."

The touch of Olivia's hand on his sent warmth through him. "My father was killed in a car accident over twenty years ago. In a strange way, I'm still trying to get over the grief. Don't know if I ever will."

Tom nodded, hoping she'd change the topic to something lighter.

"You and your wife didn't plan to have children?"

Her question jolted him. *My wife and I?* "We—you and I— planned on having children, only not as soon. But when the doctor confirmed our little stick was right, we were ecstatic. We fell in love with our baby in an instant." He opened the driver's side and put one foot on the concrete garage floor. "Let's talk about this over dinner. Can you smell it?"

She too stepped out of the vehicle. "I haven't had a home-cooked meal in a long time. It smells delicious. I'm starving."

Before he reached the garage side door leading into the house, she stopped him. "Where did we meet?"

One hand on the doorknob, he smiled at the fond memory. "In the campus library, by the entrance there was a huge photocopier. You came in and scanned the room as if searching for someone. When I saw you, I said something like, 'How can a man concentrate with so many girls around? What a gorgeous girl.'"

A grin lit her pretty face. "That was you?"

Tom gasped and hope kindled in him. "You remember?"

"I remember someone said those words, but that was it. I never dated the guy or knew who said it. Until now."

"You gave me the dirtiest look ever and left. I ran after you and we had a coffee in the cafeteria."

"See? In my life I walked away. Our stories differ. I am not your wife, but I'll pretend to be until this is over."

At his sigh of exasperation, she pursed her lips. How he yearned to kiss them. Her soft yet eager lips pressed against his throat and trailing down his chest during their last lovemaking, flashed in his memory. He wrapped her in his embrace and pulled her to him. "I don't want you to pretend."

His lips crushed hers and she welcomed him with her warmth and a soft moan, leaning into him. Her hungry kiss reminded him of their first date when he'd taught her the difference between lust and love. He pulled away, and judging by her pouty lips and closed eyes, he left her wanting more. "Why are we standing here in the freezing garage? Let's go in."

He opened the door, letting the aroma of the tarragon and sweet onion he used in the stew linger in the air and make his mouth water. Sounds of cartoons coming from the television set mixed with the piercing noises of Milo's toys.

Olivia unzipped her long coat. "Don't you think it's ironic?"

He narrowed his gaze. Uh-oh, would her story differ from his again? "What is?"

"Couples usually meet on single's cruise or at weddings, and you and me next to the Xerox machine."

Her comment brought relief to his mind and a smile to his lips. "Not ironic at all. After two years of dating and five years of marriage, we still love each other. That's what's important, not where we met."

He opened the double French doors and stepped into the living room.

Jason halted, holding his red light-saber in mid-air. Pivoting, the babysitter pulled his Darth Vader mask off his face. "Your Mommy and Daddy are home."

Lights on Milo's blue saber went out and the toy ceased making battle noises. His plastic Jedi cape swished around him as he ran to them. "Mommy, Daddy, I had fun with Jason. He knows how to play Star Wars."

"I can see that, but you'll have to continue playing Jedi some other day," Tom said, picking his son up. He smiled at the two babies in the playpen. Jason's girl must've had a growth spurt. "Looks like Rosie and Yasmin are having a ball, chewing on their teething toys, but they need to go to bed and your bedtime is soon, too. Say goodbye to Darth and Yasmin, you'll see them soon."

"Oh my God." Olivia stepped in front of Jason, creasing her forehead. "Aren't you the rebellious teenager two doors down?"

Jason's thin lips twitched in an awkward smile and his cheeks reddened. "Not rebellious since I've become a daddy. Life taught me a lesson."

She kept inspecting his face. "But you're only fifteen years old."

Bafflement reflected in the young man's expression as he frowned, but a proud smile replaced his scowl. "I'm almost twenty one and will be graduating high school. Yeah, I'm behind, but if it weren't for you and Tom, who knows where I'd be. Messed up on drugs, more than likely I'd be lost in the system." Concern filled his features as his eyebrows drew closer. "Are you all right, Olivia?"

Her breath sped and she darted her glance from Jason to Tom. "The time must've shifted when I was transported here. What year is this?"

"It's two thousand and thirteen." The words dragged out of Jason's mouth. "Are you sure you're fine?"

Tom handed money to Jason and ushered him out of the living room, puzzlement clearly written on the young man's face. "She's fine, just a bit confused."

For the first time, he doubted his own words and her theory of switching places with his real wife seemed best explanation.

"Mr. Medar, you overpaid me again." Jason's voice broke Tom's moment of doom.

Tom raised his hands and shook his head at Jason's fingers holding a twenty dollar bill. "It's quite all right. You've earned it coming here on such a short notice."

"Thanks, Mr. Medar." After pocketing the money, Jason took his jacket and Yasmin's bundle bag out of the coat closet. "We'll be off now."

Tom set the dining table while Jason got his daughter ready. Not that he needed to remind Jason of the court's order and the condition under which he was granted custody of his baby, but as his attorney, he was there to enforce it. "Stay in school and keep up your grades."

"Of course, Mr. Medar." Jason ruffled Milo's hair. "I had fun with the kids, good night." He then turned to Olivia. "Good night, Olivia. Hope you feel better."

She nodded, her stare fixed at the plain wall.

Tom placed a soft kiss on her temple. "Let's eat like a family." He turned to Milo. "Son, put your toys away, it's dinner time."

"I know him as this kid in black clothes, his face buried in the deep hood of his sweatshirt, and he never looks people in the eye." Olivia nodded toward the door of the living room Jason had left through. "What made him snap out of it?"

"His girlfriend wanted to put their baby up for adoption. He wanted to keep it. His parents employed me as his legal counselor. It wasn't easy, but I convinced the judge and got Jason into rehab. He's come a long way." Tom rubbed his palms, scanning the set table. Right, food could be served. "I'll be back in a minute." He stepped into the spacious kitchen, warmed up the jar of homemade puréed baby food and poured some in the bowl. Under the circumstances, asking Olivia to prepare a meal for Rosie might be too much.

"Hope everyone's hungry," he announced, placing the filled plates on the table. When he picked Rosie up from her playpen, he couldn't help it but blow a raspberry on her little exposed belly. His baby girl giggled, which enticed him to repeat the action.

He placed Rosie in her highchair at the table and caught Olivia's grin. His heart warmed. "You enjoyed watching that display?"

She covered her mouth with a napkin and stifled a chuckle. "I did. Usually if I saw parents do that in public it would disgust me." She leaned closer and dropped her voice to a whisper. "This life must be growing on me."

Milo stepped to her and tugged her elbow. She turned to him. He held a drawing in front of her face. "I made this for you to make you feel better. Do you like it?"

"I—" She took the picture of four stick figures in her hands and her eyebrows rose, then cast a pleading look to Tom.

He sat next to Olivia. "Mommy loves it. Why don't you tell her all about it?"

Milo didn't need further encouragement. He slapped the paper on the table and wiggled his way onto Olivia's lap. "This is Daddy and you and me and this here is Rosie in her stroller…"

Tom chuckled and scooped a spoonful of blended food, feeding it to Rosie. The baby polished off her bowl by the time her chatty brother finished describing his picture.

The initial, uncomfortable expression on Olivia's face had changed to amusement. She wrapped her arm around Milo and said, "Very creative."

Tom patted Milo's chair. "Eat now. Your dinner is getting cold."

The boy kissed Olivia's cheek before sliding into his seat. She smiled and smoothed his hair.

Holding a bottle of red wine over her glass, Tom paused. "Hmm, Gregory didn't mention if your condition would worsen with the consumption of alcohol."

She raised her glass toward the bottle. "Please pour, I could use it."

Tom smiled and tilted the bottle until red liquid filled her glass. "One drink at dinner won't hurt."

Dinner continued with its usual pace and Milo's ceaseless chatting, trying to engage Olivia in a knock-knock joke she didn't quite get, but chuckled all the same.

Tom stacked her empty bowl with his. "I'm glad you liked my stew."

With a sigh, Olivia leaned back in her chair and patted her stomach. "Do you always eat such rich dinners? I meant to hit the gym later but in all of this craziness, I forgot."

"You work out in the mornings. There's a rec room in the basement." Tom carried a stack of dirty dishes to the sink.

Olivia's hurried steps followed him across tiled floor. "I'll take care of the kitchen if you put the kids to bed."

He surveyed the counters. Baby food splattered the front and inside of the microwave. A block of parmesan cheese rested on the grater. Dirty pots and pans waited in the sink. Clean dishes needed to be unloaded from the dishwasher.

"Putting them to bed was always your duty. I come in later for a goodnight kiss and read a story to Milo. But if you're not up to it tonight, you can clean this mess." He should feel guilty for not doing the cleaning, but by offering to help, Olivia showed interest in being a part of the family and he didn't want to stop her.

Half an hour later, Tom tiptoed out of Milo's room, relieved his son had not complained much about his dad putting him to bed. Tom smiled at his sleeping child and pulled the door half closed.

Rubbing the back of his neck, he treaded across the carpeted stairs toward his study. It had been quite a day and fatigue crept over him, but he needed to go over his opening statement one more time. He peered through the glass door. A dim light above the stove illuminated a now clean kitchen. The way Olivia liked it. The still and quiet house suited his racing mind. Olivia must have retired, too.

He continued to the den, doubling as his home office. At the pull of the string on the desk lamp, soft light washed the small room. Plopping himself on the black leather couch, he raised the stack of papers to his face, but couldn't concentrate on the task at hand.

Olivia's alternative life theory wouldn't leave him. Her appearance was the same. And so was her sexy aura and her poise. The door to his study opened and he snapped his gaze from the blurry words on the page. Olivia stood in the doorframe. Her sheer nightie clung to her like a second skin. In an instant, he hardened.

She approached with slow steps, a mischievous smile gracing her lips and unmistakable hunger in her eyes. She straddled him and slid the papers from his hands. "This can wait."

Need reflected in her sultry voice as well as her kiss.

"I want you, Tom." She locked her lips with his, her tongue working magic on him.

Powerless to her passion, Tom welcomed her advances, but his mind screamed at him to stop her from coming on too strong. It was easy to shed the clothes and have sex. Hell, he'd done it in the past. Hadn't he taught her that opening her heart and soul to him meant being truly naked? He'd accept nothing less than love. With great difficulty, he cupped her head and pushed her back. Her lips were red and puffy from hard kissing. Confusion flashed in her glossy eyes and her breath caught.

"Are you still pretending to be my wife?"

She sat straight and frowned, then shrugged. "I guess."

Her nonchalant tone was like a cold shower and he sat up, too, dislodging her from his lap. "Go to bed, Olivia. I've got lots of work to do."

"What's wrong? You gave me such a wonderful kiss in the garage. I couldn't get it off my mind. I thought this is what you wanted." She wrapped her arms around her chest, hiding her erect nipples from his view.

Tom stood up and rubbed his hands over her bare arms. "I do, only I prefer love over lust. I refused you for the same reason the very first time in the university."

Her face crumpled and Olivia turned away from him.

He cupped her chin and forced her to look him in the eye. Confusion etched in her expression and she seemed embarrassed by her actions. For the first time, a sense of loss pressed on his shoulders. Had he truly lost his wife? Yes, he desired Olivia in his arms, but carnal pleasure would never be enough for him. He wanted more. "Don't feel ashamed. I promise you, I'll make you burn for me long before you have me."

CHAPTER 7

Tom's arm wrapped around Olivia's waist and her breasts pressed against his rock hard chest, but cold shivers raked her spine all the same. His words rang in her mind. *He'd make her burn for him.* Though his whisper stirred butterflies in her stomach, she tensed and she couldn't shake off the feeling he'd meant it as her punishment for coming on too strong. Could he be one of those guys who liked his woman submissive? If so, she would welcome the change in the bedroom. The guys she'd slept with in the past had proved to be all words, but when it came to action, they were spineless or had some weird fetish. Tom struck her as a man who would work her up and take care of *her* needs before he found satisfaction. Maybe she would finally get to live up her fantasies. Was it too much to ask for a man who would be bold enough to take her and have his way with her?

The mere thought set her skin tingling and coaxed a moan from her. She looped her arms around his neck. "What exactly do you have in mind?"

"Let me give you a small demonstration." Cradling her head in his hand, his lips seized hers while his tongue ignited fireworks.

She rubbed her hips on his. He must've been joking when he'd uttered his threat. His hardness pushed against her. She arched as ecstasy tightened her abdomen. Tom's embrace was balm on her lonely soul. Nibbling her lower lip, he eased the kiss. She moved her lips to his cheek, getting tickled by the stubble. "If this is punishment, bring it on."

He pulled back, unhooked her arms and swiped his hand across his lips and cheek. "Good night, Olivia." His husky whisper didn't quite match his fierce expression.

She shook her head and huffed. How she wanted to bury her hands in his warm brown hair and explore his tantalizing body. Instead, she slid one finger down the sky blue material on his chest. "Come on, Tom. You wouldn't leave me like this."

Fire burned in his honey brown eyes, but his predatory look faded. He placed an arm around her shoulders and ushered her from the office.

"Those were your exact words on our first date. Seems we'll both be reliving that night." His voice strained as if he were fighting his desire.

Her hopes rose when he cupped her cheeks in his hands and placed a gentle kiss on her forehead. "Sweet dreams."

He closed the door, leaving her gaping in the dim hallway. The nightlight cast long shadows over the walls. Every nerve in her body clamored for his touch. Not counting the neighbor with a strange obsession with married women, this had to be the first time a man refused her. How dare he deny her what she craved? *Her*, a god's gift to men. Yeah, she could seduce any straight guy and there were plenty of fish in the sea.

But she wanted *him*.

She banged on the door. "Damn you, Tom."

Muffled male chuckles sounded through the thin wood. Lips pressed and fist in the air, Olivia was prepared to pound harder. When had she become so needy? Defeated, she lowered her hand and dragged her feet back to her room. Her fury dissipated with every step. There was a time for everything and if tonight wasn't the night she'd spend in Tom's arms, the day would come. If the "little demonstration" he'd given her was an indication of the kind of pleasure she would experience, she'd wait an eternity.

She paced the floor. Carpet fibers at the foot of the bed soothed her soles. A strange nagging deep in her guts warned her perhaps she'd crossed some invisible boundary. In all honesty, she should get to know him better before jumping in bed with him. Although to *really* know a man before getting physical with him rated low on her priority list, and in the past she never bothered to find out more than basic info about her dates. Understandable. By the next morning, she never wanted to see them again. Instead of whining about it, why not treat men like dirt?

Fine, so she never won a popularity contest and along the way lost all her friends. She snorted. Some amigas they proved to be, tweeting nasty things about her, calling her a boyfriend snatcher. So she'd done what they accused her of and proved their boyfriends used them as a way to meet Olivia and get into her pants. For some, beauty was a curse. But Tom seemed to awaken something in her she'd never experienced before and for the first time she sought commitment.

With a long sigh, she stopped in front of the window. A white blanket covered the quiet street. The wind had eased, but the snow continued. The flakes in the lamplight glistened, appearing motionless. The fresh tire tracks on the road were disappearing beneath the new layer. Fuzziness filled her chest. If Tom's wife didn't return by Christmas, she would spend holidays with her little family instead of alone and bitter. Who knew the domestic bliss, the dynamics of the busy, chatty dinner around dining room table could beat eating takeout while watching the news in an easy chair? She'd have to stall finding her purpose in this life so Tom's real wife wouldn't return.

The glass fogged as she blew out her breath of frustration. This illusion would cease to exist. Could she escape the inevitability? The blinds closed at her twist of the rod.

She sat on the low stool in front of the vanity table that doubled as her desk. What had Tom said? He was of Croatian descent. Geography hadn't been her favorite subject throughout school. The black screen of her laptop came to life at the tap of her finger on the mouse. The cursor flashed inside the search box of the web browser. Unsure what she'd find, she typed Croatia. The small geographic map in the corner of the screen and the short description beneath placed it as the country at the crossroads of Central Europe, The Balkans and Mediterranean. Next, the link to "Lonely Planet" drew her attention. At the click of the mouse, the page loaded. The first paragraph read:

"Croatia's rare blend of glamour and old-fashioned authenticity make this Europe's 'it' destination, where beaches and sunshine vie for attention with cultural treasures, ancient architecture and time-tested folk traditions."

"Interesting," she murmured, clicking on the picture gallery. Clear blue water beckoned. The gorgeous towns encased in their original medieval protective walls and cloudless skies were a welcomed contrast to overcast asphalt jungle of Toronto.

Browsing through the pictures took her mind off the earlier embarrassment of Tom's rejection, but as she bookmarked the page and closed it, her thoughts returned to him. Heat pooled in her core. The man knew how to use his tongue. Would he take her to those pristine and secluded beaches where they could make love away from civilization? She shook her head to free her mind, dispelling the image of their naked bodies entwined, spread over a beach towel.

It seemed selfish of her to think only of her own needs. They had two kids and she was sure they would love to enjoy the warmth and swim in the sea.

A yawn escaped. It was getting late. She should try to get some rest. The duvet rustled while she shifted, trying to find a comfortable position. Her body refused to settle, but as her mind drifted to the place where azure water hugged the pebbled shore and Tom's wet body covered hers, her eyes drooped. *Tomorrow I'll ask him to take me to the enchanted land.*

She fell into a shallow doze, opening her eyes from time to time only to find the bedroom's furniture shrouded in a veil of darkness, not Tom as she hoped. Slipping into a deeper sleep, she floated on the gentle blue water, adrift on a vast sea. Tom appeared and she was lost in his eyes, then his lips pressed to hers.

She reached out to him and fell over the side of the bed, her body landing hard on the wood planks of the floor. Free of the bedding, cold air slid over her, adding to the rude awakening. The darkness had been replaced by a new day.

The smell of coffee wafted in the air and she sprang to her feet, focusing on the nightstand's clock. Ten minutes to seven. Tom was up. The kids would still be asleep. Now would be a perfect time for a talk. Taking off her nightie, she opened the closet. She had to admit, the feminine clothes in her wardrobe were way more fun than her dark designer suits. Fuchsia track pants and a soft pink top replaced her lacy outfit.

She hurried through her morning routine and left the bedroom. Tom sat at the table, slouched over a sheet of paper, tuned to his writing. His aftershave drifted to her and her breath caught at the sight of his toned body under the tight muscle shirt.

The pen in his hand stopped moving. He looked up at her and offered a warm grin. "Good morning, honey. Did you sleep well?"

"Like a baby. How about you?" She hoped redness wouldn't spread over her cheeks with her lie.

"Babies wake every two hours." He stood and gestured for her to sit next to him. "Coffee?"

"Yes, please." The words rushed out in an exhausted plea. She plopped on the kitchen chair and leaned her elbows on the table.

"I dreamt about you." Tom's voice held more than a tinge of desire as he set her favorite coffee mug in front of her.

He stepped behind her to caress her shoulders and her self-control shattered. She melted under his magic fingers. They worked up her neck, cradling and tilting her head back. Her gaze met his.

She licked her lips to hide her trembling breath. "Funny you should mention it. I dreamt about you, too."

"Hmm, good dream I hope." He arched a brow. His finger circled her lips.

"Tom, how long are you planning to carry on this punishment?"

"For as long as I see fit." His voice dropped to a husky tone.

She pushed her knees tight together. Naughty thoughts flooded her mind. "Wouldn't it be easier if you just spanked me and I promised to be a good girl?"

He brushed the hair off her shoulder and whispered in her ear. "Haven't done any spanking in a while, but I may still."

This time she couldn't suppress her gasp. Powerful arousal rushed heat from her core all over her body. She yanked her head free from his hold. "If you're not going to carry it out now, please stop this teasing."

To her relief, he returned to the chair where his mug and paper waited. He exhaled. A wicked grin on his face carried a certain promise. "One of these days. Maybe."

She studied him. If the deep lines on his forehead and stiff posture were indication, he must be suffering as much as her. Strange as it seemed, his delay of taking her to bed incited her lust more. Bringing the coffee to her lips, she blew on the steam and took a sip. Perfect as always. Her hunch proved right. He was dominant in the bedroom and this teasing must be some unspoken rules he had for his wife. A deeper desire stirred in her loins.

Best to change the subject. "Tell me more about yourself. Where did you learn to cook?"

"My mom." He lifted his pen and stared at her. "She still cooks enough to feed a small country."

"Does she live nearby?" Olivia savored another sip. Would a mother-in-law see right through her?

He curled his hand around his mug and sighed. "No, she's in Croatia. She took Dad's body to be buried there." A smile tugged on his lips, as if he were remembering some distant time. "She wanted to be able to put fresh flowers on his grave. Living there is healthier for her. The winters here were hard on her. She was afraid of slipping and falling on ice and wouldn't leave the house. Each year she'd put on more and more weight."

Her shoulders slumped. "My mom paraded the funeral home in her designer suit for Dad's service. I'll never forget her ridiculous, pretentious mask of sorrow under the netting of her wide brimmed hat. Mom insisted on sending Tadem to the institution for infirm. Dad fought her, but Mom did most of the yelling. He slammed the door. Early next morning, police came knocking to tell us there'd been an accident."

Tom gave a sympathetic smile and rubbed her arm. "Honey, some things can't be changed no matter how much we want them to."

"You're right. My mother can't be changed." She admired his family's togetherness, and envied it too, more than just a little. "What about the rest of your family?"

"After Dad passed away, my sister suffered a nervous breakdown. Her loser boyfriend dumped her after he drained her bank account. The guy always needed bailing out. My brother and I refused to give him a penny. Six years of stringing Mariana along, she couldn't see he had no intentions of happily ever after. Instead, he took off skydiving in Australia."

"What an asshole. I hope she's better now."

"Yes, our brother, Ante, resigned from the police force and took her home. She reconnected with her old boyfriend. They're getting married this summer." Head resting on his knuckles, he raked his glance over her. "So full of questions early in the morning. What else you'd like to know?"

"Did you always want to be a lawyer?"

He raised his head once more and Olivia caught the sadness in his eyes. "In third grade I bugged my parents to throw me a birthday party. With three kids and only my dad working, money was always tight, but they got me a bouncy castle and I invited all the kids from my class." He paused, averting his glance as if growing up poor were a cause for shame. Then he seemed to regain his proud stance and continued. "When the time came to sing the birthday song, one of the mothers started to yell at my mom, accusing her of attempted murder. Her boy had a severe nut allergy and the cake my mom baked was decorated with ground walnuts. This woman scooped her kid away and others pulled theirs before I could blow out the candles. All of them called my parents stupid immigrants and threatened legal actions."

Tom swallowed. "My mom was in tears. We had never heard of nut allergies. My dad gathered us around the table and we continued the celebration as we had for years. Just us, the family." A proud grin lit his face, replacing the sadness in his eyes. "That day I vowed to my mom I'd fight for the rights of the misunderstood and poorly treated because they didn't know the customs or couldn't speak the language enough to defend themselves."

Olivia returned his smile though doubt surfaced within her. Last time she checked, one man alone couldn't change the world. "At least you had birthday parties. My mom had money, but would not spend any on frivolous things like a birthday party for her daughter." She kept turning the mug in her hands, contemplating how to steer the conversation to Croatia. "Have you ever been to your parents' homeland?"

"Of course. Every summer mom would take us and when we got older we'd travel alone and stay with Grandma on the island." Laughter shook his shoulders and he had to set the cup down. "Our dear *Nana* Rokica was a classic. The things she used to say, ah…" He ended his chuckle with a long sigh. "They don't make them like her anymore."

Tom's laughter was infectious. Unable to resist, Olivia joined in, not quite sure what she was chuckling at. But it didn't matter. She couldn't remember the last time she had a full-blown laugh. "When was the last time you've been there?"

"Not since Dad's funeral." His voice sounded nostalgic and regretful, but a grin spread his lips. "We can't miss Mariana's wedding. You're a bridesmaid, I'm one of the groomsmen and Milo is ring boy."

Joy surged through her and she had to plant her feet on the kitchen's tile to stay seated, but couldn't hide excitement from her shrieking voice. "We're going?"

"Yes, but first we agreed to fly to Vancouver and spend this Christmas with Tadem. We want to see how Rosie will take being on a plane."

Nervous butterflies rose in Olivia's stomach. She hadn't seen her sister in over two decades. The image of Tadem's confused face lingered in Olivia's mind. Had she understood what their mother had done to her? Mother had lied when she'd promised Tadem that Olivia would go too. Her sister had obeyed the people in white coats and sat in the car. But when Olivia remained standing on the sidewalk, Tadem had broken into her rage. Tears burned Olivia's eyes, just like that dreadful day, only then she wasn't ashamed to shed them.

Tom picked up his pen and jotted a few more words on the page. The pen poised over the sheet while he tapped his finger, turning his head from side to side as if he were trying to look for some details in the kitchen.

"Are you working on your court case?"

He shook his head, his eyes filled with mischievous sparkle. "I'm compiling a list, mostly Rosie's schedule."

"Why?" She leaned closer, a distinct feeling this had something to do with her.

"I can't always be here. Tomorrow, I'll be gone all day in court. I trust you'd be able to take care of the kids?"

Her last sip of coffee went down the wrong pipe and she pounded on her chest, coughing.

CHAPTER 8

Olivia stared at the smiling face of a sunflower plush toy hanging from the highchair tucked in the corner of the spacious kitchen as she tried to re-catch her breath. Tom patted her between her shoulder blades.

He ceased tapping her back, stepped to the sink and filled the glass from the reverse osmosis tap.

"Drink some, it'll clear your throat." He handed her the water.

She nodded, taking the glass in her hand. A gulp of cold liquid quenched her parched windpipe. "For a moment…" she wheezed. "I thought I heard you saying I'm staying home alone with the kids all day tomorrow."

His gentle squeeze on her shoulder failed to boost her with encouragement. With his hand sliding down her arm, stopping at her elbow, his eyes narrowed while he studied her for a moment. "You heard me right."

At his confirmation, her stomach muscles tightened and she bit her lower lip to hide her trembling. She'd never spent a single second alone with a child, let alone taken care of one. Well not entirely true, she had played with her sister for a few rare moments when Mother had allowed. But playing with Tadem decades ago hardly made her a qualified babysitter.

"I…I can't do this." Olivia shook her head.

He pulled the seat closer, the chair's legs scraping across the floor tile. "Honey, only the judge can change the court date. It's been scheduled and confirmed for months."

"Can't you get someone to babysit?" Anxiety constricted her throat, changing her tone to a high-pitched shriek.

His eyebrows drew closer and he shrugged. "Who?"

Slouched over the table, she tapped her finger on the glass in her hand. Tom had said all his family moved to Croatia. Her mother was spending the winter someplace warm and sunny, and besides, if she was here she'd be useless. Olivia straightened.

"What about the young dad who was here last night?"

"Jason?" He scowled. "He has school all day and he better not skip a single class."

She huffed, resenting Tom's concern for a former neighborhood hoodlum. "You're not his dad. Why do you care?"

Tom's hard stare sent shivers rushing down her back. She must've said something he wouldn't expect to hear from his wife.

"I do because his dad doesn't. Jason's father is a provider. It is easier to fork out money to get his son out of his hair than to deal with his problems. I'm under an oath to make sure the young man follows the court orders or he'll lose his child."

She took another sip of water. Caring was a new concept to her, something she'd have to warm up to. "I can relate to an absent parent. At least his father didn't send him away to a boarding school, like me. I was never rebellious nor have I ever experimented with drugs."

She had stayed invisible, always pushed to the back of the room. Until her body had bloomed, then men had flocked to her like pigeons to breadcrumbs. For the first time, she'd enjoyed being the center of attention and the envy of all the girls in her school.

"There's no one but you." Tom wrapped his fingers around her wrist and yanked her back into the present. "I'll put Milo on the school bus in the morning and prepare Rosie's bottles with formula and her pureed food. All you'll have to do is pop them in the microwave for a few seconds."

"Milo's in school all day?" A hint of relief loosened the knot in her stomach, but a strange sense of loss spread through her. She would miss the little boy and his incessant chatting, but she was sure baby would occupy her time.

"Until four in the afternoon. His school bus stops by the mailbox. You'll have to be there or the driver won't let him leave. Should you run late, the bus loops around the neighborhood and passes by our house again about ten minutes later. It'll stop on the other side of the street."

Olivia contemplated. Could she take this on? She must. Something deep inside nagged her to be a perfect mom and accept Tom's children. Tomorrow would be her ultimate test. After all she'd agreed to play his wife. "Got it, four o'clock."

His chest expanded with a rush of air. Had he been afraid to breathe before she agreed? "I'll set the alarm for four o'clock. The loud and annoying one in Rosie's room we never use. There's no way you won't hear it," he offered.

Her thoughts wandered to the spare room Tom called a nursery. She had not ventured there yet, but in her previous life, she stored old stuff there. Another thought occurred and she winced. "What about changing Rosie's nappy things?"

He rewarded her with another of his mocking stares, coaxing a tight-lipped smile from her. "Honey, you taught me how to do it, so I'm sure it will come back to you."

If luck were with her, changing time wouldn't come. *Get real. Babies use nappies instead of the toilet.* "You're still mistaking me for your wife."

His exasperated exhale cut through tense silence. Though he remained quiet, the deep crease on his forehead indicated her apparent memory loss still concerned him. The thought of being his wife forever no longer surprised her, but she couldn't and mustn't start believing in a delusion that could disappear into a thin air at any moment.

"Rosie sleeps until ten in the morning," Tom continued, ignoring her previous remark. "When she gets hungry, she'll chew on things. The times on her schedule are guidelines. She can have her lunch earlier or later, same with her nap. Watch for her signs.

If she's tired she'll rub her eyes and turn cranky. Put her in her crib, she'll coo to her dollies. If she fusses, let her cry. That's how she settles down."

Tom secured the list to the fridge with magnets. Then he turned to her and pointed at a highlight on the paper. "If in doubt, refer to this list. She also loves Baby Einstein DVDs. Don't forget to pick up Milo. If there's no one waiting, the driver will take him back to school."

"I won't forget. The mailbox is right across the street." Her voice rose in annoyance. She performed complex tasks every day at work without being told twice, and getting a child from the bus stop wasn't rocket science.

"Not that one, the second mailbox down the street. Our neighbor Roy will be there getting his mail. So you'll know you're at the right place."

Puzzled for a moment, she picked up her now cold coffee mug, brought the rim to her lips, and set it back down. "How do you know he'll be there?"

"He'll be there, alright." Tom placed his hand over his heart as if giving his pledge to the Queen of England and deepened his voice. "It's his duty to rescue neglected, frustrated moms from the clutches of rotten marriages."

"He sounds just like that." Olivia's frown soon dissolved into chuckles. "I see Roy's act hasn't changed." And to think she'd found him attractive just because he resembled Johnny Depp. Tom must never find out about her crush on Roy. Now it seemed her infatuation was only due to Roy's indifference.

"You'll be fine tomorrow. It'll be easy-peasy." Tom cupped her face in his hands and brushed his lips over hers, his warm breath soft and assuring. The small gesture sent tremors to her knees.

His remark coaxed another chuckle. She wouldn't expect a lawyer to use such childish slang. "Easy-peasy?"

"I learned that one from Milo." Embracing her, he pulled her to his chest. She melted into him, inhaling his scent, reveling in every second. A danger she must not allow to happen. For all she knew he could disappear from her life any moment, the same way he'd appeared, and she'd be left alone.

"I'll call you as soon as the court is out for recess. Once the trial starts, you can text me, but I won't be able to reply right away."

"I'll be fine," she mumbled, but her words and his encouragement still failed to convince her. For the first time, it occurred to her she might fall in love with this sexy, fatherly man, only to lose him when the universe whisked her back to her real life. The idea of losing him without even saying goodbye—it made her intestines coil like cold snakes.

• • •

As every morning since her small family had appeared, Clivia awakened to the smell of freshly brewed coffee. Only today Tom brought the cup to her bed. She smiled and sat up against the cushions.

"Good morning, beautiful." He handed her the beverage and leaned closer to place a kiss on her lips.

A chuckle escaped her. Beautiful? First thing in the morning? Her hair alone must resemble a bird's nest. She set the mug on the night stand and ran fingers through the tangles.

Tom pulled a light blue shirt from his wardrobe then turned to her, holding a necktie against the fabric. "Do these go together?"

The blue letters on the face of the tie made her sit on her haunches and reach out. "What a work of art. What kind of writing is this?"

"Glagolitic." Tom scrambled into his shirt sleeves. A desire to fasten his buttons swept through her and she couldn't stop her fingers. His hands dropped to his sides and he whispered against her ear. "The alphabet was invented in eight hundred sixty-five AD and used in writing Old Church Slavic languages. Later it was replaced by Cyrillic."

God, the man could give an entire lecture on any topic and she'd never tire of listening to his sexy voice. She met his intense gaze, pursed her lips while her fingers tinkered with his bottom button. "Fascinating. Tell me more."

"*À la manière des Croates.*" He cupped her buttocks and pulled her closer. Their lips met in a frantic kiss. Olivia's pulse quickened. He leaned over her and she collapsed on the bed, his body covering hers.

"Ah, yes, Tom, show me the Croatian way," she whimpered, spreading her legs wide and stretching her arms over her head. He let out a deep grunt and trailed his tongue down her neck, raising goose bumps on her skin. At the sound of the door slamming, he halted and propped himself on his elbows.

He panted for a short moment and to her dismay, stood up. "Milo could come in any moment. But to continue, I was referring to the way Croatian hussars tied scarves, called cravats, around their neck during the European Thirty Years War. It appealed to the French and King Louis XIV. They adopted it into their fashion, hence the tie."

Blowing out a breath of frustration, she punched the mattress. The bedding rustled as she got up. In two steps she closed the distance to the full length mirror where he worked the knot on his tie. She wrapped her arms around his waist and pressed her front to his back. "I loved the history tidbit, but after you put Milo on the bus maybe you can demonstrate untying it and removing your shirt, pants—"

"Honey, I have to go." He turned and tapped the tip of her nose. "And there's something you're forgetting."

She shrugged, shaking her head. Must he remind her again? "I'm looking after the kids."

"No. There's something we say to one another before we make love." He pressed another quick kiss to her lips.

The door to the bedroom popped open. Their moment was gone.

"I'm dressed." The boy grinned.

Tom chuckled, crouched in front of his son. "Your pants are undone—wouldn't want to lose them, would you?"

Some unexplainable urge forced her to do up Milo's pants. She reached out to him, but Tom's stern voice stopped her.

"He must be able to do up his pants in school without anyone's help."

She stepped back. Tom was strict with his boy, but she supposed by doing everything for the child, never allowing him to make mistakes and learn, Milo would not be prepared for the world out there. At least that had been Mom's excuse for not helping her with anything.

"Oh." Milo flashed a row of small teeth in a shy smile, snapped the rivet and pulled up the zipper.

She gazed into the boy's proud eyes and clapped her hands. "Good work, Milo."

"Better." Tom placed his hand on the small boy's shoulder. "Let's get you into your snow suit and boots."

"Are you coming, Mommy?" Milo's sweet innocence squeezed Olivia's chest. The boy never doubted she was his mom. He'd accepted her from the beginning.

"I'll be down in a moment, love." Surprised at her endearment, she scurried to the bathroom. After running a comb through her hair, she changed into a pair of black stretch pants with a silver trim and a matching top and hurried to the foyer.

Bundled up in his black bomber, Tom helped the boy hoist his school bag on his back. Next, he tugged on the thick sleeves of Milo's red snow jacket bunched up under the ruck's straps. "Okay, say goodbye to mommy or you'll miss your bus."

"Bye, Mom." Milo blew her a kiss with his mitten-covered hand.

She pretended to catch his kiss in her hand and pressed her palm over her heart then repeated Milo's gesture. Tom opened the front door, allowing the frigid air to slide inside and wrap around her bare ankles. She shivered and squinted against the sun reflecting off the fresh snow. Too bad the footprints and tire tracks already spoiled the powder.

"I'll head out to my office to get some papers then meet my client at the courthouse. Wish me luck and I know you won't need it. You're a natural." But the melody of Tom's voice brought different memories tumbling. Images of his hard body pinning her to the mattress, the passion of his kisses, the need in his groans, rocked her core in deep trembles. She must find the magic word to Tom's passion.

First there was one small matter pressing on her mind. After he closed the door, Olivia grabbed the phone and dialed her work number. A recording of an unknown female voice said, "You've reached the extension two-five-four at Human Resources Department. I'm away from my desk, but…"

The monotonous voice continued as Olivia slid the phone away from her ear. Someone had replaced her. She punched in the extension for Jess. Her assistant answered on the first ring. "Jess Adams."

"Jess," Olivia hissed. The ringing phones and faxes and hushed voices in the background increased her sense of guilt. She missed her work. "The woman replacing me, what she's like? Good, bad, fabulous?"

"Olivia, you have to stop." Jess's whispered tone indicated Mr. Hiltorn was within hearing distance. "He can't fire you no matter how good the replacement. She's only so-so if you ask me. Got to go."

The phone line went dead. Olivia slumped into a chair. Perhaps a good workout would help her lose some of the stress. Both hands on the clock face above the door pointed at nine. Rosie would be up any minute. A book on child rearing lay on the table. She flipped straight to the page marked with a neon sticky note.

"Diapering technique?" She smiled at the absurdity. "There's a technique to it?"

The descriptions under the illustrations were of little help. This was a hands-on kind of task, not something one could learn by reading about it. She closed the book and glanced at the clock again. Twenty past nine. When would Rosie wake? On cue, cooing came through the baby monitor on the kitchen counter. Olivia's stomach tightened, but she climbed the stairs to the nursery. The baby raised her head and flashed a toothless grin, drool dripping down her chin.

Her first tooth must be cutting through. Olivia gripped the crib's rails, trying to figure out how she knew about baby teeth. Could it be her long-dormant maternal instincts? Since when had she had any? The unbearable urge to embrace the child overwhelmed her. She slid trembling hands under Rosie's shoulders, copying what she'd seen Tom do.

"Come to Mommy." She raised Rosie half way off the mattress before lowering her again. What was she doing? She could be squeezing all air out of her little lungs. No, no she couldn't pick her up. But she must. This was her baby. Why shouldn't she cradle Rosie in her arms?

"Let's try this again." Her hands steadied and she scooped up the infant. Olivia inhaled her daughter's sweet scent, a mixture of powder and milk, and finally understood what women meant by the "baby trap." Yes, she was ensnared, roped and reeled in.

The doorbell rang. She frowned. Who'd come to her house on the working day? Some unwanted solicitor? With Rosie cradled in her arms, she descended the stairs to the foyer. Her eyes widened and her mouth dropped open at the sight of who stood before her.

"Olivia," Susan stepped in, the aroma of fresh brew wafting from two extra-large paper cups on a cardboard tray. "Wow, Gregory was right. Your stunned face says it all. I hope you have something strong to put in this coffee. You'll need it."

Olivia closed the door. Stunned didn't begin to describe the anxious worry churning in her gut. "Should Dr. Mason be disclosing information about his patients?"

"Please. We're friends." Susan waved her gloved hand and set the tray on the corner table. She removed her long coat, the flowery scent of her perfume filling the foyer. "My husband didn't stand a chance. All I had to do was give him one of my truth extracting stares and he sang like a canary."

A smile she couldn't hide hovered on Olivia's lips. "Since when did you acquire one of those stares?"

"Two teenage boys and lots of practice. You'll get one, too. Takes time." Hands clapping, she approached Olivia. "I'll take my girl from you. And you carry the coffee to the living room." She wiggled her fingers at Rosie. "Come see your auntie."

A deep exhale loosened Olivia's chest. Things were patched up with her best friend and all seemed right in her world. She handed Rosie over to Susan and picked up the tray. Susan's dark curls brushed down her slender back as she bounced into the room, baby in her arms.

"You're right. I could use something strong, but it's too early." Placing the tray on the glass top, Olivia pointed to the settee across from the coffee table. The leather hissed as Susan took her seat.

Olivia scurried to the kitchen and pulled out soy milk from the fridge. Returning to the living room, she shook the carton. "I'm afraid I don't have any coffee cream."

Susan glanced over baby's head. "Just black for me. I gave up cream and sugar years ago."

Olivia sat facing Susan. "It's hard to believe you're a mom of two teenage boys and a wife to a neurologist."

Susan settled Rosie on her lap and flashed Olivia a sympathetic smile. "It's hard to understand why you don't remember any of the past six years."

"It's impossible for me to explain and you'd think I'm insane. Believe me, sometimes I feel like I am." Olivia poured a hefty amount of milk into her coffee. Avoiding eye contact with Susan, she stirred then tapped thin stick against her paper cup.

Her friend smiled at Rosie's careful inspection of her wristwatch. "I'm at loss for words, but why dwell on something neither of us can explain? Let's get this girl dressed. I hope she's big enough to wear the adorable Hello Kitty outfit I couldn't resist buying."

"You're right. Let's go upstairs to the nursery." Olivia stood and gripped the back of the chair to steady her wobbling knees. Afraid to bring the subject up, she drew in a sharp breath. "Susan, I…" Olivia licked her lips, trying to dislodge the words jammed in her throat. "My intentions weren't to hurt you when you got back to the dorm."

"Shhhh, why are you bringing it up? We said we wouldn't." Wrapping her arm around Rosie, Susan stood and pressed the baby to her chest. She followed Olivia to the foot of the stairs. "But since you brought it up, I admit I was hurt even though I knew you didn't sleep around. The girls who named you 'boyfriend snatcher' were so wrong."

"I was their scapegoat. They drew a wedge between us. Their venom means nothing now. Your understanding and our friendship is more important."

Olivia grabbed the railing for support. Was it all this love around her causing her shaky legs? She turned to Susan. "Promise you'll remember this conversation."

Susan's mouth opened, and she took a step back. "Why would I forget it?"

Tears burned Olivia's eyes and she swallowed the lump forming in her throat. "I don't belong here and I fear I'll be snatched from this life or…returned to mine without a friend."

"Olivia." Susan wrapped her fingers around her forearm. "You're serious."

"Please, I need you to promise to remember this conversation." A cold feeling knotted her insides. She couldn't be certain anyone from this life would have a single trace of memory about her.

"I promise. This is something I couldn't easily forget." Susan flashed an encouraging smile. "You're not going anywhere, Olivia. Who'd raise your family? Now let's get Rosie dressed."

Susan seemed comfortable changing Rosie and getting those chubby legs and arms into sleeves and leggings. Glad for the temporary reprieve, Olivia paid close attention to her friend's technique.

"Here she is." Susan picked Rosie up from the changing table. "All dressed and nowhere to go. Isn't she cute?"

Olivia reached out to Rosie and Susan passed her over. "Sure would be nice if you could stay until Tom gets back."

"Sorry." Susan sounded apologetic. "I have a session with my personal trainer. At my age and after two kids, it takes a major effort just to keep things where they supposed to be."

"You look fabulous." A hint of envy crept to her voice, despite her efforts to hide it. Her weak knees and lightheadedness eased. Olivia placed a kiss on Rosie's chubby cheek.

Susan tsked, her forehead creased with her frown, and she wrapped her fingers around Olivia's wrist. "It's only been ten months since you gave birth and you look great already. Give it time, your killer body will return."

Hours passed. Susan kept refilling their coffee cups and brewed another pot, even fed Rosie her lunch. Had she forgotten all about her training session? Olivia enjoyed her friend's company and help, and dared not remind her of her appointment. But a question burned on her mind. Would Susan know the password that would open the gate to Tom's heart? Maybe she'd told her in the past. No, the secret was between a husband and wife, not something to disclose even to the best friend.

Susan jumped to her feet, glancing at her watch. "I lost track of time. Gosh, it's one o'clock already."

She passed Rosie to Olivia and scurried for the coat closet. Adjusting the baby on her hip, Olivia followed her friend.

Susan bundled up and kissed Rosie then hugged Olivia. "Hopefully, my trainer can squeeze me in. We'll talk again."

From the front door Olivia waved to Susan while she backed up her Mercedes.

"Goodness," Olivia said, looking at the clock then sat Rosie in her high chair. "It's way past lunch time. Hungry?" The soft blue light inside the fridge reminded her of Tom's shirt. Soon her thoughts drifted to his chest beneath the cloth. Bet right now he was intimidating the plaintiff. She'd love to see him in action, objecting the questions from the opposing side.

Her fingers clenched, itching to feel his pecks flex under her fingertips, but her growling stomach demanded immediate attention.

A Tupperware bowl with last night's leftovers set her mouthwatering. She dished out a portion of stew and warmed the pot on the stove. Tom was right. The spices blended and the smells from the container sent her stomach on a roll of rumbles.

After warming up another portion of pureed baby food, she sat at the table. Rosie turned her head away when Olivia tried to feed her. Maybe her technique wasn't as good as Susan's. Or maybe she wasn't hungry. Baby girl had polished off two bowlfuls of her food just an hour ago.

Olivia placed a rubber toy in front of Rosie and turned to her own plate. She savored her late lunch until the last spoonful. Then she perused a fashion magazine. Every so often, Olivia glanced over the top of the publication at Rosie who cooed and chewed on her teething giraffe. The baby's face turned red, she strained. Olivia jumped to her feet, panic spreading through her. She never had to use her First Aid training she'd taken over a decade ago. Was Rosie choking?

In a next moment Rosie's color changed to normal and she grinned at Olivia, gnawing on her toy. A not-so-innocent baby smell drifted from her vicinity.

Arms askew, Olivia cocked her head. "You didn't?"

Rosie replied with a long coo.

Olivia exhaled in relief. At least it wasn't anything life threatening. Nonetheless, she faced an untried, monumental task. She paced the kitchen floor. Could she do this without gagging? What was wrong with her? In her job, she'd march straight into a boardroom full of executive suits and thrill them with her presentations. One soiled diaper should be easy to handle.

She carried Rosie to the nursery and placed her on the change table. Armed with ample amounts of baby wipes, she unfastened the Velcro straps and pulled off the nappy. She set to the task with surprising calmness. Olivia was proud of her first attempt at diaper change. She'd wished Tom could have seen her in action, patted her on the back for her accomplishment.

To snap the straps of the clean diaper into their place and make sure they weren't too tight proved harder than wiping Rosie's skin clean. "Can you stay still?"

In the next instant, the smile vanished from Rosie's face, replaced by a frown. She broke into a long wail. Olivia grimaced. Had she used a stern tone with the baby?

"There, there, don't cry." *Goodness, what can I do?* She picked up Rosie, pressed her to her chest and bounced across the room.

The alarm clock on the dresser erupted in a squealing wail. She slammed down the snooze button. How silly. Who'd need to wake up at four in the afternoon?

CHAPTER 9

Bouncing Rosie in her arms, Olivia paced the room. Her gentle movements seemed to be working. Rosie's crying softened. The baby yawned and rubbed her little eyes.

"You're tired, baby. What do you say to a nice nap, eh?" She should've put Rosie to bed earlier. Tom had left the sheet with instructions, why hadn't she followed them? Olivia inspected the diaper again. "Crooked, but it's holding."

Sadness seemed like a constant cold stone in her gut. Her instant family grew on her and no amount of fighting it off would help. Tom's real wife would return and take her rightful place next to her husband, and she'd…well, she'd go back to her empty house and share her thoughts with walls. There was no point in avoiding the unavoidable. Tonight she'd talk to him and find out if her appearance here had anything to do with his case.

A screech erupted from the digital alarm clock. Hadn't she shut that off? She must've hit the snooze. As she reached for the off button she had a distinct feeling she was forgetting something.

Now, what was she supposed to do at four in the afternoon…"Milo!"

A strong instinct told her not to leave Rosie alone in the crib, not even for a second. With the baby pressed to her hip, Olivia charged down the stairs, shoved her feet inside a first pair of shoes she found in the hallway, and threw her jacket over her shoulders.

The yellow school bus was lumbering onto her street when she ran out the door, shivering as the frigid air wrapped around her. She thanked the sleek roads and slow moving traffic. At least winter was good for something. Careful not to slip on icy patches, she sloshed down the road to the second mailbox. Rosie, snug inside her jacket, giggled with each bounce.

As Tom had said, Roy stood among moms waiting for the bus, a stack of mail shoved under his armpit.

The bus pulled up to the curb, snow crunching under its tires. With a hiss, the doors opened. Kids poured out, sometimes two by two, ignoring the driver's urges to exit one at the time.

"Hey Mrs. M., forgot to dress your baby?"

She turned in the direction of the sugar-laced voice. Roy quirked one eyebrow, his lips curved in a sordid half-smile.

"You know it's twenty-five degrees below zero." He scowled, pointing at Rosie's bare feet peeking out from under Olivia's jacket. "Thirty-two when you count in the windchill factor. Trouble in paradise?"

Olivia recognized Milo's snowsuit before his muffled greeting came through his scarf, covering his nose and mouth. She grabbed his mitted hand, throwing the best mind-your-own-business glare she could muster over her shoulder to Roy.

Frowning, Roy averted his glance then flashed a grin at a homely woman standing behind him. Her smile exposed yellowed, uneven teeth and indicated she welcomed his move.

Olivia adjusted Rosie on her hip to cover her little feet and pulled the zipper on her parka as far as the bundle under her coat would allow. What had she been thinking running out of the house with Rosie half dressed? With her mind focused on getting Milo from the bus stop, she hadn't thought of her girl and now Olivia could only hope the baby wouldn't get sick. Milo chatted all the way home, but Olivia couldn't focus on his excited tales, answering with a robotic "uh-huh" or "that's nice." She opened the door and the phone brr-inged in high-pitched demand. With a firm hand, she ushered Milo inside the foyer and closed the door on the cold.

"Can you take off your snow gear while I answer the phone?"

Milo nodded and unwrapped his scarf. Olivia reached for the handset on Tom's desk. His spicy cologne lingered in the air. How she missed him.

"Hi, honey." Though he sounded tired, Tom's voice cheered her up. "Everything all right?"

"Uh-huh." She unzipped her jacket, trying to steady her breathing. Rosie ceased chewing on her finger to flash a chin-drooling grin. "Just got Milo from the bus stop and I think Rosie is ready for her nap."

"Good." Tom's chuckles caused her to arch an eyebrow. "I set the alarm a few minutes ahead. Just in case, but you remembered. Didn't I tell you it would be easy—peasy?"

How smart of him to make sure she'd have a few extra minutes to get Milo. With his kindness, it wouldn't be long before she confessed to almost forgetting their son and running out in the sub-zero temperature with Rosie undressed. She'd excelled in business school. Surely parenting couldn't be harder than graduating with honors. But perhaps she'd set unrealistic expectations for herself. She wasn't cut out for this parenting gig. Frustration gnawed at her guts. Her attempt at being a perfect mom had failed. Despite her best efforts, she couldn't be what Tom wanted from her. But she wanted to be and perhaps she hadn't tried hard enough. Or could being a mom be one of those things women get better at with time and practice?

"Well, I can't take all the credit. I had a bit of help from Susan."

"It was nice of her to stop by." Soft music mixed with his voice. "I'm heading home. Want me to pick up take-out? I don't feel like cooking."

Here was her chance to prove to herself she in fact could be a good wife. Her husband deserved a home-cooked meal. "No, I've got dinner covered."

"Are you cooking?" Surprise laced his voice. "I think you're right, you're not my wife, but I can hardly wait to see what you'll whip up."

Oh-oh, she'd spoken too soon. What had she gotten herself into? Now she had to put a meal on the table and the kitchen scared her more than changing a baby. "Don't expect anything extravagant. How was your day?"

"Long and exhausting, Can't wait to get home. Don't strain yourself in the kitchen, soup and a sandwich will do for me."

Anticipation swirled through her. "I missed you. How long before you get here?"

"Judging by the traffic, an hour. Merging onto the highway now, got to go." A long kiss came from his end. "Bye, honey." He ended the call.

She warmed up Rosie's bottle, took her to the nursery, dressed her in a clean sleeper and sat in the rocking chair. The soft, satisfied sounds of her sucking, the warmth of her in Olivia's arms and adoring way she looked up at her mom while she fed gave Olivia a sense of belonging, yet her heart ached.

Her glance travelled to the window. Darkness descended on the street. She had an hour to prepare dinner. Her cooking skills didn't extend beyond warming up leftovers, opening a can of soup and making sandwiches. Yes, Tom said he'd be fine with a light meal, but she wanted to impress him. Somehow, staying at home and taking care of the family instead of earning an income made her feel small and insignificant. Envy swirled through her. Just a week ago, she too had ruled the boardroom as Tom must've intimidated witnesses on the stand in the courtroom today.

Damn it with these roller coaster emotions. One part of her demanded to stay home and take care of the children, while the other called for a career and to earn a paycheck. The constant war between two made her happy and miserable at once.

The sucking noises ceased and Olivia glanced at the baby in her lap. Rosie was fast asleep, her long eyelashes splayed above her cheek. She placed a tender kiss on her soft forehead before setting her in the crib, then trudged to the kitchen.

A flyer stuck to the fridge from her favorite Chinese restaurant made her reach for the phone. Ordering in was her best honed cooking skill. She dialed, but slammed the phone down. Hadn't she just told Tom not to get take-out? And now she tried to cheat her way out.

Milo sat on the stool of the breakfast bar, face cupped in his palms. "What's for dinner? I'm hungry."

Her focus zeroed in on Milo. The boy would know his dad's favorite dish. "Is there something you and Dad like?"

His grin created dimples in his cheeks, increasing his resemblance to Tom. "Chicken fingers and fries."

Okay, she'd asked for it. Not anything she'd prepared in the past. "How do I make that?"

He pointed at the fridge. "It's in the freezer. Just heat it up."

Frozen chicken fingers and a bag of pre-cut fries were stowed at the back of the compartment. She read the instructions.

"All right." She set the box on the counter. Preheating the oven didn't take a lot of brain cells. Since she'd never done it before, cooking frozen food seemed like a step up from microwaving leftovers or ordering in. Pressing the button on the stove, she set the oven to reach the desired temperature. Hmm, Tom would be here in less than an hour now. She raised the heat twenty degrees to cook faster.

"I'll have four strips. Daddy eats six of them and lots of fries. You make a salad for yourself." At Milo's voice she glanced in the direction of his pointing. "The baking sheet is in the drawer under the oven."

"Of course." She pulled the bin open and took out a flat, rectangular pan, spread the meat and cut fries, then shoved the family meal in the oven.

She turned to Milo who kept a keen eye on her movements. "Have I done this before?"

"Once." He straightened and a funny frown appeared on his face. "Dad calls it a D-day."

She quirked an eyebrow. "D-day?"

"Yeah, a disaster day. Get it?" Milo broke into gales of giggles and covered his mouth with his hand.

• • •

Tom drummed his fingers in rhythm with the upbeat song coming from the car speakers. He gripped the steering wheel when the traffic moved, only to come to a dead stop a few yards ahead. The traditional Croatian song he'd enjoyed came to an end with a long vocal solo from the lead singer. He found the next tune too slow to fit his chipper mood so he scrolled through his device in search of another fast tempo. Klapa Kampanel and their hit *Sacred Land Dalmatia* with baritone voices of the male band rang from the radio. When the guitar and drum joined in, his hand tapped the side of the steering wheel. He should download more of their music.

His thoughts drifted to the courtroom. Devils strangle them! He smiled at his mother's usual curse. But it was appropriate. That jury was impossible to read. Not one of them had blinked while he'd delivered his opening statement. With the circumstantial evidence, the prosecution couldn't prove his client was guilty any more than he could prove the poor woman on trial was innocent. Mr. Baldwin's medical team reported no change in the condition of the shooting victim, which meant no signs of coming out of his coma.

But Tom was proud of his work today. It hadn't been easy to put forth the appearance of a hard core attorney when thoughts of Olivia—the way her face softened when he'd pinned her to the mattress, her passionate cries, smooth skin, hardened nipples pressing to his chest that had tightened his boxers—wouldn't leave him.

Tom turned onto the exit ramp, leaving the crawl of highway traffic behind. He was looking forward to arriving home to his family and the dinner his wife was preparing.

He turned into his driveway. Smoke trickled through an open window sent a rush of adrenaline though him.

Inside the garage, the fire alarm shrieked, and he ran into the house. Olivia fanned the device on the ceiling with a piece of cardboard. Windows and the back doors stood wide open. Gray smoke poured out of the oven and hung in the air, choking him with the stench of burned food. Milo bounced and laughed with all his might around the chair she stood on.

The wooden seat tipped and she flapped her hands. Tom wrapped his arm around her waist.

Surprise flashed on her face as he steadied her. "You're home already."

He raised his voice to be heard over the ear-splitting sound. "I'll take care of the alarm, step down. Milo, will you please close the back door?"

"Yes, Daddy." The boy skittered away, leaving the space around the smoke alarm free for Tom to work.

At the press of the button, the shrill ceased. Olivia's expression relaxed and she slumped. Tears welled in her eyes. "I'm the world's worst mother and wife."

Laughter tickled the roof of his mouth, but he pressed his lips hard to keep it from bursting out. She was getting better in the kitchen. At least her attempt hadn't brought on the local fire department, like the last time. He wrapped his arms around her. "Honey, you're too hard on yourself."

Brushing a tear from her cheek, she cut him a guilty glance. "Hard? You have no idea. If you didn't arrive when you did, the house would've burned down. I almost forgot Milo and then I ran out with Rosie in my arms and didn't have time to dress her for the outdoors. There, I confess, I'm useless."

"You're not useless. At the end of the day, everything's fine, we're all accounted for and we survived." Tom kissed her hair, catching a whiff of smoke. "Let's see if dinner is salvageable."

He opened the oven door a crack, but at the sight of charred meat he slammed it shut. At least the smoldering from the stove had ceased, but the smell would no doubt stay for days. "Nope." He grabbed the phone. "Chinese food?"

She took a seat at the kitchen table and shrugged, her face crumpled. "My appetite is gone. I wanted to surprise you, but…" Her voice trailed off and turned into another sob.

The small buttons on the phone's dial pad played their soft tones as he dialed the restaurant. "It's all right. I wasn't in a mood for chicken fingers and fries."

She laughed through tears and his pulse quickened. His love for her bubbled up, the need to make her happy a driving force. "See, no harm done. Shall I order our usual?"

She nodded. "Chop suey, wonton soup, and egg rolls."

Tom winked, but the fact she knew "the usual" unraveled the knot in his guts. For a moment, even he'd suspected she really was his wife's double sent from some parallel world. Her mishaps almost convinced him of the theory he refused to believe.

Rosie's cooing came in through the baby monitor. Olivia stood. "I'm surprised the alarm didn't wake her. I'll go get her."

"She'd sleep through any clangor." Tom turned his attention to the phone as someone finally picked up his call. "Yes, can I'd like to place an order for delivery?"

"Where's Mommy's big girl?" Olivia's soft voice filled the kitchen through the monitoring device. He had a hard time concentrating on the menu in front of him.

With dinner taken care of, he placed his iPod on the docking station and shuffled through the songs in his library. He picked *Song Tied Us*. The band joined in with the mandolin after an intro, the male singer's deep voice sang in perfect harmony with a female vocal. Tom couldn't resist and he cranked up the volume.

Olivia strolled in, Rosie in her arms. "I like this song. What's it about?"

He wrapped his girls in a bear hug, leading Olivia to follow his steps. "The refrain tells how we are tied together through song in good times and bad, giving us happiness no matter who we are."

Her eyes sparkled. "I'm not one for poetry, but those are beautiful lyrics."

"Yes, they are. Unfortunately, much of the beauty is lost in translation."

Milo ran up to them and joined them in their slow dance. Tom hummed along with the song as it came to an end with the chime of xylophone. Three songs later, the doorbell announced the arrival of their dinner.

"Let's eat." Tom carried the bag to the kitchen and set it on the table.

Milo climbed onto his chair next to Olivia. "After, can we dance again?"

"It'll be your bed time by then." Tom sliced up a portion of chicken into bite-size pieces, dished out a spoonful of vegetables and placed the plate in front of the boy. "Mommy will get you into your pjs and I'll read you a story."

"Not fair." With a pout, Milo buried his face in his hands. "Rosie gets to stay up."

"She won't stay up for long." Tom raised his finger and stopped his son's attempt at another complaint. "You know who's coming to town and he sees you when you are sleeping and knows when you're awake."

The boy's eyes widened and he returned his attention to his plate.

Olivia's fork hovered mid-air, a piece of broccoli speared on the tines. "That song gave me creeps when I was a kid. To think some old guy from North Pole watches while you're sleeping and knows if you're good or bad."

A low chuckle rolled Tom's stomach. "It works wonders on kids. Speaking of the big guy, the kids should have pictures taken with Santa."

Milo's fork clunked on the plate and he raised his arms over his head. "Yay!"

Olivia's chewing ceased and she swallowed hard. "I never had my picture taken with him."

Milo blinked and his mouth dropped. "Why not, Mommy?"

She turned to Tom, an awkward smile on her lips. "I shouldn't say it in front of Milo."

"You can tell me later." Tom picked at the food on his plate. Her confession knotted his stomach anew. Milo was just a baby then, but they had a picture taken with Santa at Tom's office party.

With dinner behind them, Tom cleaned the kitchen while Olivia took Milo upstairs. By the way the boy's feet dragged on the tiles, Tom suspected the good night story would not be needed.

The multicolored dragon in Rosie's hands crinkled as the baby kneaded the toy's ears. Tom placed the last of the leftovers in the fridge, and picked up his daughter from the high chair.

He turned the kitchen lights off and carried Rosie to the living room. He sat her on his lap. "And how was your day?"

The baby reached for his nose. He chuckled when her little hand squeezed, blocking his airflow.

"You have one too. Right here." He tapped the tip of her nose.

Rosie's grin prompted Tom to kiss her. "You may be Daddy's girl, but you resemble your mom. And you've got her willpower."

At a soft laugh, he turned to see Olivia standing in the threshold. "It's the truth, look at her. She's a copy of you."

Olivia's hips swayed as she strolled to the couch, making Tom gulp. "And Milo's all you."

"Yes, he resembles me, but he loves his mommy."

Olivia lowered her gaze to her hands. "I loved my dad so much. Mother accused me of being too clingy and possessive. According to her, I never gave them a moment to themselves. That is why she had Tadem late in life, when the risk of having a child with Down's syndrome was much higher. She blames me."

Tom rubbed Olivia's arm. "No one is to blame for your sister's condition. You can tell me now why you haven't had a picture taken with dear Santa."

"Well." Her smile and a head shake indicated her memory was not pleasant. "My mom never subscribed to the craze of holidays. She made it clear there's no such thing as Santa. One time we cut through the mall and there he was, sitting in his big chair. I pointed at him and Mother said that wasn't Santa but some perv in a polyester suit who gets off by groping children on his lap."

Tom's mouth hung open while he struggled to process the cruelty. He placed his hand on Olivia's back. "She denied you the very essence of childhood."

"No." She scooted closer to him, her warmth spread to him. "Mother wanted to protect me from disappointment of finding the truth."

"Don't worry." He brushed her long hair over her shoulder, exposing her slender neck. Her jasmine mist masked the most of the smoke smell and filled his senses as he pressed his lips to her skin, causing her to shiver. Rosie's foot wedged under his chin and he pulled back, but continued to circle his thumb on Olivia's nape. "I have good news. The judge ordered the trial to continue in January, as I predicted. He wouldn't want to work over Christmas and miss his turkey dinner. So we'll spend our holidays with Tadem. Sound good?"

Her slow nod failed to convince him this was what she wanted. "What's wrong?"

She snapped her glance straight to his eyes. "I haven't seen Tadem in over twenty years."

The strength of her voice was all too believable. Pain stabbed his chest. Olivia had no memory of two life events. Unsure of how to reply to his wife, he smoothed Rosie's hair. "I'm sure your sister will remember you, and she'll be happy to see us. She hasn't seen Rosie yet. Milo and Tadem are best friends."

"They would be. In terms of mental age, they are about the same. Only her mind is trapped in a body of an adult. Mother's flawed daughter was a weed in her perfect garden."

Olivia's face screwed up, on the verge of tears. Tom's heart twisted. No matter how hard he tried, he couldn't undo the damage her mother had so callously done. "Honey, Tadem is fine where she is. Chances are she wouldn't get the same care from your mother."

"You're right." She sniffed. "Let's have our Christmas with Tadem."

He flashed Olivia a reassuring grin. "I already booked the flight. We'll be leaving in three weeks."

Olivia still appeared uneasy, more so when she pulled her lower lip between her teeth.

Bouncing Rosie on his knee didn't stop the bad premonition sprouting in his guts. "Visiting Tadem isn't the only thing bothering you."

Biting her nail, she shook her head. "Can you talk about your trial?"

His eyebrows drew closer. "Only what's been reported in the media. Why do you want to talk about it?"

"This could be something or nothing, but the gun used in the shooting…" She licked her lips. "I have…or had a weapon. It's missing."

He ceased bouncing his knee and pulled his daughter to his chest. "No honey. You pawned the revolver years ago. I keep the pawn shop receipt in my safe."

"I pawned it? That's a relief. I thought it was stolen. I didn't have a permit." Her chest lowered with a long exhale. But in the next instance her expression froze. She twiddled with a handful of her hair, a sure sign she was scared. "A strange uneasiness is nagging at me that same gun was used it in the shooting. The damn feeling keeps me up at night and somehow I know I'm right."

Shifting Rosie to his side, he wrapped Olivia in his arm, pulled her to his chest. She relaxed against him and he kissed her forehead. Never before had he seen his wife this worried. "Could happen, but it's a long shot. Don't be scared. It's possible to track the weapon, but I'm not a detective. This is something I should turn to the police, just to put you at ease and clear you from any possible implications."

CHAPTER 10

The speakers crackled and the singsong voice of a flight attendant announced the final approach to the Vancouver airport. Olivia gulped the air, not only to loosen the pressure in her ears, but in fear of how Rosie would take the landing. Oxygen enriched air, inside the cabin, caused fuzziness in her head and she yawned.

The takeoff hadn't seemed to bother the baby, though once strapped in her seat, she'd cried. As soon as they'd reached cruising altitude and the seatbelt sign turned off, Olivia snatched Rosie out of her confinements and rocked the child until her wails stopped. Strapping her back in the safety seat wasn't an option. A man in dark suit had rolled his eyes, then shook his head before he'd returned his attention to business section of his paper. Mere weeks ago she, too, would've frowned upon having to share a row with children. She would've demanded to be moved if sat in their proximity. Times had changed though—now she scowled at the man seated across the aisle.

She lowered Rosie to her chair. Surprise seemed to flash in the baby's dark eyes, her lips curled downward, preparing for another wail. Snapping the straps, Olivia wrinkled her forehead with sympathy. "Only for a few minutes, Rosie. Then you'll come out again."

Rosie started fussing. Like a gunslinger, Tom pulled a sippy cup from the diaper bag. "We're almost there, twinkle." He glanced at Milo sleeping next to him. "I can't believe she's still awake. I thought for sure they would both zonk out."

Straightening her seat at the flight attendant's urging, Olivia smiled at the small form under the blue blanket. "He was too excited last night. It was way past ten by the time he fell asleep. You should wake him now."

Milo surfaced from under the cover when Tom nudged him. Alertness replaced his sleepy expression in an instant. "Are we there yet?"

"Ready to see auntie?" Tom smoothed a rebellious clamp of hair at the back of Milo's head, but it sprang right up again.

Joy mixed with nervous butterflies fluttered in Olivia's stomach. She kept tapping her foot against the seat in front of her. In a few hours she would see her sister for the first time in decades. She'd rehearsed every possible scenario to justify why she hadn't come for a visit sooner. Ultimately she decided to wing it. In this life, her double had a healthy relationship with her sibling. Hopefully, Tadem wouldn't notice she was a different woman.

"I think our little travelers are ready for our trip to Europe this summer." Tom's cheerful voice cut into her musing. He brushed his fingers on her shoulder, raising the butterflies in her stomach in a different way.

The majestic coastal mountains surrounding the city and the vast, green Pacific Ocean inched closer. She tore her gaze from the window, Tom's soft smile settling her uneasiness. He always seemed to know when she needed reassurance.

"Worried about how Tadem will react?"

A long exhale loosened her tight chest and she nodded. The trembling under her feet indicated the landing gear had been lowered. The plane would touch down at any moment. She'd been through some shaky landings in the past, so she flattened her back against the seat. "I'm more worried about what to tell her. No doubt she'll have a lot of questions."

"Honey, you'll be fine." Tom tightened Milo's belt and tapped the seat for the boy to lean back.

The tires squeaked when airbus made the contact with the asphalt on the runway. A loud whoosh followed as the craft was breaking the surface speed. Passengers ignored the announcement to remain seated, the clicks of releasing seatbelts chirping through the cabin.

"Thank God for the first class. We're close to the exit." Tom unstrapped Rosie from the restraints of her seat. "She can't take another second of this bondage."

Giggles replaced the baby's shrills when Tom blew a raspberry on her belly, enticing a warmth to spread through Olivia. She took Rosie in her arms, feeling at ease surrounded by her family. If only it was up to her to decide whether she'd stay in this fantasy.

The diaper bag slung over her shoulder, she followed Tom and Milo. With a smile and a nod, she greeted the crew, something she'd never done on her countless flights in her other life.

Shuffling Rosie and Milo and carry-ons like circus jugglers between her and Tom, the four of them worked through the busy terminal, picked up their luggage from the conveyer belt and at last settled in the rental car.

From the passenger seat, she stared out the window, noting the shop windows and theaters along the way, decorated in the spirit of the holidays. How many times had she been in this city and never paid any heed to the storefronts? This time she was here to enjoy it, not to conduct her boss's unpleasant business.

She glanced at Tom, his strong profile stark against the morning sun, beaming on the window. Light danced in his brown hair. "So, which hotel are we staying in?"

"The castle in the city." His big hand covered hers, resting on her thigh. "Only the best for my family."

She gasped. In all her business travels, she'd stayed in the five stars rooms, but those were economy chain hotels. Of course, Mr. Hiltorn wouldn't splurge on a place such as the Fairmount Hotel for her. The establishment was, after all, crème de la crème. Yet he hadn't hesitated to book the executive suits for himself and his entourage. She'd seen the invoices.

At the edge of his seat, Milo tapped her shoulder. "When we can we go see auntie?"

Tom glanced at the rear-view mirror. "They're expecting us after lunch. So you take it easy, okay? Sit back in your seat."

Milo's impatient smile turned to a pout, his short arms crossing his chest and his body angling toward the window. No sounds came from Rosie, strapped in her seat. The baby must've finally succumbed to sleep.

Olivia twirled ends of her hair around her finger. In the past three weeks, domestic life had become her second nature. Who knew she would enjoy Christmas shopping for her husband and children? Anticipation of seeing their faces when they opened their presents coiled through her. Her other shelled life now seemed so empty. She wouldn't choose to trade this new existence for all riches of any world.

Tom pulled onto a long drive of the hotel's entrance adorned with round fountain. The impressive architecture resembling an English castle came into view. Olivia eased out of the car, widening her eyes at the iconic hotel's beauty and sophistication.

Tom dropped the keys into a valet's hand. The young man in the hotel's burgundy coat opened the trunk when the bellboy shuffled the buggy to grab their bags.

She pushed Rosie's stroller through the lobby, decorated in gold and burgundy trim. Tom sure knew how to surprise her. She'd splurged on his gift, but that now seemed inadequate.

After checking into their Morningside suite, which offered a spectacular skyline view of the city, Tom set to order room service while Olivia lowered sleeping Rosie in her little cot. She closed the sheer blinds, dimming the room from the bright winter sun. The four-post king-size bed engulfing the room appeared so comfy. She stripped off her travelling clothes and plopped her tired body onto the mattress. In the past two weeks, Tom had returned to their nuptial bed, but he'd yet to make love to her as he'd promised. In his few attempts, Milo had snuck in between them or Rosie had cried. By the time she'd dealt with the children and came back to their room, she'd found Tom fast asleep. Though her mind and body screamed for his loving, she'd let him rest. After all, he was the sole breadwinner now.

"How do you like the suite?" Tom closed the door behind him.

Turning onto her side, she propped her head on her elbow and offered him her most seductive smile, slow and steady. He approached her, unbuttoning his shirt. Her stomach fluttered with anticipation, and the view of his chiseled torso. Perhaps in this enchanted place things would play to their advantage.

"Love it, chic and contemporary design is my style."

"I thought you'd like it." He slid behind her. A surrendering sigh escaped her when he spooned her against him. "Milo found the Cartoon Channel, Rosie's asleep and we've got time on our hands. Now where were we two nights ago before someone interrupted us?"

His husky whisper and hot breath on her neck carried a certain promise. Olivia flipped onto her back. She managed a quick inhale before his mouth seized hers. A blaze ignited in her midriff and spread over her. She tore his shirt off his shoulders. His muscles bulged under her hands. Without breaking the hungry kiss, he yanked the fabric off, and snuck his hand under her camisole. A soft moan slipped her lips when his fingers found her nipple. She arched her back pressing her breast into his palm.

One fluffy pillow fell off the bed and whooshed on the carpet. The bedding rustled as he straddled her. Short puffs of air rushed out of her mouth while he glided her top over her head then traced his finger between her breasts, down to her panties. Her heart sped when he tucked his finger inside her underwear, dipping his face between her achy breasts. When would he unclasp her bra and release them?

"You're a balm for my soul." His low whisper sent shivers through her womb. Lips brushing on her skin raised goose bumps from her toes to her neck.

He pressed his erection on her thigh. She closed her eyes. Damn, their clothes prevented full access.

He rolled onto his back, taking her with him. Positioned on top of him, she rose up on her knees, allowing him to lower her undies below her buttocks. She met his warm gaze. Hunger in his honey eyes flooded her with wetness.

"Close your eyes." He brushed her face. She closed her own eyelids, moved by the sensation of his fingers against her skin. "Tell me what you feel."

"Ah." She gasped, sucked in a long breath and arched her back. "You're driving me wild."

Creating a slight pressure on her clit, his finger stopped its circular motions. "Not the kind of answer I expected."

Panting, her hips buckled, she licked her lips. "What…did you want me…?" She gulped. "To say?"

He continued the sweet torture. "Describe what you feel in detail."

Another moan rushed out of her. No one ever asked her to do this. How was she to respond? "I'm so tense, strung like a bow. Oh, please don't stop."

He continued finger teasing. His soft whisper infused her with more moisture. "Do you need me?"

"Yes. Oh, yes." She heaved. Never before a man forced her to beg, but beg she would if Tom asked her to. Her hips swayed, following his finger. Each time the connection broke she sought his taunting pleasure. She clasped her hand over his to keep it steady and peeked through one eye. If she couldn't give him the answer he waited on, would he cease this cajoling?

"Tell me more. What do you feel?" His narrowed gaze was unyielding.

She swallowed against her dry throat, then whimpered. Seemed the other Olivia was comfortable talking dirty to him. "I'm melting from inside."

"Better." To her dismay, he pulled his hand away and planted it on her rear. "Take off your bra." A demanding tone laced his voice.

She unhooked the clasps at the back, but his hand stopped her in pulling the straps off her shoulders. "Slowly."

Trailing fingers down her arms, he dragged the silky, pink fabric against her skin. He cupped her breasts, rubbing his thumbs over her nipples. "Mmmm, yes, love them when they pebble under my fingers."

His knuckle grazed the side of her face and she opened her eyes, meeting his. "And I love it when you're aroused."

"Make love to me. Now, Tom. Please." God, he'd stayed true to his words. She not only burned for him, she was an inferno.

Desire reflected in his eyes. "Is there something else you want to tell me?"

I love you. She wanted to scream, but the damn words wouldn't leave her mouth. Did she love him? Her heart wanted to love him, but her mind kept urging her not to rush into anything.

A hint of disappointment flashed in his eyes, he tilted his head toward the vaulted ceiling, and blew a long breath. *Damn, damn, I ruined the moment.* But if professing her love to him was what he wanted to hear from her, next time she'd force those words out if it killed her. No, she shouldn't so foolishly gush with words of her love. Her feelings confused her. Since her dad's accident, love had not existed in her life.

She sat on his now half hard cock. The three little words she couldn't bring herself to say meant so much to him. Fear of the unknown raked through her and sent a cold shiver up her spine. "Tom, my memories will never return."

A soft and slow smile stretched his lips. "Then we'll just have to make new ones."

"There's someone at the door, Daddy," Milo's small voice called out.

"Our lunch is here." Tom sat up and kissed her cheek. "After we eat, we'll head out to visit with Tadem."

• • •

Dark, imposing windows stared down at Olivia from the large, brick face of the building. The blinking multicolored lights twinkled on the two pine trees in front, but they hardly gave the surroundings the feel of Christmas. Tomorrow they'd bring Tadem to spend the day with them at the hotel and forget this dreary place if only for a moment.

She took a deep breath and pushed through the row of residents basking in the weak winter sun. Some sat in their wheelchairs while a few gathered around weather-beaten picnic table. Not one of them stopped their smattering conversations as her family passed by them.

A petite, elderly woman greeted them at the plain reception desk. "Hello, everyone." Her wintry blue eyes crinkled at the corners when she glanced at baby in Tom's arms. "And this must be Rosie. Tadem is so anxious to see all of you. She's waiting in her room." The receptionist turned her gaze at Olivia. "Doctor is amazed at her progress after the surgery. And it's nice of you to come see her so often. Many of our clients don't receive any visitations at all."

Olivia forced a smile, but guilt churned her stomach. The woman obviously failed to notice she wasn't the same Olivia as the one who visited her sister.

Her boots thumped on the carpeted floor as she followed Tom down the long corridor. Though the place wasn't a hospital, the smell of disinfectants and stale coffee from the cafeteria crept into her nose. The ever-present knots in Olivia's stomach tightened.

When Tom turned the corner, Milo ran ahead and knocked on the door of suite 201. "It's us, Auntie."

The sting of remorse slid over her. Her husband and son knew in which apartment her sister resided, yet she had no clue about her sibling's life. She halted at the entrance. The proximity of the door to the next unit assured her Tandem lived in a small place. Olivia took a tentative step into the apartment, some ten square feet with its own bathroom.

"I missed you so much." Milo rushed forward to hug Tadem's wide girth. When had her sister grown heavy? The facility might not offer adequate physical program for her to be active. Confined to this tiny space, parked in front of television, it was no wonder she put on weight. Even with her thin, black hair and small eyes in her round face, the family resemblance was undeniable.

"I missed you, too." Tadem might've grown to an adult, but her voice had remained the same, childish and slurring. She took Milo's hand, examining his temporary tattoo of a cartoon character. "This is so cool."

"You can have one, I've got more." Milo tapped her hand, indicating where to put the picture.

Tom turned the baby in his arms toward Tadem. "This is Rosie. You haven't seen her yet."

Tadem's black eyes appeared beady, but warmth filled them when she smiled. "She's so cute."

Tom extended his arms, bringing the baby closer to Tadem. "Would you like to hold her?"

"Yes." Tadem squirmed but took Rosie in her clumsy hands. Tom kept close, monitoring Tadem's movements.

"Hi, Rosie. I'm your aunt." She attempted a clumsy bounce.

Sorrow and grief overwhelmed Olivia. In an instant she relived the dreadful day when people in white coats took Tadem away.

A tight band constricted her chest and she drew in a breath. She clasped her hand over her mouth, but a yelp escaped her. Tom glanced over his shoulder then back at Tadem. "Here, I'll take Rosie. Milo boy, mommy needs a few minutes alone with Auntie. Why don't we go get some treats from the coffee shop down the street?"

The boy slapped his leg. "Aw, but we just got here."

"No buts, let's go." Tom led him to the door. "We'll be back in a few."

Unrestrained tears spilled from Olivia's eyes. With slow steps she approached the bed where her sister sat.

"I missed you all these years. I wanted to come and see you. I begged Mom to bring me, but she only kept promising, saying sure, we'll go." She leaned closer to Tadem and hugged her just like the day she'd seen her for the last time.

Tadem's finger brushed her cheek. "Tears?"

Olivia sniffed and a smile crept through her crying. "Yeah, but it's ok."

Olivia stared at Tadem's guileless face, wondering how much was she comprehending.

Tadem smiled and sat straight. "Hey, you want to see the angel?"

"What angel?"

"The one who's been visiting me. She has a message for you." Tadem's grin exposed her uneven teeth. "Want to see it?"

A message for me? Olivia frowned and shrugged. "OK."

Tadem closed her eyes, her shoulders rising as she drew in a long breath. Then her puffy face elongated. Her slanted eyes turned almond shaped, her cheekbones standing high and thick, bouncy curls replacing her scraggly hair. The transformation continued down her body, with swelling breasts, a shrinking waist and extended legs.

Olivia took a long step back, her knees shaking. "Tadem?"

Transformed, Tadem's mouth moved, but a melodious female's voice came out. "Only in body. This is what she'd look like had she not been touched."

Olivia tried to steady her racing heart by pressing hard against her chest. "Touched? By whom?"

The strange woman gave a slight nod. "By God."

"You call her condition a touch of divinity?" Anger crept to Olivia's voice despite her attempt to control the agitation. How dare this entity call her sister's infirmity a touch of God?

The angel smiled, casting a glow through the gloom room. "Now the Good Book says, 'Blessed are poor in spirit, for theirs is the kingdom of Heaven.'"

Clutching the back of the chair, Olivia steadied her trembling fingers. "I wasn't brought up in the church so I wouldn't know the meaning."

"But Jesus said, 'Allow the children, and forbid them not, to come unto me: for of such is the kingdom of Heaven.'"

The kingdom of Heaven, what a load of crap. Olivia sneered. No such place existed here on Earth or up there in sky. "From what I've heard, the Holy Bible is vague and open for interpretation. So if you're referring to Tadem being like a child, then you're right."

The brightness encircling the angel intensified. "We must help the weak and remember the words of the Lord Jesus. Whoever has a bountiful eye will be blessed, for he shares his bread with the poor."

Help the weak, share with the poor, concepts she found incomprehensible in the past, now something that came as a second nature to her. Perhaps spoken through the mouth of an angel they sounded true. "Why are you with my sister?"

"Every mortal has one guardian angel, but only those like Tadem are deserving of seeing us."

Olivia pressed her lips tight, but couldn't stop the wail building in her throat. "It's unfair to Tadem. She would've been a very beautiful woman."

In one fluid motion, the angel moved close, engulfing Olivia in tangerine scent. "She is happy in her simple life. God loves you, Olivia, and He wants you to know, your sister's state is not your fault. You must stop blaming yourself for something you have no power over."

Olivia winced with sudden realization. "Do you have anything to do with the appearance of Tom and the children?"

Sorrow flashed across angel's face. "Poor Tadem is very sick."

Olivia's stomach knotted. "No, she's fine. Her surgery was successful."

"You're in the future, Olivia. Tadem didn't have her surgery. Yet. And Tom is fighting for his life."

Cold sweat washed down Olivia's back. The angel's charged expression sent another bolt of fear through her. "What do you want from me?"

"You must choose who to send to Heaven with me. Tadem or Tom?"

"What?" Olivia gasped. "You can't make me choose."

Desperate to gain her composure, Olivia tried to recall her corporate training. What would she do when pressed by hard questions? Hit them back with questions of her own.

"Why are you making me do this?" She struggled to keep her voice strong. "You're the angel, the supreme being. Why can't you just pick one?

The angel let out a quiet chuckle. She pressed a long finger to her lips. "Shhhh, Tom is on his way back here. I have to go."

CHAPTER 11

Tom hitched Rosie a little higher on his hip and juggled a cardboard tray full of drinks in his hand. Getting a solid grip on the knob to enter Tadem's apartment was a challenge—with gloves on, it was next to impossible. The aroma of rich coffee and hot chocolate wafted from the paper cups and lessened the sharp odors of disinfectants. He tapped his booted foot on the wood, but no one answered.

"Olivia." He glanced over his shoulder to make sure Milo wasn't helping himself to sweets from the box he carried.

"Open the door, Olivia. My hands are full," Tom tried again, louder this time. Still no answer. A strange, foreboding slithered over him. His wife must have heard him. Why wouldn't she respond? He shifted the baby and turned to his son. "Milo, get the door for me." He reached out with his hand holding Rosie. The baby weighed twice as much in all her winter gear, his arm was starting to hurt by now. Served him right for not getting her stroller out the car, but the coffee shop was closer than his car at the far end of the parking lot. He made a mental note to park closer to the entrance as often as possible. "Give me the Timbits."

Milo raised his arms, a colorful box of bite size doughnuts in his hands. Tom wrapped his finger around the handle. "First take your glove off."

The boy removed his mitten by biting on the tip and sliding his hand out. He grabbed the knob, but his small hand wouldn't wrap around. "I can't open it, Daddy."

"Take the other mitten off and try with both hands."

Milo obeyed, tossing mittens onto the vinyl floor. He managed to twist the handle, but pulled the door toward him.

"Push in." Tom leaned on the wood panel before Milo could lose his grip and the door swung open.

Olivia stood frozen in the corner, her knuckles white, gripping the back of a chair. "Honey?" Tom set the tray on the small, round table and turned to glance at Tadem. She sat on the bed, where he'd left her when he'd urged Milo out of the room to give Olivia a few moments alone with her sister.

"Auntie, look." Milo grabbed the box of sweets and plopped next to Tadem. "We've got Timbits and hot chocolate with whipped cream."

"Cool, I love Timbits," Tadem droned in her lisp.

Tom set Rosie on the carpet and faced his wife, her stance rigid. She winced when he caressed her elbow, shooting him a surprised glance. Her pale face and wide eyed, she appeared petrified. "Olivia, honey, talk to me."

"I—" She gulped. "I need some fresh air."

"Alright. Let's stroll through the garden before the sun goes down." Tom turned to his son and sister-in-law devouring the Timbits, discussing with their mouths full which flavor was their favorite. "We're going for a walk, put the sweets away."

Milo and Tadem dusted the icing sugar off their hands. They sprang to their feet and the mattress coils squeaked in protest. Tadem shuffled her feet to the closet in front of the unit's door and pulled out her coat.

Dressed for the outdoors, Milo and Tadem skipped ahead on the garden path while Tom walked alongside Olivia, Rosie tucked in his arm. His wife's silence worried him. "Tell me what happened."

Olivia exhaled a misty breath on a cold wintry day. "If I didn't see it, I wouldn't believe it." She continued with a trembling voice, "After you left, Tadem asked me if I'd like to see an angel. I thought she meant some paper angel she might've made in a craft workshop, so I said okay."

Her hand shook as she pressed black leather encased fingertips to her lips. "Then she changed in front of me."

Tom furrowed his brow. "Changed?"

"Yes, she became…" Olivia frowned, gesturing with her hand as if she was desperate to find the proper word. "Normal, like she'd never had her condition. Then she spoke, but it wasn't her voice. The angel inside that took her body said it was still Tadem only in her normal appearance. She mumbled something religious… didn't make sense to me. Something about weak of mind and how their kingdom is Heaven."

"An angel entered Tandem's body and quoted the Bible?" His chest tightened, but he shook his head, struggling to comprehend and not overreact. Ever since Olivia returned from her trip, strange things had happened, most of them he couldn't explain. Though these little incidences were becoming annoying, he must remain patient and everything would snap back into its place. She needed him to believe her. He would be the one person she could rely on.

He cleared his throat before he spoke again, just to make sure he wouldn't sound untrusting. "Weak of mind, kingdom of Heaven…sounds familiar. She might've said 'Blessed are poor in spirit, for theirs is the kingdom of Heaven?'"

Turning to him, Olivia pointed her finger, her eyes wide. "Yes, that's it. You know of this saying?"

Cold wind wrapped around them as they rounded the building. He pulled a knitted hat over Rosie's ears. Bubble gum pink seemed to lighten her dark hair and eyes. He placed a kiss on her chubby cheek, but even his cherub's grin didn't stall the anxiety building in his chest. A real angel must've visited Tadem. His wife wasn't religious and never quoted a single line from the Good Book. But why would a heaven's entity hang around his sister-in-law? Unless…"It's not a saying. It's from the Bible, Matthew 5:3."

Olivia shrugged deeper into her scarf. "How do you know these things?"

"I was an altar boy." A memory of the church where he'd spent his fair share of mornings in Sunday school and serving during Mass filled him with warmth. "My parents were so proud of me when I was chosen. Mom's face beamed the first time I walked down the aisle with the cross in my hands."

Olivia shared his smile as if reliving the day with him. "What does this Matthew something mean?"

Tom shrugged, trying to recall lessons from church. Tadem was weak of mind. Therefore an angel could show herself in front of Olivia's sister. But what would the spiritual being want? His heart pounded against his ribs, but Olivia waited on answer. "Basically, tells us to be kind to those who are poor. Be it in spirit, money, or mind."

They walked along the garden path in silence. Olivia kept her gaze on the light decorations on the bushes and bare trees. Tom pondered her theory of parallel worlds. The fact she could be correct pressed on his shoulders. Even if she weren't his wife, he couldn't stop loving her. And if his real spouse returned someday and this woman vanished, would he know the difference? No, nothing would change. He wrapped his arm around her shoulder. "I should've let you get some rest when we checked in. Could it be you're exhausted and imagined her becoming an angel?"

She ceased walking and cast him a long stare, the kind that always sent shivers up his spine. How could she not be his wife?

"No, Tom. I know what I saw." A shy smile stretched her lips. She brushed his chest, dreaminess filling her eyes. With a sharp inhale, she continued, "She left and Tadem's appearance returned. She seemed to have no recollection of what happened." Olivia swallowed then continued. "I wasn't scared of this...entity." Her lips twisted and she averted her gaze to the gravel on the path. Could she be omitting something about her encounter with the divinity? "Oh, but Tom, my sister would've been beautiful. It's so unfair to her."

"Life is unfair." Tom cast her what he hoped was a reassuring smile. "We're luckier than some. Come on, honey, cheer up. Tomorrow's Christmas."

Olivia glanced at the brown brick building. "We should get her into a better place."

He cringed at yet another inconsistency in Olivia's story. "We already tried that. She's spent most of her life here and doesn't like being away from her room."

"I don't think her room is cozy at all. The bed looks like it's on its last leg." A smile lit up Olivia's face. "Well, I'll go shopping and get her a few nice things."

"I'm sure she'd like that." Tom kissed Olivia's cheek. With her mood improved, the weight lifted off his chest. "You must be feeling better."

She nodded. "Um-hmm." A slight frown replaced her small smile. "Can you hear Milo and Tadem? When was the last time you saw either of them?"

His eyes widened and panic engulfed him. How could he forget those two? He handed the baby to Olivia. "Hold her, I'll go look."

Gravel crunched under his pounding boots. His breath misted as he called out. "Milo, Tadem! Where are you guys?"

He stopped and listened. A child's laughter echoed in the distance. Tom followed the sound and the chuckling grew louder. The path ended and a lone tree stood in the small clearing, its bare branches decorated with frosty Christmas lights. Milo giggled while a young woman spun him in her arms. The curls of her raven hair bounced on her back. A soft glow radiated from her.

Milo pointed at him. "Look Daddy, Tadem's angel came out to play with me."

The woman placed Milo on the ground and faced Tom. Her glow seemed to intensify when she scanned him.

"Tom." The voice called his name with urgency, but the angel's lips didn't move.

Dizziness spun him. He pressed his hand to his temple. *What is that buzzing noise?* The presence of others surrounding him pressed on his awareness, but he saw no one—just Milo and the angel.

"Clear," a male's voice shouted.

Coldness pressed to his torso and a second later a strong, electrical current seared through him. He clenched his chest and fought for every breath. A steady and monotonous tone replaced the broken bleeps.

His heartbeat steadied, the searing pain in his chest dissipated and those invisible presences seemed to leave his side at the change of the sound.

He still clutched his chest when he raised his head toward Milo. Tadem, looking her old self, stood beside to the boy, a wide grin on her face.

•••

A pained groan drifted from the garden. Olivia straightened from her crouching position behind the bushes she'd been searching. She clenched Rosie to her chest and broke into a run on the gravel path.

Her feet slowed down with the sight of Tom, Milo, and her sister seated on the bench.

"Thank God you found them." She panted, approaching the trio. "You two scared us. Why did you wander off on your own?"

No one spoke, but Tom's eyes, round as plates, were red rimmed and his face pale.

Olivia caressed his shoulder. "You've seen the angel, too."

Tom's slow nod stopped her heart. He gasped before he spoke. "She spun Milo in her arms when I found them."

His voice, though steady, seemed awkward. Did he hide something? No, he wouldn't keep anything from her. Seeing the angel had spooked him. Hell, it had thrown her for a loop when it happened to her.

"It's getting late, let's head back." She took Milo's hand. "Tomorrow we'll bring Tadem to our hotel to celebrate Christmas."

"Yay." Milo grabbed Tadem's hand. "Santa's coming tonight."

A dimple on his chin formed with Tom's frown, and made him adorable. "What about this angel?"

Olivia shrugged one shoulder. Perhaps she was experiencing some of that marvel of the season she'd heard about all these years, but never believed in. "It's Christmas, miracles are supposed to happen."

A slow smile replaced Tom's grimace. "Yes, you're right." He pushed off the bench and wrapped her in a bear hug. "I'll love you no matter what."

And she loved him. The words formed in her mouth, but her tongue froze. Damn it, why couldn't she bring herself to say them?

"I know you love me, too." His whisper brushed her neck. The warmth of his breath spread heat through her on this cold evening. "It was difficult for you to admit it for the first time."

Her throat closed and she blinked fast, pushing back stinging tears. A long breath loosened the knot in her chest. Why couldn't she listen to her heart? Her soul wanted her to love him. She always thought a life without love was better. No one could hurt her. How was she to change her firm belief?

Tom released her from his embrace and took her by her hand. "It's been a long day. Come, this will all make more sense in the morning," he said, leading the way back to Tadem's apartment.

•••

The next morning, Olivia woke in a spacious bed next to Tom. He slept on his side, his powerful arms crossed over his chest.

She smiled at his peaceful appearance and slipped from under the covers.

She leaned over Rosie's cot. The baby sucked her thumb noisily, but continued sleeping. The tip of Milo's head peeked out from beneath the blanket. Olivia flipped the corner, uncovering his face. He inhaled deeply and turned to his side, hugging his teddy bear under his elbow.

She scrambled from her nightgown into a pair of tight jeans and a sweatshirt, then scribbled a note for Tom.

Gone to get Tadem. Don't open any presents without us. Love, Olivia.

Car keys jiggled on their ring when she grabbed them off the counter and she snuck out of their hotel suite. During her drive, she kept thinking about yesterday's events. Neither she nor Tom brought up the topic of seeing an angel after they left the facility. Had Milo known of this entity overtaking his aunt's body? Why had he never mentioned a thing?

A coffee shop with an open sign caught her attention. She pulled over and grabbed her purse. The line extended from the counter to the front door, but she needed a quick wake up. The service was fast and some ten minutes later, she left with a large cup, the heat from the beverage warming her hand.

The front of the home where Tadem resided stood empty in the early morning. The front door was open, but the reception decorated with a string of paper angels was unattended. She continued to Tadem's unit and found her sister ready and anxious to go.

The roads suddenly turned busy on their way back. The stores were closed on holidays. Where were all these people going? Must be a church-attending crowd.

Olivia blew an exasperated breath as the traffic light ahead changed to red for the third time. There must be an accident ahead. She turned to Tadem in the passenger seat. Her sister had her head turned toward the window, but Olivia wanted to find out more about the angel.

"Tadem," she croaked, not knowing how to ask the delicate question.

Tadem whirled her head around, facing her with a grin.

Olivia forced a smile to her face. She raked her brain, searching for right words. "Does the angel visit you often?"

"She's always with me, since I was little." Tadem turned her attention to the window again.

Tadem's casual tone baffled Olivia. Her sister must be used to this entity if she'd been with her all these years. Of course she wouldn't know, she never visited nor cared.

"And she enters your body every time she appears?"

"No." Tadem traced her finger on the fogged glass. "Last night was the first time. She said it's the only way you can see her."

The sedan in front crept another few feet. Olivia eased her foot off the brake and let her car follow the flow. "Why did she show herself to Tom and Milo?"

"I told Milo about her long time ago and he wanted to see her." Tadem shifted in her seat, tagging on the belt. "Last night she told me her secret. She's Tom's guardian, too."

Olivia swallowed a lump. Tom had appeared ill when she found him slouched on the bench, but she dismissed his shaky voice and trembling hands as fear of what he'd experienced. Could it be his days were numbered and his angel waited for him to die and take his soul? No. It was Christmas. Bad things should not happen on this joyful day.

"Ah, there's the hold up." She raised the hand over the steering wheel when the flashing lights of a squad car came into her view. The two officers in navy blue uniforms dragged a handcuffed woman toward their vehicle. They struggled to contain her while she shouted and jerked, trying to free herself of their hold.

Everyone stopped and gawked at the early morning show. Olivia pulled up alongside the police car just in time to see one of the officers press his hand on the captured woman's head, attempting to push her into the back of the cruiser.

The woman froze and raised her head. Olivia shuddered when the scraggly captive seemed to glare in her direction. She'd seen her before, but where? An odd, familiar feeling slid down her back. She'd experienced this only once before and she would never forget the woman's tired yet accusatory eyes. It happened the moment she'd fired her last employee from the list. Right here in Vancouver. What was her name? Nela something…starting with L. Larkin, Larin? Yes, Larin. That was her, getting forced into the police car. The foreboding filled Olivia's head. What connection could she possibly have with all this confusion? The first time Olivia had seen the woman her life had gone amiss. Though she couldn't complain now, what if the woman's reappearance was meant as some sign?

The traffic light turned green and Olivia pushed her foot on the accelerator. She was acting on her gut instinct, but beyond that, she had nothing to go on. In this future life, she had to take everything as a warning.

CHAPTER 12

The memory of pain swarmed Tom before he opened his eyes. His hand flew to his chest. The bed shook as he jolted and sat up with his spine rigid. Through the thin cotton of his t-shirt, his heart drummed against his palm. He heaved a heavy sigh. The fear sent his heart into overdrive. He turned to Olivia and spotted a vacant pillow and flat covers. A pang of emptiness swept him. Every morning for the past three weeks she'd greeted him with her enchanting smile. He missed placing a kiss on her face, warmed by sleep. Today however, his rude awakening would've startled her. Perhaps it was for the best he woke alone.

Still, the strong and steady thumping under his palm failed to convince him he was fine. The dread of a heart attack shattered his cheerful Christmas mood. God, the presence of the others closing in on him and the cold, slimy pads against his skin weren't something he wanted to experience again. During the incident, someone had definitely called "clear"—he didn't imagine that— but that could've come from the frozen pond beyond the tree line where youngsters played hockey.

The door to his suite room popped open. Milo bounced on his toes at the threshold. "Good morning, Daddy." He held his arm up, pointing behind him. By his round eyes and a grin stretching his lips wide, Tom knew what the boy would say next. "Santa came."

A chuckle shook Tom. It'd been close to midnight by the time the boy finally succumbed to sleep. Olivia and he had tippy toed, putting the presents under the small Christmas tree by the window. Now, their son's joy caused him to forget his gloom for a moment. This was the first year Milo grasped the whole Christmas splendor and seeing him this happy made Tom relive his childhood holidays all over again—an incredible thing he had thought a thing long gone.

His eyes zeroed in on a neon yellow sticky note on the footboard. The bed cover rustled as he reached for the paper, reading and eyeing Milo. Not that the boy would notice his father's preoccupation with chest pain, especially on Christmas morning, but Tom couldn't shake off the guilty feeling. "Can't open the presents yet." Frowning, he waved Olivia's note in his hand. "Mommy went to get your favorite auntie."

A pout quickly set on Milo's face and he lowered his head and arm. "Aw, can I open just one?"

Tom shook his head, feeling his son's disappointment. "Mommy said not to open any until she gets back. Let's wait for her." He glanced over Milo's cowboy pajamas. "But she'd like it if you change."

"Then can we open the presents?"

Tom had to chuckle at his son's persistence. The boy was strong willed, just like his mother. "If Mommy and Tadem are back by then."

Milo scratched his head, but retreated to his room. With him gone, Tom's gloom returned. He drew in a long breath, held it in, then exhaled slowly. He waited. No burning pain and none of the numbness or tightness of last night.

He eased out of the bed and grabbed his favorite faded jeans off the floor. Pulling his pants on, an idea turned in his head. Maybe he should use the hotel's gym to reassure himself. Do a bit of cardio exercising, bring his heartbeat up and see if he could keep it steady for twenty minutes.

Sliding his arms through the sleeves of his sweatshirt, he pulled the hoodie over his head. Nah, he should trust his body and not jump to conclusions. The whole thing could've been just a fluke. Tadem's angel must have had something to do with the occurrence of his near heart attack.

Tom cautiously ambled to the living room. Milo hummed a tune from *The Polar Express* and pranced around the Christmas tree. His frolicking pulled Tom out of his mulling. The boy had seemed remarkably comfortable around his changed aunt. Maybe he knew more than Olivia or him. Careful now, he warned himself. He must proceed with a delicacy of hostile hostage negotiation. *Ease off, Milo's just a five- year-old boy.*

"Come here." He patted his leg for the boy to sit in his lap.

Milo glanced over his shoulder, but didn't let go of the big box he was examining with zeal. *Good luck figuring out what is under the wrapping.*

"What?"

"Rosie's still sleeping so we can't talk too loud." Tom tapped his leg again.

When the boy approached, Tom picked him up, sat him on his lap, and wrapped his arm around his small shoulders. "Auntie Tadem looked different last night. Did she scare you when she changed?"

Milo's eyes lit at the mention of Tadem's angel, but he shook his head.

The boy was hiding something. Maybe the angel frightened him. Tom had seen abused children so terrified that nothing could get them to speak out. He stared at his son, thinking of his next question, but Milo kept his keen gaze on the presents. "Have you seen her change into an angel before?"

Milo tapped his finger on his cheek, his eyes slid from right to left. A proud grin sprung on his face. "No, but Auntie told me stories, and last night, she said the angel wanted to see me."

Had Milo ever mentioned Tadem's angel? Tom couldn't remember. It was possible the boy had chatted excessively about it, but he might've replied with an absent-minded aha and um-hmm, while he'd paid attention to anything else. "What did angel tell you?"

"Nothing." The boy's guilty face matched the tremor in his voice.

Tom cocked his head, fixing Milo with his best speak-up-or-else stare. "I can tell when someone's not telling the truth."

Milo slouched. A frown replaced his sunny smile. "I can't remember."

So the angel had spoken. Tom tickled the boy's ribs, making him squirm and giggle. "Try to remember."

Milo face crumpled, lips scrounged. "I don't know what she meant." He dragged his words out. "But she said you and mommy will be happy when I and Rosie get born."

When they get born? What kind of riddle does this angel want me to solve? Olivia's theory of alternate worlds pressed heavy on his mind—with every revelation it made more sense. Tom clamped his molars before he blurted out something and scared Milo. Instead, he cleared his throat and grinned at the fond memory. "Of course we were crazy happy to have you, and always will be. Wouldn't change a thing for the entire world."

Milo's small eyebrows arched, he beamed at the opportunity. "Can I open one present, then?"

"Nice try, kiddo." Tom ruffled his hair and lowered the boy.

Pouting, Milo picked up his teddy bear and plopped in front of the television.

At Rosie's cooing, Tom got up and stretched. "Tell you what. Continue examining the boxes and try to guess what each one is. Mommy should be here any minute. Then I'll order us a nice, big breakfast and we'll open the presents."

Milo's face lit up, he dropped his stuffy toy and flew to the piled wrapped boxes.

The door to their suite swung open. Olivia rushed in. The rubber soles of her boots squeaked on the tile floor as she halted by the entrance. Relief washed away fear on her face, her shoulders relaxed.

"Mommy's here," Milo announced, shaking a box and making the contents rattle. But his head turned as she made a beeline for Tom. "Mommy?"

"Oh! Thank God," she gasped, rushing to Tom she wrapped her arms around his torso and pressed her body on his. The coldness still clung to her coat, seeped through his shirt.

He embraced her, rocking from side to side. "I missed you, too." His glance travelled to the suit's door, left wide open. His wife trembled and tightened her hold. Could something have happened to Tadem? "Hey, hey. Honey, what is wrong?"

"Auntie Tadem." Milo pointed at the big box as Tadem stepped into sight. "This one's for you."

Her shoulders rose and fell with her fast breathing. "Olivia ran out of the elevator and I couldn't keep up with her."

So, other than out of breath, his sister-in-law was fine.

"You left Tadem alone in the hallway? She can't run." Tom tried to sound casual, but an accusatory tone crept to his voice. "Something happened?"

Olivia pulled back, her mouth dropped as if she just now remembered her sister. "I held her hand when I shot out of the elevator, but it slipped out."

Worry spiraled though him. Olivia's alabaster face appeared ghostly. He cupped her cheeks. "Were you mugged?"

"No, God. Nothing like that. I—" Her chin shook, breath quivered when she opened her mouth as if to say something, but a whimper choked her words.

Tom pulled her to him, nestled her head under his chin. "You're safe now. Take a deep breath first."

"I can't bear the thought I'd lose you one day. You and the kids." On the verge of tears, her quivering voice ripped his heart.

He hugged her tighter and kissed her head. "Why would you fear that? I'm not going anywhere." But the guilt pangs of hiding his possible heart attack stung him all over again.

She pulled back, bit her lip and stared at him. Her brows drew closer. Tears glimmered in her steel eyes. "Just…I saw something… someone…I'm not sure."

His guts twisted with her words. Maybe she'd detected his sudden fear. He thought he'd hidden it from her, but he was only fooling himself. They'd always shared a special connection. Guilt stirred deep in him. He hated keeping things from her, but the pain had only lasted for a few seconds. Knowing her, she would worry over something that could be trivial. Soothing circles of his palm on her back eased her breathing. "Everything's fine, honey." He placed another kiss to Olivia's temple and released her from his hold.

She nodded, wiping her eyes. Doubt crept to his shoulders with her silence.

Rosie's cooing grew louder. The baby demanded attention. He welcomed the distraction and stepped into the room. "Come to Daddy." He picked up Rosie from her cot. Bouncing the baby in his arms, he returned to Olivia while she hung her long coat in the small foyer's closet. "Chin up, honey, it's Christmas. Milo can't wait to open his presents and a great day is ahead of us."

A soft smile lit her pretty face, but her stiff shoulders still nagged him. "I shouldn't have burst in like this."

"There's nothing to worry about. I think changing Rosie would help you take your mind off this. I'll warm up the bottle for her, but first let me call room service." Tom handed the baby to Olivia and reached for the phone on the wall. "Or would you rather eat in the restaurant?"

Slouched over the bed, Olivia glanced over her shoulder without ceasing the diaper duty, a funny frown on her face. "Two kids and Tadem, I don't think you need to ask."

"Room service it is." He dialed and shoved his free hand deep inside his jean's pocket to refrain from checking his heartbeat.

• • •

They are fine, they are fine. But Tom's jittery. He kept his hands shoved deep in his pockets and every so often he pressed hard on his chest. In the beam of sunlight casting through the suite's window, his complexion seemed sallow.

Olivia settled in the recliner with Rosie eagerly sucking, the warm formula disappearing from the bottle.

Tom perched himself on the sofa next to her, steam curling from the mug of cocoa in his hand. "Okay." He turned to Milo and Tadem. "You can open one present each before our food gets here."

"Can I open this one?" Milo raised a square in white wrapping with candy canes.

Her son's enthusiasm brought a smile to Olivia's face, but a sting of loss extinguished her kindle of hope. One day she would come home and find an empty house. Not a single trace of her family left. "Is your name on it?"

Milo examined the tag and nodded. "It's for me from you and Daddy."

"You can open it." Tom blew on the surface of the dark liquid then set the mug on the stand by her seat. Her mouth watered at the cocoa and milk mixture. "Should be cooled off by now, but be careful."

Milo ripped open the wrapping and revealed his first gift of Christmas. "Oh wow, look Mommy." He shoved a book under her nose.

"*A Dangerous Book for Boys.* Nice." Olivia darted her glance at Tom, raising a questioning eyebrow.

"Don't worry, honey. It's a Canadian edition." Tom cupped one hand around his mouth and whispered, "It's pretty tame."

Olivia joined Tom in his chuckling. The knot in her chest loosened and she sank deeper into the recliner. Her husband always knew how to lighten any situation and cheer her up. His tender care had long shattered her strong protective walls. She turned to Milo. "Show your gift to Auntie until Rosie's done eating. Then we'll open more presents."

While Milo and Tadem were absorbed in flipping through the pages, Olivia grabbed the opportunity and turned to Tom, who studied her through his narrowed eyes. "I tried to ask Tadem about her angel, but didn't get far. All I found out was that she's around her all the time and that you share the same guardian with her."

Tom's eyebrows twitched and fear crossed his eyes. He straightened. "I'd think there are an infinite number of angels in Heaven. Why would I share one with Tadem?"

"Tadem stopped talking after she blurted it out." Olivia studied her sister, trying to find any trace of the angel. If she was with Tadem all the time, that meant she could be here right now. "As a baby, she'd be looking at me, then her glance would snap away and she'd stare into empty space, grinning. I tried to see what grabbed her attention, but never saw a thing."

Tom placed his hand on her knee. "Babies often do that. Remember Milo and Rosie smiling at the ceiling? When we looked up there was nothing there."

Tom's question should infuriate her, but his gentle rub on her knee helped dissipate the last bit of Olivia's fear. "Tadem continued this activity long after her baby days. Should I ask her to show us her angel again? Maybe she can change at will."

A mask of fear settled on Tom's face. "I don't think it's a good idea. It would scare the kids." He leaned closer, propping himself on his elbow. "This upset you? That I share her angel?"

"Yes, that and…" Olivia cocked her head. Could she tell him about the bad feeling she'd gotten when she saw that wicked woman getting shoved into the police car? No, they already had lots of inexplicable stuff to deal with. The woman seemed to have fallen on bad times after she'd fired her, but Olivia was only doing her job. But that excuse was growing old. Nothing prevented her from showing some compassion. Instead she'd chosen to get on the same wagon with Hiltorn and his bullies who treated people like trash.

"And what?" Tom's voice drifted to her.

"Not important." She sat Rosie upright and patted her back, but his stare implied he wouldn't let her off that easy.

"It had to be important." He glanced at the Milo and Tadem then faced her again and dropped his voice to a whisper. "I've never seen you shaken like that."

Guilty shame rushed heat to her cheeks, but she had to lie to him to get him off her back. "There was an accident. I didn't recognize the part of the city I ended up in due to heavy traffic. I panicked."

His shoulders slumped, he exhaled loudly. Had he bought her story? Not likely, but it seemed he, too, wanted to drop the issue. "I asked Milo about the angel, too." A reluctant tone laced Tom's voice. He might've pushed the boy for answers. "Didn't get far. Last night was the first time he saw her, though Tadem told him about her. He said the angel mumbled something about our kids will be born. None of it made any sense."

Olivia shook her head. The angel had mentioned she was in the future, though the year stayed the same. Maybe the entity had sent her ahead but couldn't actually shift the time. Desperation overwhelmed her, but she swallowed the rising lump. She wouldn't be able to take much more of this mystery. "The knot gets worse the more we try to untangle the mess. I feel there's nothing we can do here but play along."

"You could be right." With a loud sigh, Tom stood and took the empty bottle from her hand. Then he slid a narrow box wrapped in silver in her palm. "From me."

She placed Rosie on her play mat and the baby reached for the hanging toys. Olivia opened the box. Her breath caught at the sight of a princess-cut diamond solitaire pendant hanging from white gold necklace. "It's…stunning."

"It will be once you put it on." He kissed the top of her head, sending soft tickles to the center of her belly. "Hope this jogs your memory."

She pierced him with her questioning stare. He crossed his arms over his chest, one hand massaging his left side. "The words you cannot seem to remember each time we start to make love."

"So diamonds should help me remember? Well, I always said that diamonds are a girl's best friend." She curled her lip, trying to remember an old movie she'd seen long ago.

"Yes." A hopeful expression filled his features and voice. She may be onto something.

She pondered the saying while he nodded, expecting her to blurt out the word or words. So the secret to his sweet loving wasn't a simple "I love you" as she had thought. Girl's best friend, best friend. Damn it, what could it be? She glanced at the diamond, as light danced in its cuts, casting shapes on her palm. The answer flashed in her mind. "Dazzle me," she whispered, hypnotized by the beauty of the stone.

At Tom's soft gasp, she snapped her head, meeting his beaming face. "You remembered." He pulled her to his chest and seared her lips with his. The friction of his stubble on her skin and the whisk of his tongue on hers coaxed a moan from her. "Tonight you'll get dazzled out of your wits," he murmured against her cheek, his soft voice and breath carried a certain promise, sending trickles of desire to her core.

• • •

Christmas wrappings, ribbons, and bows covered the hotel's suite floor and hung from the chairs. Dirty dishes covered the table. Olivia tucked her hand under her legs suppressing the itch to tidy the room up. Just a month ago, she would have expected maid service to do the job, and the thought to clean up would never cross her mind.

Enya's "Silent Night" came from the speakers of Tom's laptop, filling Olivia's chest with the warm, fuzzy feeling of the season. Christmas with her family, the way she'd heard people around the water cooler describe year after year. She much preferred this over playing catch up with her paperwork while the cleaning crew paid her no heed. If only Tom would stop checking his email.

He rubbed his palms. "So, all presents unwrapped? My hands are so chaffed from prying the toys out of the packaging. I don't think I can open another one."

"Yes, Daddy. I checked it twice. No Rosie, the dolly is the present not the box." Milo's attempts to engage Rosie with her new toy were unsuccessful.

"Alright. It's a nice day, how about a walk?" Tom turned to Olivia. "We should get out so the maids can tidy up the suite."

"Yes, by all means." She stood up. Now would be a great time to present him with her gift. Though the anticipation had been brewing in her for weeks, a sudden bout of nervousness stirred her. What if he didn't like it? "Not all the presents have been opened." She reached behind the tree, pulled out a small box from its hiding place and handed it to him. "This one is from me."

"Thank you, honey." He beamed, ripping the golden paper. His jaw dropped at the sight of the vibrant tile inlaid into the lid of the ebony box. "This is Glagolitic." He traced his thumb over the intricate, white letter on the red background.

"Neoglagolitic actually." A smile stretched her lips, and pride filled her. She knew she would stun him with her gift. "The closest thing I could find. Open it, there's more inside."

He popped the lid open and stared in silence for a few moments, then picked the item in his fingers, examining the golden tie clip from every side. "I love it. How did you know?"

"Just a hunch. Since I saw your tie, I couldn't stop thinking about it." But it was the constant, burning desire for him that had started her creativity. In the past, she certainly had not put any effort into buying presents. Nor had she ever given or received any. But now with her family, she'd spent hours scouring the malls and fighting the crowds in search for that perfect gift. Milo already couldn't put his action figures down, Rosie's booties fit her perfectly and would go nicely with her new winter coat, and Tadem loved her sweatshirt and matching pants.

"This deserves extra dazzling tonight. Hope you're up to it." His slow wink rushed heat to her face. What was wrong with her? She never blushed at a man's advances.

"You have no idea just how up to it I am." She rubbed her neck to ease her pent up passion. A walk in the cold air would help. "Let's go."

Though Milo complained about leaving the pile of his new toys, he got dressed for outdoors and settled for a small action figure to take along.

Tom pushed Rosie's stroller to the play area.

"Watch me slide." Milo ran to the climber on the hotel's ground, and scrambled up the ladder to the top of the slide. Tadem plopped herself on the bench. Her residential center must put very little effort in engaging the residents in physical activities. Olivia would make sure to have her sister get into some type of fitness activity.

Tom stopped and ogled monkey bars. Olivia's eyebrows arched when he grabbed the bars and preformed chin ups. Was he training for tonight's promised marathon, or reliving his childhood?

"Good," he said, jumping down. "Twenty reps and still not out of breath." He pointed at the stairs leading out of the play area. "I'm going to run up those steps."

She glanced over her shoulder at the two flights of steep steps then back at him. "I know the meal was heavy, but you didn't eat that much."

"Don't worry. I'll be ready for tonight if I can run up a flight of steps." He tapped her arm and took off.

"Run up a flight of steps"—hadn't she read an article about this just the other day? Didn't doctors advise their patients who'd suffered a heart attack that if they were able to run the up the stairs without getting winded, they'd be ready to have sex?

"Oh my god." She lowered to the bench, her legs suddenly wobbly.

Tom ran up to her. A peculiar grin on his face suggested he wanted to take her right there and now. "Running up those steps warmed me up." He grabbed her wrists, pulling her up. "Come on. You should try it."

"No, Tom." She managed to whisper through her tight throat, "Did you experience chest pains?"

His grin vanished and he lowered on the bench. "No."

But the tremble in his voice failed to convince her. The anticipation of tonight's dazzling abandoned her. "Please, tell me."

His exhale came out long and loud, and a reluctant, lopsided grin formed his mouth. "When the angel showed up, a debilitating pain in my chest, like I've never experienced before, sent me to my knees. From all I've heard about heart attacks, I'd say it felt like I was experiencing one." At her gasp and stern gaze, he straightened and put his hands up. "I'm fine, really I am. The pain hasn't returned and it only lasted for a few seconds."

Tears she could no longer control filled her eyes and blurred her vision. She couldn't take this anymore. She wanted answers, but things were getting more complicated. Tom didn't want her to worry, that was why he lied, but a lie by omission was still a lie. The angel had said he was fighting for his life, maybe he just didn't know it yet. "Are you sure?"

"Yes, I don't feel anything." This time his voice didn't falter and a reassurance relaxed her, but tears still kept coming.

He removed his glove and wiped her tears. "I screwed up, I know. I should've told you."

Damn it, she should stop this water works display, if not for Tom then for Milo. Her son wouldn't like to see his mom this upset. She drew in a long breath. "Pent up frustration, I needed to vent it out. But, if we're going to find answers, we must work together. No more withholding."

He squeezed her hand and nodded. "In that case, you should come clean, too."

Yes, she should. She sighed. Of course he hadn't believed her story. "The night you came to my life, I was here, in Vancouver, on Mr. Hiltorn's firing mission. The last person I laid off gave me the creeps, which never happened before. I'm positive I saw her again today. I've got the same awful feeling under my skin."

His eyebrows drew closer and he gazed into her eyes. "You think this person has something to do with our situation?"

She shrugged and shook her head. "I don't know. I just want you to believe me."

"I'd dismissed your theory as some farfetched nonsense and refused to believe it. But now you've convinced me there's much more here." His confession brought a sense of relief to her, and for the first time she trusted him with her heart. She leaned her head on his shoulder. Time seemed to slow down, the sounds grew distant. Lost in the peaceful oblivion washed in the rays of setting sun, she smiled at Milo racing up the ladder to slide once again, and Tadem clapping her hands.

Tom reached into his coat pocket and pulled out his cell, shattering her tranquil moment. He read a text from the screen. His eyebrow twitched and he scowled, but wrapped her in his arm all the same. She drew a long breath, taking in the fresh sea breeze scent he seemed to carry with him.

"Don't tell me. More bad news." Her gaze darted to the phone in his hand, hoping to catch a glimpse of the text message, but he was faster and shoved the mobile back to his pocket.

He brushed his lips against hers and she shuddered. His tongue teased and prodded her mouth to open, then met hers in a whirlwind. A moan of desire slipped her lips. Damn it, never before had she gone this long without satisfying her physical needs. Milo's giggling brought her back to the moment and she pulled back. They shouldn't get carried away in front of the boy.

A devilish smile tugged corners of Tom's mouth, but faded fast as if he remembered something. "The case just took an unexpected turn. We'll have to return sooner than I wanted." That same smile he'd worn a minute ago returned, and two sparkles danced in his eyes. "But not before I fulfill my promise tonight."

CHAPTER 13

The doorframe dug into Tom's back. He uncrossed his arms and pushed away from the wooden trim. His heart liquefied as Olivia placed a soft kiss on Milo's head. The boy drew in a deep breath and tightened his arms around the teddy bear. She turned to the playpen, pulled the fleece blanket, covering thumb-sucking Rosie up to her shoulder, and stroked her dark hair.

The warm, fuzzy feeling moved to Tom's stomach. Whether the woman taking care of his children was his wife or her double from some other world, he loved her. And tonight he would show her just how much.

"I thought Milo would never go to sleep." At Olivia's husky whisper, Tom blinked fast. Anticipation surged through him, sending blood to his groin.

She stepped to him and wrapped her arms around his waist. His abs instantly flexed. He kissed her forehead, taking in her subtle floral scent. She shuddered against him, the unconscious reaction telling him she'd too waited for a night of passion. His arm wrapped around her shoulders, he led her out of the children's room and into the main bedroom of their hotel's suite. Vancouver's lights twinkled in the frosty Christmas night and reflected on the ten-foot windows hidden behind sheer curtains.

She gasped and stared, wide-eyed, at the candles flickering and casting the dancing shadows on the walls and ceiling. Just the kind of reaction she'd had on their wedding night. Could the ambience he'd created have jogged her memory? No, it couldn't, she was some other woman, and he must stop hoping her memories would return. Hands resting on her shoulders, he dismissed the thought and pulled her to him. Finally a time for them.

He nuzzled her neck and nibbled her earlobe.

A husky moan slipped from her lips while her head rolled to the side, allowing him better access. He trailed his lips to the hollow of her delicate throat.

"I need you, Tom." The harshness in her breath rushed the blood to his already tight groin. "Dazzle me."

"And you'll have me." Placing his hands over hers, he stopped her from taking off his shirt. "But patience, dear. It won't hurt to take it slow."

If his angel waited to take his soul to wherever it was destined to go, he'd enjoy this one night, make it last.

Her forehead creased and surprise zipped across her beautiful eyes. She parted her lips as if to say something, but he sealed them with his. While his tongue explored her mouth, he cupped her buttocks and raised her off the carpeted floor. Her graceful legs wrapped around his hips, while she hung to him by his shoulders. By now she was his playful kitten. Her hard, hungry kiss spurred him. His passion fused and merged with hers. He fueled her need by plunging in his tongue, nibbling her bottom lip, barely letting her come up for air.

He pressed her backside against the wall, rubbing his erection on her abdomen. Damn it, she was so hot he could explode before he had her naked. In the past, he'd always savored every second of their lovemaking by taking it slow and postponing the climax.

She broke the kiss and arched her back, jamming her breasts against his chest. Her fingers dug into his hair and pulled him to her bosom. "Take me, Tom. Make me scream your name."

He smiled at the urgency in her voice. She was exactly where he wanted her. Hot and wanton. He lowered her feet to the floor then wiggled a remote from his jeans pocket. The cool leather of the chair caressed his skin. At the press of a button, soft music filled the room.

"Strip for me," he demanded.

She stiffened. Her frown made her appear uncertain of his order. He questioned his method—after all this was a different woman. Nonetheless she must earn her orgasm.

A wicked grin appeared on her face. She stood in front of him, her hips swaying in beat with the sensual tune. She undid the row of buttons on her shirt. Then she flipped her hair from side to side, brushing his chest and face. She allowed her shirt to slide down her arms, and slid her bra straps off her shoulders. He stopped her when she was about to unclasp the hooks on the back and reveal her breasts.

"Leave your bra like this." He reached for her swinging hips. She paused, scooping her hair on the top of her head, while he popped the button on her slacks and slid the zipper down. He tugged the jeans to her knees.

She turned and bent over, her legs straight, and stuck her taut ass in his face. He got on his feet, pulled her lacy panties just below her butt cheeks and rubbed his palm over the firm globes. He slapped one side then the other, coaxing a yelp from her. She threw him a stunned look over her shoulder, confirming his speculation that her cry came at his unexpected action.

"Not long ago you asked me to spank you." With circular movements, he soothed the hot skin of her buttocks while she freed her legs. "Now turn around and undress me."

She obeyed, raising his shirt up his torso. He scrambled out of his tee. The soft cotton dropped from her hand and brushed his bare back on its way down. Hands gliding on his chest, she kissed him slowly, working her way down his chest and abdomen. Her fingers brushed an old scar on his right flank. When her gaze met his, a question hovered in her black depths. Why did she feel uncomfortable asking him straight out?

With a long inhale, he placed his hand over hers to stop her from tickling him. "The mark of an emperor."

Her eyebrows knitted, but she remained silent. Hmm, how to make a long story short and not break this enchanting moment? A quick explanation would be the best, just as the first time she, or her double, had seen his scar. "My brother always dared me and I tried hard to prove I wasn't a snotty brat he took me for. So I climbed the statue of Emperor Augustus, slipped, and it took twelve stitches to close the nasty cut." Tom frowned and shrugged. "Roman emperors still have powers to hurt you."

"Looks good on you, though," she whispered after a short chuckle, and traced her tongue over the hardened skin. He pulled his stomach in when her fingers darted to his waist. She worked fast, unbuckling his belt, undoing the zipper and button. Once she freed him of his trousers and boxers, leaving them heaped around his ankles, she kneeled and reached for his hardness. Her fingers wrapped around the base of his stiff cock. She slid the tip between her succulent lips, suckling along his erection, causing tightness in his balls.

"Ah…yeah." A gruff moan slipped out of him. He cupped her head and she took his full length in her mouth. His toes curled into the lush carpet, locking his stance while his pelvis thrust slightly. The urge to slam her on the mattress and plunge himself into her heat almost crushed him. *Exercise self-control, man.* And to do that, he must stop her before he exploded in her mouth.

He hissed, and despite raging fire in his soul, pulled back. "Easy, honey. We have the whole night."

She stood and locked her lips with his. Her tongue tasted salty and mixed with her own sweet flavor. With one arm behind her back, he struggled to unhook her bra as he backed her against the bed. On his third yank the clasp came undone. "I must be out of practice."

Her soft chuckle tickled his ear. "You're quite skilled. The clasp is bent."

He slid the lace down, and her breasts perked. "That's better," he murmured, and closed his mouth around her nipple while he pinched her other hard nub.

Her knees must've given in, for she lowered herself to the bed, pulling him along. She stroked his hair as he brushed his lips back and forth along her downy skin, from her sensitive area around her belly button, down to her flank and hip. He blew on her flesh, causing goose bumps to rise. Then he slid her panties to her knees and traced a "v" at the top of her legs, fluttering her pubic hair. He spread her legs and knelt between them, one finger exploring her swollen folds.

"Yes," she cried, arching, and pressed her body to his. "That's the spot."

She kicked her feet, flicking her underwear off, then opened her legs wide, inviting him in, but he swallowed hard and pulled back. Damn it, it was difficult to exercise this much self-control. Her arousal was powerful tonight. It would be, after a month of romancing, tempting and not fulfilling her desires. How long would he be able to push her before she erupted in his arms? He'd have to slow down her pace.

"Not so fast." The ice bucket cooling the bottle of champagne on the headboard came into his focus. Coldness seeped in his fingers when he reached in and extracted one ice cube. She closed her eyes while he slid the chilled rime from her lips, down her chin, neck, torso, between her breasts, leaving the cube to melt, pooling inside her belly button. He licked the racing drops and sucked the liquid from her hot skin.

"Ah, please, please." She panted, clutching to the pillow under her head. Her back arched when he trailed his tongue down her inner thighs. "I'm ready."

He coaxed her to suck in her breath with his teasing finger, brushing her mound. "Soon, love. I'll have you scream my name."

"I've been good." Her legs wrapped around him, locking him in her magic. "I've waited long enough."

Yes, she had been and had not attempted her pushy way since the night he'd refused her. He studied her rosy cheeks—her panting and writhing all told him her body and mind were taut. She needed him—hell, he needed her. He'd give her what she wanted, craved. She deserved their union.

With his fingers wrapped around the base of his shaft, he glided inside her wetness, filling her.

She arched higher and sucked in a breath. "Oh, god, I knew you'd be big."

Her muscles closed around him, tightening, engulfing. He pumped inside her, her hips rising to meet his thrusts. Her cries grew louder as she climbed higher, her breaths quickened.

"Tom." Her gasp indicated she was on the verge of climax.

"No pet, let's come together," he grunted, allowing his orgasm to mount. "Hold it for another second. You can do it, love."

"I can't." Her fingers slipped off his sweaty shoulder, down his back and stopped on his butt.

"Yes, you can. Another second. Do it for me." Plunging deeper into her, a guttural moan escaped him.

"Tom," she cried, her voice nearing a scream.

"Go for it." His body stiffened and he rose on his elbows. "Let me watch you."

The tips of her disheveled hair stuck in the corner of her mouth and made her extra-sexy while her body rocked hard.

"Tom." Another moan pushed out of her along with his name.

A rush of wetness flooded his cock and drove him over the brink. He slammed his hips against hers, his climax taking him on a roller coaster ride, his hands molding her buttocks, holding her locked in place while he thrust her body into the mattress again and again until finally collapsing.

Her eyes opened, she cupped his face and pulled him to her so his chest lay flush with hers. He uttered a satisfied groan and slid one arm under her, legs intertwined with hers. His face buried in the crook of her neck. He reveled in her quick breaths and soft moans. As his heart steadied, he placed a soft kiss on her temple. He'd planned to bring her favorite toy at some point, but decided to test her and wait for her to beg him to use it on her. Judging by her relaxed face, his performance had been better than gratifying.

A smile stretched her lips, lighting her face. She played with his hair then shuddered.

"Are you cold?" He reached for the covers.

"No, just experienced an unexpected ripple of passion."

He pulled her closer to him and held her tight, taking in her softness and warmth.

Her palm pressed on his chest. "No pain?"

"None." He sat up, reaching for the bottle in the ice bucket. "Are you up for a glass of bubbly?"

"Crack it open." She reached for the flutes from the floor and turned to him, holding the glasses for him to fill once he popped the cork.

He took one long-stemmed glass from her and raised it. "To us."

She cast him a dazzling smile. A sharp sound of their crystals clinking together filled the room. "Couldn't ask for a better Christmas."

"Neither could I." Though sweet champagne wasn't his stuff, he drained the glass, soft bubbles clinging to his dry throat.

She placed her empty glass on the nightstand and nestled in his arms. He brushed his knuckles over her shoulder while basking in the afterglow of their lovemaking. Soon, his fingers found her hardened nipple. Her soft moan filled the silence, and she pressed her arching back on his chest.

She slid down the pillow. "Not sure if I can go for another big one."

"That is why I brought this." He reached for the toy inside the drawer of the nightstand.

Her finger traced along the purple silicone and stopped at the curved tip. With her mouth dropped open, she shot him a lustful grin. "Oh."

He pressed a wet kiss on her skin and nibbled her neck. "Oh indeed. It's the name of this incredible device. Oh! Rabbit."

"The shape alone promises some wicked arousal." Her thumb tapped the soft ears of the clit stimulator. "Does it have multiple speeds?"

"Of course." He flicked an eyebrow at her provocative tone. "Care to try it?"

"Oh yes, just looking at it makes me wet." She spread her legs wide. He poised the toy at her entrance, denying her the pleasure of penetration. At the press of a tiny button, the dildo buzzed to life.

Her face reddened while he slid the "Rabbit" inside her. Once fully inserted and in place he kneeled between her legs. "You want it to go faster?"

"Yes," she panted, crumpling bed sheets. "Faster."

"Uh-uh, did you forget to say please?" His fingers brushed her tender mound.

"Oh, please, Tom."

He indulged her, speeding up the stimulator. Her body tensed and she sucked in a breath. "Ah, sweet Jesus, this is good."

Her immense pleasure and coarse voice hardened his cock to painful levels. "Describe what you're feeling."

"God, my pussy, all of me is…burning for your…ah…" Moans swallowed her words and nothing coherent came out of her mouth. Her knee under his hand shook. There'd be no way of controlling her orgasm when she seemed on the brink of climax.

He eased the toy out and she yelped at the loss of the contact, but squealed as he slammed inside her, and she closed her legs around him. In a few hard thrusts, he couldn't stop from climaxing. She stiffened too, while her muscles closed on his shaft buried deep inside her. Her simultaneous orgasm took him on a wild ride, rolling and jerking his body like he was standing on a deck of a ship caught in a wild storm. Once again, he wrapped her in his arms and pulled her to him, holding her there until his breathing calmed. Then he placed a kiss on her forehead, and another one on her lips.

"Sleep now," he whispered.

He listened to her even breathing, but sleep failed to take him. Sheets rustled on his way out of bed. Heat from the vent below the window crawled up his bare legs, and he stared at the twinkling city. Olivia's loud inhale and a soft moan made him turn to the bed. She flipped to her side, her naked back ending in firm buttocks set on top of the sexiest legs. He turned to the window, extinguishing his desire. His woman needed rest. Later perhaps. Waking her up to make love just as it dawned was always his favorite.

CHAPTER 14

Lack of sleep added to Tom's displeasure. His fingers drumming on the metal table echoed in the empty visitation room of the women's correctional facility. A glance over his shoulder at the square window at the top of the door confirmed no one stood on the other side. It had been over fifteen minutes since the prison guard had gone to fetch Maria from her cell. The metal cuffs on the burly woman's belt had clanked with her slow gait, and told him the officer would take her time.

At the clunk of a heavy door opening, he turned his head just as Maria strutted in wearing her neon orange suit. With the bright sun and the neon his eyes hurt, or maybe he was tired from a night of passion and an early flight to Toronto. At least the kids and Olivia had gotten plenty of sleep on the plane.

The young woman dragged her feet across the polished vinyl floor then threw herself onto the empty chair. She squared her jaw and put on that I-don't-give-a-crap expression. Could she be picking up an attitude in prison?

"Un-cuff her," he ordered. The guard woman shot him a look of surprise, but obeyed all the same. She quietly withdrew to the back of the room, taking her spot by the door, hands on her wide waist. For a moment he contemplated insisting she wait outside, but he'd be conducting the interview in Croatian so the prison guard wouldn't understand a word.

Braced on his elbows, he leaned over his papers on the table. "How're you doing, Mar—"

"I spent the last two days in solitary confinement. How do you think I'm doing?"

Yep, the girl had fallen under some bad influences. Three months ago, she'd been a frightened little mouse and he'd worried she'd die in prison before her trial date. Seemed she could hold her own now. But he knew her kind—all phony and easy to break under pressure.

He exhaled slowly before he continued. She should be on her best behavior instead of getting into more trouble than she already was. "Tell me you're kidding."

"They took the picture of my boy away." Her voice cracked and veins on her neck popped. She swallowed and straightened. "The guards on duty are known to turn their backs. I was afraid of Fat Bertha…" And indeed fear flashed in her wide eyes. She tucked a loose lock of her sandy hair behind her ear. "I haven't seen my boy in almost a year. He's with my mom and my sister. I haven't sent them any money since I've ended up here."

Tom's insides mellowed. He flipped to the blank page of his note book and made a memo to himself. At least he could take one worry from her. "I'll send them a few bucks."

As if a load of bricks fell from her shoulders, she slumped. Tears freely poured down her pale cheeks. "Mr. Medar, it's nice of you, but you really don't have to do this."

Tom nodded, pressing his lips into a tight smile. The girl had chosen the lesser of two evils, between being taken advantage of by an inmate and the safety of isolation. "It's alright, Maria. No trouble at all."

"None of this is alright." She spat. "I believed I'd find a better life in this country." With a heavy sigh, she leaned back in her chair. "Did you know a roll of toilet paper has more value than my degree in economics?"

His heart sank. Many had fallen prey to same trap. They'd read someplace about honey and milk awaiting them in a foreign country, only to find a different fate. They gave up the last bit of possessions to secure a plane ticket and maybe a bit of cash. Maria, more than likely, had more to lose here than in Croatia.

"I understand diplomas from other countries are often not recognized here."

She twisted the cuff of her sleeve. "Had I known that, I never would've left home. I was shocked at first, but I needed a job and so I chose Mr. Baldwin's domestic employment."

"Was there another choice?" He twirled the pen between his fingers.

Redness spread over her face, indicating she wasn't comfortable with what she was about to disclose. Her voice was barely audible when she said, "Stripper."

"You chose wisely." The gravity of his words hit him as he said them.

She let out a shrill laugh "Look where it got me."

Now rolling the pen between his palms, he arched an eyebrow. "Worse things can happen in the strip joint. I'll get you out of this and you must trust me. I'm your only friend now." Paper crinkled when he pulled out a copy of a report. "You need to be honest with me and tell me everything you know, no matter how insignificant it seems."

Maria switched her glance from him to her hands resting in her lap. "Yes, Mr. Medar."

Better, she was back to her soft self. Maybe now she'd be willing to talk. "Mrs. Baldwin caught you in his room, sniffing her husband's underwear."

Maria didn't answer immediately. Instead, she cocked her head, her lips curled downward, her glance slid to the side. "I didn't."

"So you were in his room when she caught you." He shifted, trying to get Maria to look at him. Knowing the girl's traditional upbringing, he understood she was conditioned to stare at her feet during hard questioning.

"Mr. Baldwin sent me to fetch him some clean clothes."

Tom stared at her, gesturing with his hand to continue.

"He spilled his drink on his shirt during their fundraising barbeque."

"Why did you grab his underwear?" The girl was hiding something. Though her eyes seemed to light up when she spoke of Mr. Baldwin, she avoided looking at Tom and he couldn't read her face.

Clearing her throat, she shrugged. "I…don't know. Just did."

He leaned forward, shooting her his most uncompromising glare.

She buried her face in her hands. "I can't tell, Mr. Medar. Please, don't make me."

"Maria." He reached for her wrists and pulled her hands down. "It is admirable you're keeping Mr. Baldwin's secret, but you have to understand. The evidence is mounting against you, and I have nothing to refute the charges."

Her eyes reddened and she swiped at the fresh tears. Sandy blonde hair fell over her face when she shook her head. She clamped her lips tight.

Frustration seized all the muscles in his back. He wouldn't be able to defend her if she didn't tell the truth. "Don't be daft, Maria. Mr. Baldwin's secret will stay safe. I can be discreet."

Still, if she said she grabbed her boss's underwear in error or he'd requested she bring him the fresh pair, Tom would have to investigate.

She wiped her tears with the sleeve of her orange jumper and heaved. "Are we done here?"

"No, we're not. Sit." Irritation made his voice harsh. OK, the girl wasn't about to let her tongue loose. Time to redirect. 'Did you have an affair with him?"

Her face crumpled, but she returned to her seat and said a firm, "No."

An affair between an older man and a much younger woman, eighteen years, wouldn't make the evening news. He shook his head, expecting her to continue. When she remained silent, he banged his hand on the table. She flinched and shot him a scared glance. "Care to elaborate?"

"It's nothing like that, Mr. Medar." Her high-pitched voice indicated her throat was closing in again.

He took a calming breath. It would do no good if he lost his temper, but damn it, the woman challenged him. "Then shed some light on how it is. To the world, it seems exactly like that."

"He was like no man I've ever seen. You know how the guys are back home, wearing the same pair of jeans until they disintegrate on them." She sniffed.

"At least they wouldn't put you behind bars." Hopefully his firm tone would tell her she had crossed her line and fallen for a man way out of her league.

"No, they'd do worse. Knock a girl up and split." After a short pause, her face mellowed. "Mr. Baldwin, he smelled nice, always in fine clothes, he was kind to me. Understood me."

Interesting. He leaned over the table. Mr. Baldwin would've been the first gentleman Maria had encountered. She could've mistook his kindness and caring for something more. "Has he ever touched you…inappropriately?"

"I wish he had. He only talked to me, told me about his life and…" She frowned as in disgust. "His loveless marriage. Poor man."

So Mr. Baldwin poured his heart out to Maria. And if Mrs. Baldwin suspected, or worse, had known about her husband's innocent yet deep connection with Maria, she would act out of jealousy. No wonder the lady fought to keep Maria behind bars for good. He wouldn't forget her cold and plastic appearance—too much Botox and not enough brains. He straightened. "If the staff stayed in their own building, why were you in the house the night of shooting?"

"Erich, I mean, Mr. Baldwin asked me to meet him in his study. He said he had some great news he wanted to share with me." She lowered her head, her shoulders shook and a wail ripped out of her mouth. "That's when I found him on the floor in the pool of blood." Her voice was raspy as she continued after drawing in a long breath. "I screamed and grabbed the gun. Stupid, I know, but it was an impulse. The next thing I know, Mrs. Baldwin came down yelling. Calling me names. Oh, Mr. Medar, it was awful. I didn't know what to do."

Okay, Maria had made a big mistake by grabbing the gun, but she had not pulled the trigger. The prosecution was trying to account the lack of gun residue on her hands with the gloves theory, but she wasn't stupid. Why would she dispose of gloves then incriminate herself by placing her fingerprints on the weapon? Besides, she wouldn't have the motive, not when she obviously harbored some strong feelings for the victim, unless she'd mistaken Baldwin's kindness for love. As for opportunity, that was something Tom would have to prove she didn't have.

He slipped the pawn receipt under her nose. "Care to explain why your signature is on the purchase of the gun?"

She raised her glance at him, her mouth agape. "Mrs. Baldwin drove me to this shop. Gave me the piece of paper and said to show it to the man—Steve, she said his name was. He gave me a box and pointed where to sign. That's all. I swear."

His mind worked in time with the fast tapping of his foot. If the Mrs. was trying to pin the shooting of her husband on the hired help, she was doing a lousy job. It was time for her to go from a person of interest to a suspect. "When Mrs. Baldwin caught you in her husband's bedroom during this barbecue, was she alone?"

"No, she had a man groping her all over, shameless hussy that she is. They both laughed when they barged into the room. She said she loved fucking on her husband's bed or it would never see any action." Then, as if startled by her words, Maria gasped. "You didn't hear this from me. Please, she can have me deported. She did it to one maid. Sent something called La Migra after her."

He raised his hands. Poor Maria had heard one too many stories. "You can breathe easy. There's no immigration police in Canada. Do you know this other man?"

"He came to the estate often, mostly when Mr. Baldwin was away. The staff called him, uh…it sounded like Hill Torn. It was a silly name, I thought because he was so curt."

"Hiltorn?" Tom's pulse quickened. Olivia's boss? From what his wife had described, the man was rude and abrupt in manners. This was something worth looking into. How could he prove Mrs. Baldwin's infidelity?

His cell vibrated. He pulled it out of his pocket. The message on the screen was from his intern. *Baldwin out of coma, doctors will allow a brief questioning. Meet you at St. Michael's.*

• • •

Tom stomped his feet on the black carpet in the hospital's lobby, shaking fresh snow off his boots. He'd made it from the women's correctional facility at the outskirts of greater Toronto to the downtown's St. Michael's Hospital in record time. It was a miracle the police hadn't pulled him over for speeding and unsafe lane changes. His intern ceased his frantic pacing and approached him. "Finally."

"Sorry, Alex, traffic was a murder." Tom tapped the young man on his shoulder, nudging him onward. "Fill me in on our way."

"Mrs. Baldwin is here trying to stop the interview." Alex disposed of his empty coffee cup in the nearest trash bin and pushed his fashionable eyeglasses up his nose.

"I was afraid she might." Tom sped down the long corridor. The squeaking of his wet soles sounded in time with his strides.

At least the noise took the edge of sharp disinfectant stinging his nose. A small group of journalists gathered in front of Mr. Baldwin's room, guarded by a uniformed officer.

"Preposterous," Mrs. Baldwin's voice boomed in the narrow hallway. "My husband barely opened his eyes."

When she spun in Tom's direction, not a strand of her hair moved. "Ah, here comes the shooter's lawyer."

Reporters flocked to him, thrusting microphones at his face. He shielded his face from the blinding flashes of their cameras. They all seemed to shout the same question. "Mr. Medar, any new development in the case?"

Damn, how did the media get a hold of this? Good thing he'd grabbed the moment and called Olivia on his way down. From the look of it, he wouldn't have a chance to talk to her any time soon. He missed her and the kids already. They were supposed to be enjoying their holidays. After a wild night of loving in the luxurious Vancouver hotel, the peck on her cheek he'd given her this morning seemed inadequate. But he would make up for his absence when he got home this evening, if the day's events didn't drain his last ounce of strength.

As if waiting for his permission to speak, he raised his hand. When the reporters continued to shout, he hollered over the clamor, "No comment."

He pivoted on his heel, nodding to the cop, and with Alex on his heels, slipped inside the hospital room, leaving the media to the mercy of Mrs. Baldwin.

Two doctors kept keen eyes on the machines surrounding the raised hospital bed and monitoring the patient's vitals. The detective on the case acknowledged his arrival with a single nod. Mr. Baldwin's lawyer, decked in his Armani suit, tore his frowning gaze from Tom, leaned over the frail body barely visible beneath the tubes delivering fluids and medication and whispered in Mr.

Baldwin's ear. Tom knew his corporate type. What would this guy know of a criminal case?

Tom glanced down at his faded jeans and snow boots. Well, he really must learn to keep a suit and a pair of nice shoes in his car. But for now, his casual attire would have to do, despite the attorney's disdain.

Alex flashed open the page of his notebook. Tom scanned over the bullet points, nodding to his intern. He had to admit, the youngster would make an excellent lawyer one day.

"Listen here." One of the doctors in crisp, white coat turned to them. The man raised his rimless glasses and rubbed his bloodshot eyes. "You've a few minutes. Try to ask yes or no questions and keep your voices low."

Quiet nods followed the doctor's announcement and Tom tiptoed to Mr. Baldwin's bedside. Pen poised over the blank page of the notepad, Alex waited next to Tom.

"Mr. Baldwin," the other lawyer said "Detective Maloney is here." He pointed to a mustached man and moved his finger to Tom. The corporate's blank expression changed to disgust. "And the lawyer representing the accused, Mr. Medar, and his intern will be taking notes."

"Gentlemen, please." Detective Maloney spoke, standing at the foot of the bed. "Mr. Baldwin, did you see the shooter?"

Baldwin's eyelids fluttered, but he steadied his gaze on Tom. "No," he panted, but continued with a weak voice, "It was dark. Maria?"

The question caught Tom unprepared. Had Mr. Baldwin cared about the young woman as she seemed to care about him? Tom cleared his throat, and stepped closer to the bed. "She's held in the women's correctional facility outside Toronto."

Fast beeping filled the room. Doctors rushed to the monitors in a flurry of white coats. After a moment, they faced the gathered crowd. "You will have to leave."

Baldwin tapped his lawyer's hand. The snarky man's bald spot glistened in the ceiling light as he leaned over the patient and listened. Then he tilted his head, settling beady eyes on Tom. He straightened and tugged on the sleeves of his jacket. "Are you sure, Mr. Baldwin?"

Baldwin managed a small nod, his eyes closed. The lawyer pressed his lips in a tight line and succeeded in restraining his tongue.

Tom turned for the door, following the detective and Alex.

"Mr. Baldwin wants a word with you, Mr. Medar." The corporate's indifferent voice stopped him in mid-step. He turned to the bed, his eyebrows drawing closer.

"Should I stay?" Alex's whisper pierced Tom's confusion.

Tom locked the glances with the corporate's cold eyes. "I need my intern here to take notes."

A grimace of disapproval appeared on the lawyer's face, but to Tom's surprise the man pointed his long, thin, finger at the chair and shrugged, as if it was all the same to him if the intern stayed or left.

One of the doctors with glasses spoke. "Mr. Baldwin. This is highly unadvisable. You're too weak to conduct an interview."

Baldwin's hand twitched and he attempted to raise it, but the tube attached to the IV restrained his movement.

Tom leaned toward the bed and spoke over the din of the buzzing machines. "Mr. Baldwin, do you have a question for me?"

"Why…" Baldwin rasped. "Why is Maria in prison?"

"She is the prime suspect in your shooting."

"No." Baldwin gave a weak shake of his head. "She's innocent."

Baldwin confirmed what Tom knew all along, yet this confession would not clear her name, not when all evidence pointed to her. Still, he must proceed with caution and choose his words wisely, or this exclusive interview would be short. "We need to prove her innocence."

"My wife said I had an affair with Maria?" With a slow exhale, Baldwin squeezed his eyes tighter. His voice cracked. "There's nothing funny about getting old, you know…and it's even less amusing if you have to do it alone."

So, that was it: Baldwin was afraid of aging and he found Maria to confide in. He'd lost body mass while in the coma, but at forty-eight, he couldn't be considered old. Well, for some, passing a certain age meant a death sentence.

As if expecting a long confession, Tom lowered to a nearby chair. He sat motionless, allowing the weak man a moment of silence. The scratching of Alex's pen mixed with the machines' droning.

Baldwin's tired eyes met Tom's. "Maria didn't tell you?" He closed his eyes again and rolled his head, letting out a short moan of pain. "No, she wouldn't say a word. She's a good soul."

Tom pulled the chair closer to the bed, its metal legs scraping the tile floor. "Mr. Baldwin, she'll be found guilty if she doesn't speak. And whatever it is, I assure you, your secret will stay safe."

"No, my wife will sell the story to the first journalist if I file for divorce." Baldwin tapped his fingers. He glanced at his lawyer and the man nodded, then his deep set eyes settled on Tom. "But, I did it anyway."

Another piece of the puzzle fell into its place. Baldwin had filed for divorce and Mrs. hadn't liked it. Now what was it she held over his head? "Maria, so pure and innocent. She taught me the importance of being honest. Nine years of hiding is long enough." He lowered his voice as he continued, "An embarrassing medical condition…" His swallow filled the long pause. "I had gallbladder removed…I…well…often I can't hold it."

The frail man's furrowed face told Tom he wasn't comfortable disclosing the details of his humiliation.

"It's alright, Mr. Baldwin. I understand."

But Baldwin licked his parched lips and went on, his voice gaining in strength. "The doc said 'happens in ten percent of cases.' Wouldn't change a thing if I sued him. There's no cure for my benign condition. Not so harmless in the circles I move in. This is…unacceptable. But to live in constant fear of discovery is worse. Let them know and if they want to report on this…" He waved his hand, dismissing the subject.

Tom drew in a sharp breath and leaned on his elbows. The tangled yarn of his first major criminal case had begun to unravel. Until today he felt like he'd been spinning in circles. Now the connection between this case, Olivia and her long pawned gun seemed stronger.

Why turn Mr. Baldwin into a laughingstock when they could use so many excuses and keep this man's condition a secret? He wasn't a sacrificial lamb to be thrown to the lions with flashing cameras so that they could sell the snapshots and stories to the highest paying tabloid. Tom would come up with a feasible story.

With a heavy sigh, he pushed away from the chair. "No Mr. Baldwin, we can do this without disclosing your embarrassment. Right now your priority is to get well and on your feet so you can take the stand and defend Maria."

A weak smile tugged the corners of Baldwin's lips. "Tell her to stay strong. For me."

Tom nodded to Alex and the young intern pocketed his pen and writing pad. "She'll be glad to hear from you." With one hand on the knob, he cast one more look at the patient. "I'll see you again."

Baldwin blinked his heavy lids and nodded once. Tom turned the knob, but let it go and spun to face the man in the bed. "One more question. Do you know a man named Jim Hiltorn?"

Baldwin's eyes snapped open, rage flashed in them. "He pushed for a merger, but I wasn't up to inheriting his company's debts. Hiltorn took it pretty hard when the deal fell through."

CHAPTER 15

After Milo and Rosie succumbed to sleep, Olivia turned off the lights in the house and stood in front of the bay window, overlooking the empty street. Where was Tom? He never took this long at work. Each time a car's headlights cast beams on the pavement, her heart sped, only to drop in disappointment when the vehicle continued on.

She slid the diamond along the necklace. The whirr-whirr of the pendant against the chain calmed her nerves and brought the memory of their passionate night. Not that the images ever left her. Her husband had given her not two, but five soaring orgasms. The little sex toy, both delightful and wicked, had driven her crazy. What else could he be hiding in his closet?

He would be home any minute, and hopefully, ready to show her his collection. If he had one. By now the anticipation soaked her panties. In the last hour, a single car passed by. Should she call him? No, she was just a temporary wife, she couldn't appear that needy. But what she shared with Tom was nothing like her previous one-night stands. Her whole body tingled with life, however surreal. For the first time, she was in a relationship that was going somewhere. But where? She refused to return to her lone existence now that she'd fallen in love with the family life.

The garage door rumbled on its way up, and the sound thrilled her. Tom was home. She ran up the stairs, shed her house coat and slipped under the covers of their bed. Back propped against the pillow, book in hand, she waited on him, shifting her eyes from the blurry words on the page to the doorway.

A moment later, he entered the bedroom. His slumped shoulders and long yawn showed his exhaustion.

He closed the door, exhaling loudly. "Still awake?"

She thumbed the corners of pages. "I couldn't sleep."

In one swift movement, he removed his jeans and shirt as he headed straight for the bed, leaving his clothes scattered on the floor. "Baldwin's lawyer scrutinized me for showing up in my casual clothes."

"He wouldn't know you rushed to the hospital from the jail." So much for lovemaking tonight, but at least they would snuggle and maybe he'd muster enough energy after he rested for a bit.

"Eh, the guy is a jerk, took me for an amateur." Tom's hand slid under the blanket and caressed her bare thigh. "Sorry, lost the track of time going over the notes with Alex. What a day."

Her libido nosedived as she closed and placed her book on the nightstand. She laced her fingers with his. Her poor husband pulled a double shift today, the least she could do was give him time to rest. "Are you hungry? I can warm some chicken soup."

"No, thanks, we ordered in." He yawned.

"I figured you'd be in the office, but didn't want to disturb you. So, Baldwin's out of his coma. Wow, after how many months?"

"Three. He's very thin, but otherwise normal and doctors seem optimistic."

"That's good." She tried to sound enthusiastic, but a tremor crept to her voice. She couldn't shake off the premonition once the trial was over, she'd be yanked away from this life. After all, the entity that sent her had placed her here at the beginning of the trial. She held a key to solving it. The cold gut sense that her old gun had been used to commit the crime increased.

He propped his head on his arm and stared at her. The same hunger of last night burned in his warm eyes. She shivered imagining the possibilities. Yet she couldn't ignore his tiredness.

He ceased circling his thumb on her hand. "Did you know Hiltorn wanted to merge his company with Baldwin's?"

"There were some rumors over a year ago on the executive level. Intelcorp was supposed to be C-Two's division. But then all the talk died down when it started. How did you find out about it? I mean, even I never knew if it was real."

He rubbed his temple and groaned. "Baldwin said so today."

"What prompted you to ask this?" Why would Baldwin disclose something like that? Maybe his meds made him babble about the unsuccessful merger.

Tom rolled to his back, slid his hand under his head, and blew out a breath. "I can't discuss it."

She wrapped her arm around his hard chest and nestled against him. He nuzzled her neck. His warm breath brushed her skin. "You know, you never did tell me how you obtained that gun."

She froze. They were back to the weapon discussion. She had known this would surface at some point. "A couple years ago, I attended a corporate retreat. We played a business edition of truth or dare, but the game quickly turned to the teenager's version." She swallowed in anticipation of spilling this next part, but anger flared in her. How stupid she'd been, willing to do anything to please her boss, even accept an unregistered firearm. "I got encouraged by the dares of others, and I confessed more than I should. A few days later, my boss handed me the gun. Said it was for my own protection. To scare pushy guys from getting what they wanted. Seemed logical at the time so I took it—he was my boss—how could I say no? But I refused the bullets."

She closed her eyes. It was time to tell the truth. "In my world, I still have that gun and didn't have any intention of turning it in."

"You do?" Surprise in his voice and his furrowing brow stirred sharp nails in her stomach.

Afraid where Tom was going with these questions, she wrapped a lock of her hair around her index finger. "Did the ballistics prove where the gun came from?"

His pause turned into foreboding silence. "Yes, it's your old gun."

She stifled a whimper in her throat. Her forewarning was correct. He tightened his hold around her waist. The warmth of his body calmed her unease. "You didn't have a motive or the opportunity to shoot Mr. Baldwin. The only thing you could be charged with is illegal possession of a firearm. Not even that since in this life, you got rid of it long before the shooting. All I know is before you returned from Vancouver all confused, my case was going nowhere. Do you think that gun has something to do with this alternate world happening?"

Surrounded by his arms, her body relaxed. "Yeah, I think so. Does this mean the trial will be soon?"

"This is a high profile case and all involved parties share connections. They can pull strings and set the trial for next month if Mr. Baldwin regains his strength. Even then, trials of this nature could take months to close."

She pressed her lips tight, stifling a whimper. A month before the beginning of an end. That was all she had left with her wickedly skilled husband and two wonderful children. She resolved to find a way to buy more time, to search for a way to stay with them forever.

• • •

Tom crept to the kitchen door and stared in silence. Olivia lowered the cell phone next to the address book on the table and glanced at him. A nostalgic smile danced on her lips. She placed the pen down and cocked her head, sending her raven hair cascading over her shoulder.

"How long you've been watching me from there?"

Tom pushed away from the doorframe and stepped to her. He kissed the top of her head, inhaling her floral shampoo. "Less than a minute. And how long you've been up?"

"About an hour. Even made a pot of coffee, but it's weak." She scowled, tilting her cup.

He lifted the lid of the machine and peeked in. "The filter flipped, that's why. I'll make a fresh pot."

"Thanks, I'm sure you wouldn't drink this." She stuck her tongue out.

After dropping six scoops in the fresh filter, he poured the water into the compartment and pushed brew button. Soon, thick, dark liquid trickled into the pot and rich aroma drifted through the kitchen.

He joined her at the table, taking his usual seat across from her. "What are you writing there?"

"Just phone numbers and addresses, emails and such." She kept her face glued to the paper.

Curiosity sparked in him. "Whose?"

"Everyone's. Friends, family, you know." She scratched her cheek with the tip of her pen.

"Don't you have them already in your contacts? Like in your email or cell phone?"

"I do, but electronic files can be damaged, or corrupted and can easily be lost or deleted. I feel better if I write them as back up in my little book."

Four short beeps indicated the coffee was ready. He stood and tapped her arm. "Good idea. Something my mom would do. She doesn't trust technology either. You should see how appalled she got when my brother showed her some grocery app on his cell."

Olivia's lips stretched in a grin, matching his. "Why would she get upset over that?"

He chuckled at the memory and she joined in, but her meek smile and the flicking of her eyebrows indicated she expected him to explain. He ceased laughing with a long sigh. "Ante was so proud showing mom his new cell, but she just looked at it and said, 'Unless that phone washes my dishes and cleans the kitchen, it's still a phone.' Then he showed her the grocery app and she scowled. Mom likes to shop on the piazza with her friends. They must squeeze every *pomidoro* before buying. No app can do that."

Her baffled expression replaced the grin. "What's *pomidoro*?"

"Tomato." He took two cups from the cupboard and filled them with coffee, the potent scent promising a rich brew. The mugs' bottoms clinked against the table top and he angled the chair toward her. "Here's a fresh cup of my joe."

She took a sip and smacked her lips, making them glisten. "I can never get enough of your morning brew."

A memory of their wild night tugged on the corners of his mouth. He leaned closer. "There was something else you couldn't get enough of."

Her white teeth flashed when she bit on her lower lip, but it was her sucking sound that sent a rush of blood to his groin. A mischievous smile lingered on her face, and she cradled her mug in her hands. "Are there more toys in your closet?"

"No toys only scented oils and creams." He studied her. Had she rummaged through his bag? No, she would've found the feather tickler. A stimulating toy she couldn't stand for him use on her. Not without breaking into gales of giggles. But someday soon, he would try again.

"No ropes or handcuffs?" Her tone carried a hint of disappointment.

Hanging out with his boasting university buddies he had learned a few tricks on bondage and dominance, but his mama had taught him to respect a woman, not demean her. Plus he'd grown bored of the constant stream of girls throwing themselves at him and their eagerness to submit to humiliation. Olivia's resistance came as a much needed relief. If only she had had enough guts to refuse the gun from her boss. Well, people tended to act in unpredictable ways when it came to pleasing the management in fear of losing a job or getting passed on for the promotion.

He tilted his head in suspicion. This was after all a different lady seated across from him. Good thing the kids were still asleep so they could carry on this conversation. "Do you want to try all that stuff?"

"No. I don't think I'd go for bondage and submissive slave thing. Some role playing and use of gentle toys is as far as I'd go."

"Phew, I can't picture you as a submissive. And though you turn me on when you take control, I don't want to be dominated all the time. So our happy medium is perfect."

She drained her coffee and handed the empty cup to him. "Yes, it is. Refill."

"Yes, ma'am." He stood, brushing his finger along her hand as he took her cup. "Tonight you should draw me a bubble bath and we'll play, as you put it."

Her eyes sparkled with desire and once again she drew her lower lip between her teeth, flashing a wicked grin.

A long sigh failed to loosen his tight throat. How he hated taking a rain check, though postponing the pleasure promised hotter sex and a mind blowing orgasm. "I have to transform to a lawyer, then I have to go to jail and start prepping my client for a trial. Poor girl has no idea what kind of grueling questions she'll be put under. Every bit of dirt from her life will get dug out and put on display."

"Poor indeed. I cannot even imagine what she must be going through." Olivia closed her notebook and stood. "I'll make you some breakfast before you head out."

He took off for the stairs, heading to master bedroom. "Toast me a bagel and spread some cream cheese on it."

A perfectly golden bagel waited on the plate in the middle of the table. Olivia's toasting skills had improved. He heard her soft cooing through the baby monitor. She was getting Rosie ready. Switching from a passionate lover to a mom came so naturally to his wife.

He gobbled his breakfast in four bites and washed it down with a few sips of his coffee. With his travel mug filled, he grabbed his briefcase and opened the coat closet.

While he scrambled into his coat, Olivia came down the stairs, Rosie on her hip. "Daddy has to go."

"But I always have a moment for my girls." He took Rosie in his hands.

Fear flashed in Olivia's eyes and her face crumpled. She turned away from him and walked away. Shifting Rosie to his side, he reached for Olivia's elbow, pulled her close and placed a reassuring kiss on her temple. "You wrote the contact info because you're afraid all of this, me and our kids, will disappear one day and we'll never see each other."

She sniffed. "I found that address book tucked in my drawer. I had it before you came to my life and if my fears turn out to be correct, I somehow know I'll still have the info." She swallowed. "If I leave, I can still find you."

Her trembling voice and shivering body told him he should give her fears some merit. "If we do get separated, I'll tear this planet to shreds to find you."

She pulled back and wiped her tears. Her short chuckle chipped a morsel of his worry away. "What if you don't remember me? If we're strangers to each other?"

"Honey, you will never be a stranger." He cupped her chin. How could he show her his love was strong enough to keep them together? "What we share is not something I can forget."

Olivia stared at him. The pleading in her wide eyes ate at his heart. "How will you find me?"

"I don't know, but I can promise you, if it comes to that, I will not stop looking for you." His assuring gaze should put her mind at ease. Rosie's fidgeting broke his stare. The little girl was picking up on their emotions. He placed a kiss on his baby's head. Her soft frizzes tickled his nose.

Olivia took her in her arms and gave him a watery smile. He cupped her face, her tears squeezed his chest. "No more tears. I'm here and nothing will pull us apart."

She nodded and drew in a long breath. "Will you be gone all day like yesterday?"

"I don't think so." He buttoned up and with one final peck on Olivia's cheek he headed out.

During his hour's drive to the women's correctional facility his mind drifted to Olivia's fears and his failure to assure her. Hell, he'd failed to convince himself. Anything he'd said were mere words. Perhaps he should think of an alternative. If she was right, he should have some way of finding her, remembering her and the life they shared. But what could he plant as a reminder?

Snow crunched under the tires as he parked in front of the institutional brownstone building. He flashed his card, signed his name in the visitor's book, clasped his badge to the jacket of his suit and followed the guard down the long corridor.

At the press of her meaty finger on the button, the loud buzz filled the air and the metal rod door slid open.

This time Maria waited, seated at the table. Her face lit up when he entered the large room. "Is it true? Did Mr. Baldwin pull through?"

"He did, Maria." Tom placed his briefcase on the small table and scrambled out of his coat.

Maria clasped her fingers and raised her face toward the ceiling. "Thank you, God, for answering my prayers."

If only. Then again, Baldwin had seemed taken by this simple country girl. Matters of the heart would never make any sense. Tom pulled his notebook and a pen out of his leather bag. "Maria, Mr. Baldwin sends his…" How should he phrase it? Love? Tom frowned. Maybe. But he didn't want to give Maria a wrong message. "Well, he said to stay strong and he gave you permission to speak freely. So whatever you know, now is the time to come clean."

She froze, and stared at him wide eyed. "He said that?"

"Yes." Tom cocked his head. Baldwin had been vague in his explanation about the embarrassing condition he suffered. Since the day of her arrest, Maria refused to speak out. Why else would Baldwin give her the permission if she didn't know his secret? "Could he be impotent?"

Her gaze dropped to her hands. "I wouldn't know anything about that."

"I can find out what kind of permanent complications could arise after a gallbladder surgery. It must be something rare. His doctor said it only happens in some ten percent."

"He lost control of his…" She swallowed.

He remained silent. Maria averted her eyes elsewhere. He finished her sentence. "Bladder control?"

"No," she shouted, shooting daggers at him from her eyes.

His client tested his patience with her hesitation to talk. "What then? His bowels?"

Perhaps it was his raised voice or angry tone, but Maria burst into tears. So that was it, Baldwin had messed himself during the fundraising barbecue. The man must've tried hard to hide away from the crème of society. Her shoulders relaxed and she wept as if a heavy weight had been lifted off her back. Someone else shared Baldwin's secret.

Tom mellowed. He tapped her shoulder. "Don't worry. In court we'll say you were sent to fetching clean clothes because he spilled a drink when someone bumped into him."

She sighed and attempted a shy smile. "Thank you, Mr. Medar."

He leaned on his elbows. It wouldn't be likely that Baldwin just told her. "How did you know?"

"My mother suffers the same. I recognized his symptoms."

He nodded. At least she had shown Baldwin compassion. Not something the magnate would experience from his gold digging wife or corporate world. "Now, the hard work begins. The jury will buy none of your pretentious tough girl attitude you put up the other day. You must look the naïve, pure-hearted village girl. When you're on that stand, I want you to cry, sob if you have to, plea, show them how frightened you are."

Her breath quivered and sweat beaded on her brow. "I understand, Mr. Medar. Will I see Erich before the trial?"

"I don't think so." But knowing Baldwin and his connections, everything was possible, though Tom didn't want to raise her hopes.

He reached into his pocket and pulled out his cell. Another text message from Alex displayed on the screen. Trial set for three weeks from today. Damn, less time than he hoped for, but when one had connections the world moved at their speed.

CHAPTER 16

The cement highway divider passed in a blur during Tom's drive home. The Narnia soundtrack coming through the car speakers couldn't chase away his morose thoughts.

He lowered his hands on the steering wheel to ease the ache between his shoulder blades. His sticky eyes glued on the taillights of the car ahead. The trial, which had promised to catapult his career as a defense attorney, barely held his attention. Was he about to lose his wife and family? If his "real" wife returned, would he know the difference? Easy now, he might be single in his "other" life. Yeah, that alternative held more appeal. If this was a fantasy of a sort, he could find Olivia in the other world. If only he could convince his mind he'd have memories of her and the life they shared.

How would the switch happen? More importantly, when? Olivia seemed certain the re-altering would occur after he won the case. How could she be so sure either would happen? In recent days, he'd been getting the same premonition, but he never told her. She'd only worry more. He should do something to secure his promise to remember her in his other life. In the alternate world the photos of his family, her Christmas present might not exist, but it wouldn't hurt to try and store it someplace secure.

He pulled into the garage and cut the engine. The music continued and he reclined in his seat, allowing his mind to drift on the sounds of the battle song. The chords of drums and trumpets alternated with magnificent voices and lifted his spirit. As the rhythm sped, he reaffirmed his determination to fight for his family. He wouldn't forget them. Not that he could, they were his.

As he entered the house through the side door, warmth caressed his face.

"Daddy's home," Milo announced. Tom snickered at his son's continuing coloring activity in front of the cartoon-blaring television.

Olivia stepped out of the kitchen, Rosie snuggled in her arms. Tom's chest squeezed at his wife's widening smile. This perfect picture of the ideal family confirmed there was too much at stake. He wouldn't survive without them. If some supernatural entity pulled at their strings, how was he to protect what was precious to him? *By loving them more, that's how*. He would savor every second with them. Spend time with her. Memorize the sound of her voice.

Her soft lips touched his cheek, leaving a tingle spreading on his still chilled skin. "How did the prepping go?"

"Hmm?" Oh yes, the trial. He mustn't forget about his work. "It will take more than one session to get the desired results. I hope she doesn't fall apart on the stand."

He put his coat over the hanger inside the closet and removed his boots. One thing he'd have to prove was Mrs. Baldwin's infidelity. So far the always well-put-together lady eluded them all with her "concerned wife" talk. True, Mrs. Baldwin had jumped Hiltorn's bones at the barbeque and it stood to reason folks talked about the affair around the water cooler, but so far no one was talking to him.

Tom stood in the kitchen doorway, ruffling Milo's hair as he passed by him. The conversation may not be appropriate at the dinner table. With an ever observant five-year-old boy present, he should watch his choice of words. Good thing Olivia waited for the microwave oven to beep, out of Milo's hearing distance.

In a few strides, Tom reached her just as a long sound announced the baby food was warmed up. Her closeness steadied his thoughts. "Do you think your boss is capable of an affair?"

Amusement flashed in her eyes as she stirred the steamy portion of blended food in the baby bowl. "He's divorced for the fourth time as I recall. So it wouldn't be him who committed adultery."

Tom glanced at the kitchen table to make sure Milo wasn't paying any attention. The boy seemed busy making Rosie giggle by wriggling his tongue at her. His little princess found amusement in everything.

He turned to Olivia. "Would he go after the wife of another man? A man he planned a merger with?"

Olivia ceased stirring the orange mush and shot him a surprised glance. "He had an affair with Mrs. Baldwin?"

Tom put his hands up to curb her eagerness to dig for details. "This bit of info came my way yesterday. I need to find out more about this before I can put her on the stand."

"I've been on maternity leave for the past ten months. Even if I'm in the office, I doubt I'd care about stuff like this if I heard it. Employees saw me as all work and no fun." She spooned out another scoop of the baby food from the jar and into the dish. While stirring she let out a short gasp. "Isn't it a bit strange I'm finding this intriguing now?"

Tom nodded. He could number a few times she'd come home with some juicy gossip from the office, but that had been her double. "Maybe if you ask around you won't appear suspicious."

Her gaze wandered around the kitchen and finally settled on him. She traced her index finger down his tie. "I think I can find out."

He wrapped his arm around her waist and pulled her closer, careful of Rosie's dinner in Olivia's hand. "You're not all work. I should vouch for that. Now tell me, how are you going to find out?"

She set the bowl on the kitchen counter and wrapped her arms around his neck. "Well, it seems in this life my assistant and I are friends. If anyone knows a thing about office affairs, it's Jess. I'll call her tomorrow."

She licked her lips, making them glisten in the overhead light. He slid his hands down her waist and tucked them inside her jean pockets, cupping her buttocks. "If you're in the mood tonight, I'd like to cash in that rain check from this morning."

Her lips met his and she cupped his face. "Can't hardly wait for the kids to fall asleep."

Tightening his embrace, he whispered. "I love you, Olivia. Always remember no matter what happens."

She laid her head on his shoulder. "Our life is not something I'll forget."

"You have my promise never to give up." He cradled her face in his hands, trying to memorize every detail. Those long lashes encircling her beautiful black eyes, ruby lips, raven hair, framing her soft features on her alabaster skin.

Rosie turned her giggles of delight to cries of protest. Her little, chubby feet pounded against the footrest of her high chair.

"Dinner's coming." Olivia scrambled out of his embrace, grabbed a cracker and plopped it in front the hungry baby.

Tom turned to the stove and inspected the simmering pots. Though the smell of chicken broth made his stomach rumble, the prospect of losing his family shut down his appetite.

• • •

Olivia poured the milk over Milo's cereal, phone receiver tucked between her ear and shoulder. She put the carton back in the fridge and rubbed her neck while the monotone sound filled her ear. The sensation of last night's lovemaking and Tom's lips gliding on the back of her neck refused to leave her since she'd awakened to the sound of a running shower and the fresh scent of his body wash.

"Mommy, the milk tastes funny." Milo grimaced and pushed the bowl away.

She slid his breakfast back in front of him. "I bought the milk yesterday, can't be sour already. One more spoonful. It'll be long time before you get to eat your morning snack at school."

He scooped a small amount and frowned, eyeing the spoon in front of his mouth.

Olivia chuckled at his funny frown. "You can't go to school on empty stomach."

His face fell as he chewed then swallowed fast. "Can I be excused now?"

"Fine, go get ready. Daddy will walk you to your bus stop." She turned her attention to an automated greeting message that came through after the sixth ring. Mr. Hiltorn's idea of having a real person answer the phone had not lasted long, as she suspected. Over a year ago his accountant had calculated the receptionist's salary and come up with the cheaper solution.

At least she didn't have to chit-chat with an overly pleasant receptionist and answer all her questions about Rosie's development. Nor listen to her motherly advice on child rearing. Olivia hoped poor Beatrice was offered a retirement, but knowing Hiltorn, no one was safe.

"If you know the extension of the person you're trying to reach, please dial it now," the mechanical voice droned.

Finally, Olivia punched four digits on the pad.

Her assistant answered on the first ring as always. "Jess Adams."

"I'm so glad you're at your desk, Jess." She contemplated how to bring up the subject of office affairs, but maybe in this life she was as nosey as the rest of them.

"You're lucky and caught me between meetings. What's up?"

Unsure how to ask, she cleared her throat. "This may sound weird, but I have a question."

"Go ahead." Jess's voice took on a curious tone.

"Do you know if…" Hell, snooping was never her thing. "Have you heard of…um…"

"I'm in a bit of hurry. Spit it out," Jess hissed.

"Are there any talks about the boss having an affair with Mrs. Baldwin?"

The chirping of fax machines and ringing phones filled the silence on Jess's end. "Jess? You still there?"

"I'm here." Her heavy breath came through, her voice somber. "Not over the phone. Meet me at the Bistro for lunch?"

Olivia frowned. Since when had she met with her staff for lunch? Especially at the greasy spoon place serving cheap meals, plates piled with greasy fries as the only side order. But she lived a different life now, so she better get used to the idea. "See you then. I'm bringing Rosie."

"Oh goody, I get to hold the baby," Jess chirped.

Olivia replaced the receiver and turned to Tom and Milo in the foyer. She would never get used to see them go, not knowing if they would return. "All set to face your day?"

"If Daddy would hurry." Milo hoisted his backpack. She placed a kiss on his cheeks. "Have fun at school."

Then she faced Tom as he tucked his scarf inside his black coat. Creases formed at the corners of his mouth when he smiled. His wink sent a trickle to her core. He placed his hands on her shoulders and gave her a peck on her lips. The pine scent of his aftershave drifted to her. "I'll be at the office all day if you need me."

She swallowed and nodded. What she needed was him naked and tied to the bedpost for an entire day. "I'm meeting Jess downtown for lunch."

"Say hi to the queen of gossip. Have fun. I'll fold the stroller and put it in the trunk before I head out." He hugged her one more time.

Olivia held him closer. "You seem to know Jess well."

"She's quite a character with her innocent flirting." He tapped her bum and, after another kiss, released her from his embrace. With one hand on Milo's shoulder, he opened the front door. "Let's go, boy."

Olivia waved them goodbye, wondering if Jess ever made a move on Tom. No, she might have enjoyed teasing, but she wouldn't cross the line and neither would Tom.

After rummaging through the diaper bag and finding all the items necessary for an outing with a baby, Olivia zipped the duffle. At Rosie's cooing coming through the monitor, she climbed the stairs to the nursery.

The baby's sweet smell melted her insides, but at the sight of her daughter, her jaw dropped. "Look at you. You're standing up."

Olivia took out the camera from the dresser's drawer. "Look at Mommy."

Rosie rewarded her with a grin and babbling, drool dripping down her chin while she clung to the railing.

"Daddy's going to be so sorry he missed seeing you on your feet for the first time." Olivia snapped a few pictures then returned the camera to the drawer. She picked Rosie up from her crib and cradled her small frame in her arms. Would the angel keep her family together long enough to see Rosie walk? If the entity had tried to teach her a lesson, she learned it. She was no longer that heartless monster.

Tears stung her eyes and she blinked them away, then placed a soft kiss on Rosie's head. "We're going out, yes just the two of us. Let's get ready."

After changing and feeding Rosie, Olivia bundled her up and strapped the baby in her car seat. She deserved a pat on her back for her first attempt at an outing with a baby on her own.

Finding parking in downtown Toronto proved harder than packing Rosie with all her gear, but Olivia squeezed her family van in an empty spot on the street. She got Rosie out of her seat and into her stroller, then dropped a few coins in the parking meter on the sidewalk. Cold wind slapped at her face during her half a block walk. Chatter, clinking of cutlery and the smell of fetid frying oil surrounded her at the Bistro's doorstep. Wait staff bustled in and out the flapping kitchen doors. Had everyone taken their lunch here?

She spotted Jess's flaxen, long hair before her assistant waved from the booth at the back. "Olivia, over here."

Pushing the stroller through the narrow aisles seemed tougher than fighting the downtown traffic. How witless people could be, babbling away and ignoring her request to make room, then giving her dirty looks when she rolled the wheel over their feet, yet they'd seen her coming. Her perspective had changed. Not long ago she'd been one of those people angry at mothers who forced strollers down rows where there was no room.

Jess jumped out of the booth, a grin on her face covered in subtle yet perfect makeup. "Here's my big girl."

Her remark stunned Olivia. Yes, she still struggled with her weight, but by no means was she "big."

Jess proceeded to unbuckle Rosie and take her out of the pink bundle bag attached to the stroller. "She's getting heavy."

Oh, Jess had directed the initial greeting to the baby. Her shoulders relaxed and she took the seat on the burgundy booth, facing Jess. "She's a growing wonder."

Jess pushed a mug filled with coffee her way. "The service is slow here, so I ordered for you."

"Thanks." Olivia took a sip and shuddered at the abominable taste. The weak brew resembled something she'd make, then dump out. Couldn't compare to Tom's.

"Why do you ask about the boss's affair with certain Mrs.?" Jess bounced Rosie on her knees without glancing Olivia's way.

Olivia pushed the cup aside. She couldn't discuss an ongoing case, so answering Jess's question would be difficult without lying. But she could be vague. She moved in the same circles of people. "I've heard something from a mutual friend."

"Oh." Jess's shaped eyebrows arched and she ceased bouncing Rosie. "So gossip is a number one priority in higher society, too?"

Aware of her overgrown eyebrows, Olivia made a mental note to make an appointment at the spa. "As if you didn't know."

Jess gave her a light slap on her hand. "Of course I did, silly. Just teasing you. Anyway, this is what I know." Her face paled under the makeup and fear flashed in her soft blue eyes. "I did something I shouldn't and Beatrice got fired."

Olivia placed her hand over Jess's and furrowed her eyebrows. "What did you do?"

Jess swallowed and glanced around the Bistro to make sure no one listened. She turned to Olivia and lowered her voice to a mere whisper. "We have this neat telephone feature installed. The reception has a button that allows you to monitor phone conversations. We're not permitted to use it, though. When I filled in for her lunch break, the boss's line light lit up and I couldn't help myself. I just wanted to see if I could find out about payment of the overtime as was promised. Then a woman's voice came through, sounded like the Mrs. you mentioned. I recognized her voice from the news. Anyhow, they were talking about some hit job and how much money the man asked. She called the boss darling and he replied to her with sweetheart. It was sickening and I should've stopped, but couldn't." Jess shook her head, staring at her mug. "The computer log showed the monitor was used from the reception desk and Beatrice was sent packing. I never told a soul about this. You know what, now that I've told you, I feel better."

The noise in the dining room seemed to fade into the distance. Hit job. The man wanted money. Words repeated in Olivia's head. Dear God, if Jess had gotten the conversation right, Mr. Hiltorn and Mrs. Baldwin had planned to hire a hit man to kill Mr. Baldwin. Somehow the job must've gone amiss, because a professional killer would not do the job half way. Could be the pro's price was too steep. The only way to use this information would be for Jess to testify, but she could lose her job and gain a permanent stain on her résumé as a whistleblower.

Jess still stared at her coffee, fear etched on her face. Knowing her assistant, Jess could've gotten the thing all wrong and out of context. For all anyone knew, the boss discussed a movie he'd seen the night before. Olivia leaned over the table. "It could be nothing."

Jess nodded and exhaled loudly. "I hope you're right." She picked up the menu tucked at the metal holder in the corner. "They have good salads here."

The coffee was abominable so Olivia had doubts about the food. She opened the menu and scanned through the pages. God, the menu listed the meals the restaurant served in pictures, barely any words to describe them. If it weren't for Jess, who still had not calmed down from her confession, she'd leave. However, the new Olivia needed to start making friends in this world and the next one, and Jess seemed like one already.

Olivia lowered the cardboard on the table. "When did we become friends?"

One eyebrow on Jess's face arched and she flashed half a smile. "When you first started with Intelcorp and lost your presentation, I saved the day and your ass. Everyone thinks me strange for keeping copies of copies, but it proved right more than once."

Olivia remembered that panic stricken day, yet not the way Jess described it. "Have I ever thanked you?"

Jess tweaked her head. "No, but it's never too late."

"Accept my belated thanks."

Jess's smile bloomed to a full grin and she nodded, then made a funny noise at Rosie busily inspecting beads on her necklace.

Olivia flipped through the glossy pages of the menu. What to do with the boss? Though many had threatened to sue Mr. Hiltorn in the past, his conduct had been unethical, not illegal. This time however, he might not stand a chance.

Should she disclose Jess's information to Tom? What if it proved right and brought the trial to a quick end?

CHAPTER 17

The digital display on the parking meter counted down the last minute of Olivia's time. Misery coiled through her with every decreasing second. Jess's confession kept repeating in her head. Without it, the case could drag on for months. Hiltorn had been very careful and covered his ass well, but he'd overlooked the obvious—the unpredictability of the office bimbo. Unfortunately, poor Beatrice had now lost her job a couple of years before retirement.

Rosie's babbling drifted from the back seat and made Olivia chuckle as she stared at the phone in her hand. At the press of the green button, a blank message screen lit up. There was no telling how far Hiltorn would go. Someone needed to stop him. Her thumbs worked fast, typing the text. *The boss and Mrs. Baldwin seem in cahoots on killing their victim.*

She hit the send button and pulled out of her parking with three seconds left on display. A small car slipped into her spot and the driver of the van waiting for her space screeched its brakes. A horn blasted, shrill and furious. Oh, how she missed downtown.

The light turned red at the second intersection and her cell chimed. *The detectives pressed him hard in an interview yesterday, but he played dumb. Talk soon.*

The blue numbers on the clock read twelve twenty. Almost three hours before she had to meet Milo's school bus. She hadn't had lunch this early in months, well since she had "stopped" working. She responded to Tom. *Got the list you left on the fridge. Going to stop at the grocery store.*

The extensive list took longer than she expected. Back home more than an hour later, she pushed the garage door button. Tom's sedan sat parked in its spot. He was home early. She eased her van next to his vehicle and got out. With Rosie in one arm and diaper bag in the other, she paused by the door, doubt over whether disclosing Jess's information was a wise idea clouding her thoughts.

Olivia shook her head. No, she'd done the right thing even if her action would cause her to lose her family sooner. What was done couldn't be undone. She must not impede the trial for her selfish reasons. The angel had been clear in her demands. Tom or Tadem. But would it be fair to trade her sister's life for Tom's? Her life with Tom and their children would come to an end—keeping the information to buy another day or two was wrong.

She stepped in the foyer. Milo's crying, the sound broken up with retching, drifted from upstairs. The school dismissal was at three thirty, the bus should drop him at the stop by four. Why was he home over an hour early?

"Tom." Her voice echoed in the hallway with high ceiling. She set the diaper bag on the wooden bench.

"Upstairs bathroom." His voice carried urgency.

She took the stairs by twos and froze in the doorway. Tom held Milo's head over the toilet. Heaves convulsed Milo's thin shoulders.

"Oh god." To see her child this sick dropped her heart to her stomach.

Milo's vomiting ceased. Tom cradled his small body in his arms, wiped his mouth with a damp cloth, and kissed the boy's head. "You'll be fine, buddy." When he leveled his eyes with hers, concern flashed in them. "School called me after lunch. They called the house first, but got the answering machine. I've sent you a few texts. Did you get them?"

"I..." she swallowed the lump in her throat. "I forgot my cell in the car then didn't check it when I got back in. I wanted to get home. I don't understand—he was just fine this morning."

Worry edged Tom's face. "Kids can get sick quickly, but this is not normal. School said they don't have any cases of a stomach bug going around. I've lost count of the times he threw up in the past hour. If it's food, I hoped it would stop by now. We should get him to the emergency room."

She nodded, her eyes refusing to blink. "Let's go."

She followed Tom as he rushed from the bathroom to the garage, a whirlwind of worry.

She tried to calm down with a long sigh. But her hands wouldn't stop shaking and strapping Rosie into her seat proved impossible.

Tom took over the job. "He's quite limp. Did he eat something no one else did?"

Olivia's mind raced to the breakfast time. Her hand flew to her lips. "Oh god. He said the milk on his cereal tasted funny. But he never likes to eat in the morning and I forced him to take one more spoonful."

Without another word, Tom ran into the house and re-emerged with a carton of milk inside the plastic bag.

The mad dash to the hospital passed in worry and constant turning to check on Milo in the back seat. His pale face and dark circles made him appear sicker by the second. What could make him this ill this quick?

Tires screeched in front of the glass entrance. Tom's shoulders rose and fell as if he had run to the hospital. "Take him in. I'll park and come back with Rosie."

Olivia scrambled out of the car, scooped Milo in her arms and dashed for the triage station. "Quick! He's very sick."

The thin nurse waved her hand at the orderly, her expression blank. Must've reached her quota of caring. "First, we need to enter the boy in our system. I need his health card."

Of course, the protocol first, saving lives second. Screaming frantically and causing trouble would solve nothing. Better to behave and abide by the rules. Olivia reached into the diaper bag and pulled out her wallet. Did she even carry the kids' health cards with her?

The orderly rolled the gurney close to the station. "Ma'am, you can put the boy down."

She eased Milo onto the bed, his skin white and cold. Then she pulled his health card from her purse and handed the green plastic rectangle to the nurse.

"Take the seat in front of that window." The nurse pointed to the clear, divider on the side of the waiting room filled with rows of blue vinyl chairs occupied by a few individuals.

Olivia reluctantly stopped brushing her son's hair and stepped away from him. Another nurse took the card from the triage and sat in front of the computer. She proceeded to ask questions about Milo's health history. Olivia somehow knew the answers to what childhood diseases and vaccinations her son had, and that he had never been hospitalized before.

Tom came in through the sliding doors, pushing Rosie in her stroller. "What did they say?"

"Nothing yet, just entering his info into their system."

Rolling onto his side, Milo moaned, his arms wrapped around his stomach. His knees bent, he rocked.

Tom stepped to the nurse behind clear glass window. "My son's in pain, please hurry."

Her ponytail bobbed with her nod, but she didn't turn her head from the computer screen and the click-click of her typing never stopped. "I'm working as fast as I can."

The printer behind her buzzed to life and spit out three bracelets. The nurse pulled them from the tray. She squeezed her large frame through the narrow break between partitions and wrapped one white, stiff paper around Milo's wrist and handed the other two to Tom. "These are your IDs so you can enter and exit the E.R. area freely. The kids' express clinic hasn't closed yet. We paged the pediatrician to see him right away."

The same orderly reappeared and pushed Milo's bed to the examination room. Moans of pain replaced Milo's cries. Olivia chewed on her nail while her stomach tightened with every passing second. She glanced at the clock above the bed. Thirty minutes since they'd been shown into this square room and still no one had looked at her son. What was keeping the doctor? The nurse had said they paged him. Every second was important.

A young, black man in green scrubs knocked on the frosty glass door and introduced himself as Milo's doctor.

He stepped to Milo's bed. "How're you doing, buddy? Not too good, I see."

With a sigh Olivia lowered to the chair next to the bed. The doctor's arrival seemed to loosen her spine a bit. At least he tried to sound cheerful, but she caught a concern in his voice.

"No one else sick?" The doctor pulled on Milo's lids and flashed the light in each eye. Milo blinked fast and jerked his head to the side. He then lifted the boy's shirt. Milo cried out when he pressed on his stomach.

"No, thank god." Tom's worried stare at his sick boy squeezed Olivia's chest.

The doctor turned to her. "Did he ingest something no one else did? At home or school?"

"We think it could be the milk. I take soy milk, Rosie is on formula." Olivia shot a questioning glance at Tom. He shook his head. "My husband didn't have any."

"Do you have the milk?" The doctor pushed the glasses up his nose.

"Yes," she shouted in unison with Tom while he raised his hand holding the bag.

"We'll run tests on Milo, but his swollen stomach suggests some kind of poisoning." The bag rustled when the doctor took it from Tom. "Our lab will confirm my suspicion and find out what type of poison could've been used." Then he turned to Milo on the bed. "In the meantime, we'll get some fluids into him. A nurse will set him with the IV."

After the doctor left, minutes stretched like hours. Olivia exchanged a few words with Tom, but couldn't stop blaming herself for forcing Milo to eat more of his breakfast. A nurse attached an IV in Milo's pale hand, took his blood sample, then left the tiny room.

The heavy silence, punctuated with the uncaring tick-tock of the clock on the wall, finally pushed Olivia over the edge. She broke down into sobs. "It's my fault. I should've smelled the milk and dumped his breakfast. Instead I…"

"Stop that." Tom placed sleeping Rosie on the edge of Milo's bed and surrounded her with pillows. He stepped close and pulled her into his embrace. "Not another word of this. You couldn't have known."

The warmth and closeness of his body, coupled with his sea scent and his gentle swaying calmed her storm of guilt. With one last snivel, she wiped her eyes and locked her gaze with his. Getting hysterical wouldn't help Milo.

The doctor knocked on the door and peeked in. "I need to talk to you."

Tom pulled away from her. Cold air crawled into the space where his closeness had warmed her.

Creases on the doctor's young face worried her, but in the next instance, he flashed them a reassuring smile. "Milo's color is returning and his breathing sounds less labored." He paused, glancing at the floor, then raised his head, a serious look on his face. "However, we found a few pellets of Ratoxin in the carton."

Tom scowled. "Rat poison? We don't have anything like that in the house. How the hell did that get into the milk?"

A whole new fear stiffened Olivia. Her shaking hand pressed to her trembling lips. All words left her mind. In cases like this parents were held responsible for endangering their children. She already blamed herself plenty for forcing him to eat.

"The good news is there are only traces of it in Milo's blood. But enough to make him quite sick." The doctor turned to her. "You didn't shake the carton before you poured the milk?"

With one hard swallow, she mustered enough voice. "No, I never do."

The doctor shrugged one shoulder. "That in itself is good, since the pellets fell to the bottom and didn't dissolve completely. I was correct to administer a dose of vitamin K. Milo will be fine but we need to keep him overnight for observation."

Tom's shoulders and chest rose and fell with his fast breaths. "I'd say this was targeted to all of us. Whoever did this assumed we all consumed milk. If I catch the person, I'll pound the shit out of him and I don't care if I lose my lawyer's license."

Whether from the doctor's good prognosis or the rage burning in Tom's eyes she didn't know, but Olivia's tears streamed freely down her face.

Tom yanked the cell out of his jacket pocket. "The doctor may have reported this to the police, but I need the results now."

Phone pressed to his ear, he paced at the foot of the bed. "Detective Maloney, please...yes, I can hold...detective, Tom Medar. Sorry to disturb you, but the matter is pressing. I'm in the hospital, my son's been poisoned. I suspect it was meant to kill all of us."

Tom nodded and after a few minutes added, "Thank you, detective. I appreciate your help."

He lowered to a chair next to her. He took her hand in his and laced their fingers, his face mellowing. "Detective Maloney will take this personally. We can't go home until his men are done. Our house is now a crime scene."

"Oh god," she cried, burying her face in her hand.

"We'll check into a hotel for the night." He wrapped his arm around her and pulled her close.

"You take Rosie, I'll stay with Milo."

"Honey, he'll be fine and you need to rest so you can help him tomorrow when he wakes." Tom gestured toward the baby. "And Rosie needs her mom, too."

With heavy heart, Olivia rose to her feet, kissed Milo's now warm forehead, and grabbed the diaper bag. "You're right."

• • •

The next morning Milo welcomed them with a big smile. "Mom, Dad, Rosie!"

Dark circles framed his eyes, but he was cheerful and even had a glass of apple juice. With the threat gone, tiredness settled over Olivia. She barely kept her eyes open while yawn after yawn stretched her mouth wide. Though Tom had checked them into a cozy hotel, her worry hadn't allowed her a wink of sleep.

Tom kept glancing at his cell phone, but no calls came.

Just before noon a tall, burly man in dark suit knocked on the room's door.

"Detective Maloney? Come in." Tom gestured with his head, then pointed at Olivia. "I don't believe you met my other half."

"Correction, she's your better half." The detective nodded to Olivia and pulled off his leather glove then extended his thick hand. "Pleasure to meet you, ma'am."

"Detective Maloney's an old school gentleman." Tom pointed at the chair in the corner and the unexpected guest took his seat. "Any news?"

"There's a sign of forceful entry on the patio door." Detective Maloney took off his tuque and smoothed his graying hair.

Tom hammered his fist into his palm. "Damn, I thought I checked that sticky lock before going to bed."

A loud breath through his bulbous nose rustled the detective's thick mustache before he spoke. "We interviewed the neighbors and turns out the young man down the street saw someone snooping around your house at wee hours. Your neighbor gave us the description of the suspect and the vehicle he left in, along with the license plate. Didn't take long to locate him. The guy had many priors for petty crimes and was already in custody for drunken and disorderly conduct. He played dumb at first, they all do, but when I told him his daddy won't save him this time, he squealed how his old man put him up to it."

"Who's his daddy?" With narrowed eyes, Tom cocked his head as if he knew the answer already.

"Jim Hiltorn. We're searching for him as a person of interest, but the man is nowhere to be found. He must be getting desperate to pull a stunt like this." Detective Maloney turned to Olivia. "You worked for him. Do you know where could he be hiding?"

Olivia's mouth dropped open, her gut clenched. Her boss had sent his son to poison them all? "Just yesterday I discovered he had an affair with Mrs. Baldwin. Maybe he ran to her. I had no idea his company is in such dire straits he'd resort to this. The financial reports showed a steady growth. The company is among the top one hundred."

Detective Maloney pulled his cell out of his pocket and stood. "Covering one crime often requires committing another, and keeping a high profile attorney on a retainer for the past fifteen years would drain the biggest accounts. I'll send a unit to Baldwin's estate." His gaze settled on Milo. "I'm glad your son's fine."

"Thank you, detective. Can we return home?" Tom patted the big man's shoulder and extended his hand.

"Yes, my men are done." After their handshake, Maloney saluted by pressing his two fingers to his temple and left the room.

To think Mr. Hiltorn would stoop so low and resort to premeditated murder just to get what he wanted—or rather to get even for what he had not gotten. How long had he been lying to the world about the financial stability of the Intelcorp? Was the life of his corporation truly worth more than lives of all people he'd ruined by cutting them from the payroll? Where would this stop? Olivia stuffed the thought away and returned to her son and daughter, playing on the bed.

Tom packed the last of the items into the diaper bag. "Well, Hiltorn didn't kill us, but we'll have to clean the house top to bottom to make sure no pellets were placed where kids could get them. The job will pull me away from the case for a day, but it won't stop me." He straightened and squared his jaw. "No doubt they'll be all well lawyered up, but I'll be ready to face them in the courtroom."

CHAPTER 18

Sadness mixed with pride inside Tom. Maria never should've seen the inside of a prison. This was why he became a lawyer, to defend the innocent. Had not taken much effort from the detectives to put heat on Ike Hiltorn, the bragging idiot confessed without realizing what he'd done. Confession had concluded Tom's involvement in the case. His client was free. From now on, he'd be handed larger cases. No more closing mortgages and finalizing divorces.

He pulled his cell out and dialed Olivia.

"Hey." The sound of her cheerful voice sent warmth racing through his blood. For the past two days she'd been depressed, focusing on cleaning. Thankfully, no more poison pallets had been found.

"I have some great news for Maria, so I'll be a little later than usual. I should tell her personally."

"Interrogation went the way you predicted then?" Behind Olivia's voice was Rosie's loud babbling.

"Yeah." He yearned to be home with his loved ones. The trial may not take place if Hiltorn turned himself in and it could mean his time with Olivia was running out. Milo's complaint about computer not co-operating drifted to the phone from the distance.

"Got to go. Our son messed up my laptop."

Tom chuckled. "Oh the joys of staying home sick. He'll be back at school tomorrow." Never having to miss so many days in a row, their son longed for structured activities. Tom glanced at his wristwatch. "I have to go too so I can get home soon. Get in a celebrating mood."

Olivia moaned and smacked a kiss in the receiver. "I can hardly wait."

"Wear something nice under your house coat." He'd love to take her out, but with two kids the best he could get was dinner at a family restaurant. And with Hiltorn still loose, he decided against asking Jason to babysit. Besides, it was mid-term. Their neighbor would be buried under his books. The young dad must've stayed up all night studying when he spotted Ike snooping around. And bottle of an expensive wine and a takeout from her favorite steakhouse, followed by hours of slow pleasing her in front of roaring fireplace, held lots of appeal.

"Only the best for you, but I have to go now." She rushed the words out as he heard Milo return. Frustration edged the boy's voice. A click and the line went dead.

Tom pocketed the cell just as Maloney entered the room. "I spoke to the warden of the women's prison. She wants something in writing of course, but she'll have Maria transferred to a single cell."

"That was fast." Tom scrambled into his coat.

Maloney shrugged. "Baldwin pulled his strings."

"That explains it." Tom shook his hand with the detective. "Thanks for all the hard work."

"Can't take all the credit. Your help was crucial to the case."

•••

Olivia stood glued to the news report on the television. Rosie had fallen to sleep over an hour ago, but Milo kept creeping out of bed and whining to switch the channel back to cartoons. She tucked the remote in the back pocket of her jeans and kissed his forehead. "Enough TV for you today. Your eyes look tired. It's late. You should be in bed, love. School's tomorrow."

The boy hung his head and headed for the stairs. "Fine."

The Hiltorn case, as media now called it, developed with every passing minute. Photos portraying smiling, beautiful and happy

Maria flashed on the screen. Media had turned her into a darling at the flip of a dime. Just yesterday they hadn't hesitated to show her prison pictures.

"Hi, honey, I'm home." Tom's cheerful voice reached Olivia from the foyer, but she could only spare him a quick glance over her shoulder before her eyes flew back to the screen.

Cameras flashed, microphones were shoved in detective Maloney's face. Uniformed officers struggled to keep overzealous reporters at bay. Hiltorn stepped out of the police vehicle, his hands handcuffed in front, suit jacket covering his head. Maloney grabbed his elbow and led him through the crowd.

Olivia clapped her hands, her heart pounding. Had she never lived this life, she would side with her now incarcerated boss and defend his actions, thinking he only wanted best for the corporation and the greater benefit. There had been multiple options to bail out his business. Attempting a murder shouldn't be one.

"I missed you, too," Tom teased as he handed her a glass of red wine. "How long have you been stuck in front of the television?"

She gulped the tangy liquid, a nice vintage meant for sipping, but with everything happening today, she needed something to steady her nerves. Then she chuckled and pressed her body on his. He took the glass from her hand and placed it on the coffee table. In the next instant, his lips crushed hers, his tongue licked them, coaxed them open. With a sigh, she surrendered to him, holding him tight in her arms. Heat pooled in her core with every flick of his tongue. For all she knew, this could be the last opportunity she'd get to make love to him and she wouldn't waste another minute. The thought made her frantic and in a strange way horny.

His hand cupped her rear, and he pulled out the remote to turn off the blaring television. "Enough of this damn thing. What do you say we finish this bottle in our bedroom?"

He took her hand and led her upstairs, shutting the door of Milo's room on his way to the master suite. The boy spread over the bed was fast asleep.

"He couldn't wait for you to get home, and neither could I." She unzipped his pants and reached inside. His hard cock sent a rush of wetness between her legs.

Tom set the bottle and two glasses on the dresser. With a swift movement, he pressed her back against the wall, and gripped her wrists above her head. Soft moans puffed from her mouth with his kissing and licking of her neck. She wiggled one hand free and unbuckled his belt. He spread her robe open, driving her wild with desire.

His hands caressed down the side of her breasts and slid lower to settle against her waist. "Nice teddy. Love how it covers you in lace."

Seeing a fierce desire flashing in his eyes, she was glad she kept the undergarment on. The outfit hardly left anything to imagination, especially the roll on her stomach, which for some reason Tom found very sexy.

Electricity charged the air around them and boosted her arousal. She pushed away from the wall, backing Tom towards the bed. He slid his tie over his head and she gripped the fabric of his shirt, then yanked it apart, sending tiny buttons in all directions. Her hands glided on his rock hard chest.

She stripped off his ruined shirt and pushed on his bare shoulders. He dropped to the bed and raised his hips, allowing her to slide his pants off. She straddled him. "We'll do it my way this time."

He teased her nipples through the thin lace by brushing his palms over her hardened nubbins. "Oh, yeah, tonight you take charge."

Her breath stuck in her throat and she let out a cry of surprise when he slid his hand to her crotch and pulled the snaps free. His finger found her tingling clit and gave it a satisfying rub.

She panted, rose to her knees and poised her entrance over his erection. His hands gripped her hips while she eased down until his hardness filled her.

"Oh…" Moans overtook her voice as she ground her pelvis against his. He matched her pace with his thrusts, and her cries with grunts. Her climax peeked and passion snapped in her core, releasing the waves of pleasure through her. Tom tightened his hold on her hips, holding her firmly while his plunges deepened.

"Yes, oh, yes." Holding the scream in her throat, she threw her head back and surrendered to sweet trembles, hoping they would never cease. The quivers led to exhaustion. She collapsed into Tom's arms and he cradled her against his chest. He kissed her forehead and brushed her hair. Sleep crept over her and strange images formed before her eyes when she started to doze off, but she shook herself awake. With Tom's case solved, if she fell asleep, he'd be gone by the time she awoke. No, she must not sleep tonight. She could make it.

Tom's slow and steady breathing confirmed he was asleep. Fuzziness filled her head and her eyelids dropped. Damn, it must be the wine. She never should've slurped it so fast. The quiet house and soft bed along with Tom's warm body lulled her to sleep.

A female's voice whispering her name woke her. She propped herself on her elbows. "Someone there?" she whispered back.

"Hmm?" Tom rolled to his back.

"Go back to sleep. It's nothing." But her curiosity drew her out of bed. She grabbed her slacks and a sweater on her way out of the bedroom.

"This way, Olivia." The voice coaxed her to follow it down the stairs, through the hallway and into the garage. "There's something you must see. Get in the car and drive."

"Are you the angel I saw overtaking Tadem's body?" Olivia put on a pair of old runners she kept on the garage shelf.

"Yes."

"Maybe I should leave a note for Tom." She turned toward the door.

The voice stopped her. "No time. We must go. Now."

The driver's door to her van opened. Olivia narrowed her eyes. She swallowed a lump forming in her throat. Her feet carried her closer to the vehicle. A nagging deep in her gut told her she must do as requested. No backing out.

CHAPTER 19

Olivia gripped the steering wheel in a feeble attempt to steady her trembling hands. The cold air and her shivering assured her she wasn't trapped inside a nightmare. The angel's whispers had lured her out of cozy bed and Tom's embrace. This was the reality.

Reality? For the past three months, her perception was distorted. She stared at the rear-view mirror, hoping she'd catch a glimpse of the angel. "Why can't I see you?"

"We only show ourselves to those worthy of seeing us." The soft voice seemed to come through the car speakers, but the key wasn't in the ignition and no lights lit the dashboard.

She licked her parched lips. "Worthy of seeing you? Like Tadem?"

"Yes, like her and…Tom."

Olivia's blood froze and her heart dropped. "Tom? Why him?"

What the hell was she doing in this freezing garage instead of snuggled in bed with her husband? This was absurd. She grabbed onto handle, but the door wouldn't open. Jamming her shoulder against the stiff metal produced the same result. The entity had trapped her.

Her heart sped and she jabbed her elbow at the door panel. Pain ripped through her arm. Wincing, she cupped her joint in her palm. "Are you doing this? Let me out. I'm not driving anywhere."

"You must. It's time."

"Time for what?" A strange lethargy set over her, and she leaned back in her seat. She stood powerless against the higher being, and things may get worse if she didn't cooperate. "I forgot my key inside the house. The car won't start without it."

The engine roared to life and the dashboard lit up. Her hands flew away from the steering wheel. "How the hell?"

Heat poured out of the vents and for a moment calmed her chills. She watched her hands on the steering wheel reversing out of the garage and onto the road. Her mind screamed to stop, run away, do something, anything, to get back into the house, but her body no longer answered to her commands. "So where to?"

"You know. You always knew."

"I do?" She dragged the words out, but a picture of her destination formed in her head and she shifted into drive. "But what's there, other than a spot on a winding country road?"

"It's where your future begins." The whisper behind her head rose hairs on her nape.

Drifting snow blew over the road as she drove on, glancing at the reflection of her house in the mirrors until she no longer could spot its brick siding.

She drove in silence and merged onto almost deserted highway. "You still here?"

"Keep going." The voice filled the interior. If this was God's messenger, its ways were mysterious.

"Mind if I put on some music?" No reply came from the angel. Olivia pulled a CD out of the case and inserted the disk. Sounds of pipe-organ from *The Phantom of the Opera* startled her, but she burst into ironic laughter. How fitting. Hadn't the heroine believed *an angel of music* taught her to sing? When in fact the angel was a demented man with disfigured face.

Maybe the angel in Olivia's car was some lunatic hiding in shadows. She should sing along to pass the time, hide her fear or scare her personal phantom away. Her stab at the soprano could raise the dead she'd been told. Then there was something to be said about prudent silence.

Oh what the heck, it just may work. After the opening piano chords, she joined in with the lead soprano. The words tightened her throat and choked her singing. Her voice tapered off. The lyrics hit too damn close to home. Would Tom think of her?

Would his love fade? No, they had promised each other many times. She must hold on to the vow. All she had to do was drive to the destination and then…what? What waited for her there?

Snowflakes whirled in the beams of her headlights, stirring the darkness as her car sped ahead. The last track on the CD played when she took the exit ramp.

She took note of the road signs and the landmarks. Waterloo County. She was outside the city already. *Enter the roundabout and take the first right.* The voice boomed in her head.

"Blair Road." She read the green sign. After passing a few scarce houses lining the narrow and winding asphalt, her surrounding dissolved into darkness. Her foot pushed on the brake pedal. Her instinct told her to go back. She grabbed the gearstick and tried to shift into reverse, but the transmission wouldn't budge. *Past the point of no return* …the phantom's singing warned her to follow the road ahead and find spot where she could make a wide turn.

Through the veil of darkness, dense forest loomed over the road. She must've passed the last sign of civilization some fifteen minutes ago. The angel remained silent or maybe had abandoned her. The Phantom CD started playing from the beginning. She flipped on high beams. The glistening snowflakes blinded her and she switched back to regular headlights.

The heavy snowfall and wiper blades racing at full speed back and forth across the windshield made it hard to see the road ahead. This was crazy. What was she thinking when she left the safety of her home? When would she learn to listen to reason? And now she was hopelessly lost. Served her right.

If Tom woke and found her gone, he'd be worried and livid with her for heading out into the night alone. She should call him. He'd come to her rescue, or send help considering she was over an hour's drive away from the city.

She slid her hand inside her coat pocket. Her fingers grasped the liner, and her breath caught. Impossible, her cell had to be in there. She wiggled her fingers, inspecting the pouch, hoping the phone would appear. Where could she have left the stupid thing? She slapped her leg. "Top of the microwave."

That was where she'd placed her cell after talking to Tom. Damn, her head must've been in a gutter. What should she do now? The GPS! The device only gave garbled static and displayed squiggly lines. *What the hell? It worked a minute ago.*

A pickup truck pulled up behind her. She blew out a breath of relief. The driver could help her turn the car around and direct her back to the highway. She squinted at the intense lights mounted at the top of the cabin roof illuminating the interior of her car. What was going on?

The vehicle slowed down and its lights sunk in her rear-view mirror. Scenes from the horror movies involving the lost women on the abandoned road flashed before her eyes.

The pickup sped up and came to her rear bumper, flashing those bright lights inside her cabin. Shouts of young males reached her. The guys must be drunk or high, or maybe both.

"Oh god," she gasped. Fear sent needles down her spine, stiffening her arms and shoulders.

The truck's lights faded into the distance again. Maybe they'd had a bit of fun with her and would leave her alone. Then it began again. At the fast approaching beams and roaring laughter, a scream ripped from her throat.

The shouts grew louder. A bottle thrown from the truck shattered against her trunk. "City folks don't belong here."

"Please, don't do this." Her chin trembled and she barely uttered the words. Her eyes glued to the rear-view mirror. The combination of letters and numbers of the pickup's rust covered license plate on the front bumper stood out in the intense light. Her panic stricken mind screamed to write the plate number. She tapped around the dashboard, hoping she would find a writing instrument and found a marker under her palm. With a shaky hand she scribbled the plate numbers on her forearm, felt tip digging into her skin.

Three bright yellow signs ahead warned her she was entering a sharp bend. The truck sped to her rear bumper again. A piercing scream tore from her mouth. She slammed on the brake. The truck rammed her car and pushed her off the road.

A deafening sound of screeching metal ripped through her ears. The van shook and groaned on uneven ground. She cradled her head in her arms. The airbag deployed and the impact knocked her hard.

Her head swam. She fought to hold on and not slip into inviting darkness.

"Who will it be, Olivia? Tom or Tadem?" The angel's calm voice dissolved into silence.

"I can't choose. Don't make me." She mumbled with the last of her strength, surrendering to oblivion while the Phantom's voice grew distant, or maybe it was Tom's.

• • •

"Miss? Can you hear me?"

Olivia's lashes fluttered, but she couldn't open her eyes. She coughed. A sharp pain ripped through her chest. Her head was propped. Something stiff was fitted around her neck. At least she didn't have to struggle to find a comfortable position to relieve the agony. Darkness opened up in front of her once again. She wanted to slip there.

"Stay with me, Miss Owen." The woman demanded, clapping her hands above Olivia's ear. "Stay with me."

Olivia moaned. Why did the woman keep addressing her by her maiden name?

"I'm Amira. We're from the local EMS. We'll get you out of here." The woman's demanding voice yanked her back to the cold and uninviting world.

"Medar," she whispered.

"I'm sorry?" Amira leaned her ear over Olivia's mouth.

Latex covered fingers pulled down on Olivia's lids. Amira flashed the light in each eye. "Pupils are normal."

"I'm Mrs. Medar." Olivia tried to scan the scene through her lashes. The flashing lights of the emergency vehicles parked on the road above stood out in the dim light of dawn.

"Your driver's license identifies you as Olivia Owen."

Olivia's heart sank. She was back in her old, empty world. There was a time she'd give anything for this chance, now she'd give it all away to be with Tom and her children.

Still, a sliver of hope lived in her mind. "Please, find my husband."

Amira patted her arm. "Let us get you out first."

A firefighter approached her. "Miss, can I get you to cross your arms over your abdomen? That's great. Keep them like that."

He grabbed her shoulders. "I'm going to sit you upright and my colleague will slide the board behind you. If you experience any pain, let me know right away. Are you okay to proceed?"

"Yes." She answered with a weak voice. All she wanted was to find Tom and the sooner she was pulled out of this wreck, the sooner she could start.

"Easy now." The firefighter pulled her up. "Any pain?"

She bit her lower lip and whimpered. "No, I'm fine."

"Are you sure?" Doubt crept into the man's deep voice. "'Cause we can pull the car apart to free you."

"I'm sure." Her words came out with a whoosh of air.

He studied the writing on her forearm. "What's this?"

"License plate of the pickup that rammed me into the ditch." Good thing her scribbling had not wiped out. She wrote it with

Milo's washable marker. "The road was covered in snow. Airbag hit me hard in the face."

"Airbag? Snow?" The man gave a reluctant cough. "Your Mercedes is a vintage. It's not equipped with airbags. There has been no snowfall in over two months." He continued to work around her. "I'm glad you kept your wits and wrote the plates down. Catching them won't be hard. Clever guys have done this before."

Her old Mercedes? If she mentioned she drove a van when she got pushed off road, they may book her into psych ward.

Amira reappeared next to her. "Ready?"

Olivia nodded. Their hands grabbed the board attached to her back and in a fluid motion pulled her out. The stretcher seemed to expand under her legs and in the next instant the four EMS personnel carried her to the road and placed her on a gurney. An oxygen mask lowered over her nose and mouth. Blankets were wrapped around her. The mobile bed was pushed at the back of the ambulance. The back door slammed shut and the vehicle drove off with blaring sirens.

"Please, can you notify my husband?" Olivia pleaded with Amira, but deep down she knew better.

"A constable will take your statement in the hospital." Amira turned her head at the driver's divider. "We'll be there in a few minutes."

The ambulance pulled up at the entrance. A morsel of Olivia's worries chipped away. At least the pain in her neck and shoulders would be alleviated, and meds would knock her out cold. She craved the glorious oblivion.

The rear door popped open and Amira jumped out. "Thirty-five-year-old female with multiple contusions and abrasions, no obvious fractures, BP is one-ten over seventy, heart rate normal." She placed the clipboard on Olivia's legs and continued to shout her condition while the crew of two nurses and a doctor rolled her down the long corridor. When the gurney came to a stop in front of the double glass door, she squeezed Olivia's shoulder. "You're in good hands now. Take care."

Olivia nodded and stared at Amira's back, her black hair pulled in a thick braid bouncing against the white EMS letters of her deep navy jacket.

The rest of the day passed in examinations and x-ray rooms. The doctor couldn't explain why her bruises were consistent to that of a deploying airbag, yet there had not been one in her car. They considered her very lucky for not sustaining serious injuries. At last, she was left alone in her room. As time passed she grew more anxious to get out of the hospital and return home. Before supper time, a police officer came to take her statement. She filed an accident report, describing the pickup truck, including the license plate.

"Have you notified my husband?" She handed the paper back to the uniformed officer.

The man tilted his head toward the tiled floor then leveled his eyes with hers. "Sorry, miss. We're still looking. Thank you for your co-operation. Get yourself some rest."

He replaced his cap and left her room.

Right, they're still looking. They all must think her a total wacko, with her crying for a husband and children who didn't exist. If she didn't stop, they would send her to a shrink and she would never get out of here. What if her double was with Tom and he couldn't tell the difference? *Stop it. He said to trust him. Besides, you know there is no double.* The meds kicked in and pulled her into a blissful sleep.

• • •

The next day, a nurse handed her the large, clear plastic bag with her belongings sealed inside. She shook them out of the sack onto the bed and shifted through them. The notebook where she'd written all the phone numbers and addresses came into focus. With a shaky hand she picked up the thin item and flipped through the pages. They were blank. All her efforts in the other life were useless. She threw the book onto the pile as tears stung her eyes. An item slid out of it. She clasped her hand over the shiny object to prevent it from falling off her bed. And exhaled a shaky breath at the sight of Tom's tie pin, the one she'd given him at Christmas. Maybe he'd placed it in her notebook. If she could bring an object from the future perhaps that explained why had the license plate of the pickup remained on her arm.

"The doctor is discharging you today. You won't need this anymore." Her nurse removed her IV oblivious to Olivia's astonishment. "Is there anyone who can take you home?"

"No." She was alone again. Once that had suited her just fine, but now…she wouldn't survive her solitude. Numbness gripped her and her will for living was dying, but she wouldn't allow her memory for Tom and their children to wither.

An hour later, she left the hospital with a few prescriptions in her pocket. Strange, snow didn't cover the ground and the grass had turned green. It was warm in the cab. She leaned toward the driver. "Would you mind turning the heat down?"

"Heat's not on. Do you want some a/c back there?" He threw his question over his shoulder.

"Yes, please." She leaned back and stared out the window. Spring.

Her house mocked her with empty and deadly silence. And worst of all, everything stood in its place. No toys lay scattered on the floor. No scents of Tom's cooking wafted in the air. No blaring cartoons or Milo sprawled on the carpet in front of television. No sweet giggles of her beautiful baby girl.

Olivia's arms ached to hold her children, to cover them in kisses, to tell them how much she loved them. Pain in her heart exploded and shattered her chest. She wanted her family life back, all of it. Even her weight gain.

"Tom. Milo. Rosie." She stumbled through the house, calling their names, looking for any sign of their existence. The nursery once again served as storage for the boxes with her old junk. Tears streamed down her face.

"Give them back to me, they're mine." Her shouts echoed around empty walls. No answer. Anger flared in her. "Damn it, did you hear me? They're mine."

A speck of light twinkled in the darkness and expanded until the room filled with its glow. She flattened her back against the cold wall. The angel heard her.

"You're seeing me in my purest form." The light shimmered with angel's voice. "Can you see it? Without love, there's nothing. You want to give up this future for your career?"

"No, I choose love. Please, I'll do anything you want," Olivia uttered through her tight throat. The angel was testing her. A vision of Rosie's baby fingers wrapped around hers flashed before her eyes. No money in the bank, no property or expensive car could measure up to what had been taken away from her. "Return them to me. They're so little. They need me."

"Your children have not been born. To see Tom your soul must enter Heaven."

Her chin dropped and her quivering breath filled the silence. "I'd have to die to get there."

"You said you'll do anything. He's waiting for you."

She shook her head, her back slid down the wall. Her mind refused to accept the angel's words. Yes, she'd agreed to do anything, but not to commit suicide. "No, he's not dead. I know he's not."

Frustration forced her to raise her voice, but the light continued to intensify and the same daze settled over her. On her wobbly legs, she staggered to her bedroom and collapsed in the bed. With her face buried in the pillow, now devoid of Tom's sea scent, she broke down and surrendered to sobs. Tom was out there, somewhere, probably searching for her. But just as her address book turned up blank, all the records about them could disappear. The angel had to have something to do with it.

"To hell with you." She tossed the pillow at the fading light. "I'll find Tom."

Her eyelids drooped and she hovered between sleep and wakefulness for a few moments. The light shrunk and vanished, leaving her in darkness.

•••

The sound of a phone ringing pierced through her sleep. She flipped to her side, but the shrill clangor reverberated in her head.

"Tom." Her eyes snapped open. She closed them fast as the sunbeam piercing through open blinds fell across the bed.

She glued the receiver to her ear, hoping to hear his voice.

"Olivia?" Jess's whisper came through.

Olivia's heart sputtered, but hearing a familiar voice gave her some assurance that things weren't hopeless. "Yes?"

"Mr. Hiltorn's livid. You didn't come to work or call or email again. Are you sick?"

Of course, in this life she worked, not lived a life of a stay-at-home mom on maternity leave. And Hiltorn was a free man. "I was in a car accident. I spent almost two days in the hospital."

"Oh my god," Jess shrieked, then lowered her voice. "Are you okay?"

"Just bruised. My car is totaled, though." She sat in bed and propped her head on her hand. If Hiltorn was livid with her, it could mean he was making everyone's lives a living hell. No need for her co-workers to suffer because of her. She would dose up on pain killers and drag her sore body to work. "I'll be there in a few."

"Are you sure you want to come in?" Hiltorn's growling drifted from Jess's end and confirmed Olivia's decision. Jess continued when boss's barking ceased. "Not your Mercedes, I hope. You love that car."

"Yeah, but was told I'll get good money for parts. Tell Hiltorn I'll be there." She replaced the receiver and stepped in the shower. Warm water helped loosen up her stiff muscles and she wished she could stay under the spray forever. Her thoughts were constantly with her children and husband. Kids she never had and if she couldn't find Tom, she wouldn't have them. Sadness swept over her, tightening her ribcage. A long wail wrenched her body. No point dwelling on that. She needed to get her ass into gear and not stop until she accomplished her goal. The corporate world had taught her a tough life lesson she planned to use.

She shut the water and stepped out. Wrapped in a towel, she opened her closet and found all her business suits hanging. Her girly, fun wardrobe she'd come to adore was gone. No amount of makeup would cover the bruises. And why hide them? Let the employees see Hiltorn forced her to show her face at work so soon after the accident.

Her convertible two-seater sat in the garage, its key hanging on the rack by the door. Everything was in the same place, as if she'd never left this life.

At the office people's eyes widened and many turned their faces away at her approach. Some asked if she was okay, others wanted to know what happened. But it was the genuine concern in their voices and eyes that touched her. Wasn't she the corporate slut?

Jess's crumpled face met her at the door. "He wants to see you in his office. Right away."

Olivia put her purse on the desk in her office and squeezed Jess's shoulder. "Don't worry. It's all right."

"It doesn't look good. You don't look good."

"Looks worse than it is." A long sigh filled her with calm and she stepped into Hiltorn's office. "You wanted to see me?"

"Owen, close the door and sit." Without looking at her, he flicked his hand toward a chair across from his desk. She took a seat, but he kept his eyes glued to the computer screen. If he did this for fear effect, it was wasted on her. To think how much she had respected him not so long ago.

He swiveled his chair, facing her, his forearms flat on the desk. "I have had enough of your tardiness. For the past three months, I've been watching you drag your sorry ass around here, when you granted us with your presence. You are, or were, the best of the best so I figured you'd snap out of whatever gripped you." He paused and leaned back in his leather high back recliner. "I've fired people for less. No. Wait. I had you fire them for me. But I can't have you fire yourself, so consider *me* dismissing you a privilege."

"Yes, I'm honored you extended me the courtesy." She couldn't hide the sarcasm in her voice. Not that she tried.

Deep creases formed around his mouth with his frown. "How dare you show such impertinence?"

She stood, slowly and ground her molars. "How dare you kick me to the curb after I did your dirty business for years?"

He slapped his hands on the desk and pushed to his feet, leaning over the table. "I never asked you to spread your legs for any of my business clients, but who am I to meddle in your stuff? Helped me score a few deals and got you a promotion or two. Now clean out your office. You could've been a part of something special."

She dug her nails in her palms. Those days were nothing to be proud of, but at least she had cast her promiscuity away now and wouldn't go back. Her hand almost flew to his cheek, but she had to show him she was better than that. He probably wanted her to slap him so later he could accuse her of an assault. After five years, she was ordinary and unimportant. Just as the countless employees she'd dismissed whose hard work and dedication to the company went up in smoke.

"No, you can't fire me. Because I quit. And I am a part of something special." At least she would be once she reunited with Tom. She stepped to the door.

"One more thing." Hiltorn's irate voice stopped her on her way out. "The gun I gave you is company property."

Holding onto the knob, she snapped her head toward him. Of course, the gun. In her misery she'd forgotten about the pistol in her closet. "You can't expect me to bring it here. I can't be caught in public with a concealed weapon."

"Didn't bother you when you took it home." He grabbed the pen from the holder on his desk.

Okay, he had a point there. Still she would be dammed to let him have that gun.

He scribbled on a sticky page and handed her the neon note. "Take it to this pawn shop. Ask for Steve. Say I sent you."

She flicked an eyebrow. So this was how she ended up pawning the gun. "Should this shop be buying illegal weapons?"

"My…acquaintance will take care of it." Hiltorn straightened and shoved his hands inside his trouser pockets. She gave him a once over. His smug expression confirmed her suspicion. He was putting the blocks in place for shooting Mr. Baldwin. Her heart sped, but she maintained her current appearance.

"Yes, boss, anything you say," she smirked then pulled the door open and bolted out of Hiltorn's office.

Cleaning her space took no time. There were no family pictures or any personal items. She stowed her framed diploma under her arm and grabbed her purse. Jess stood in the doorway, her brows knitted. At least she granted her silence.

"I'm out of here." Olivia flung her purse over her shoulder.

"What are you going to do?" Jess's voice quivered and her chin trembled. Her assistant should rejoice to see her go. She had made the poor girl's life miserable with her demands. But her actions in the past were mimicked by her boss's. The corporate world was cold and unforgiving. For five years, she fooled herself that she belonged here in that cut-throat environment.

"I'll think of something." Olivia gave an exhausted laugh. "Strange, but I'm actually relieved. This place is no longer my problem."

Jess's shoulders rose with her long inhale. She nodded. "I know what I have to do."

Olivia took a moment to scan the walls of her office that doubled for her second home. How many days had she worked here from early mornings to late evenings, oblivious to the world outside? No more. She closed the door and left. Her legs couldn't carry her out fast enough, making her heels click on the polished stairs. She peeked at the reception, where Beatrice swung her chair around, stretching the telephone cord attached to her earpiece connecting her to the switchboard. The woman's motherly face dropped. "Olivia, good Lord. I heard you've been in an accident. How are you doing, dear?"

"As to be expected." Olivia attempted a smile.

"Good grief, I cannot believe you still made it in to work. If only our boss would value your dedication. Are you going out for lunch?" Beatrice scanned the telephone lines through her thick glasses.

Olivia ceased buttoning her jacket. The receptionist didn't know she was no longer an employee. Should she try to explain or let it go?

"I haven't had my break since I came in. You know how it is. I will lose my job if I left the reception unattended. Would you mind filling in for just a few minutes while I run to the ladies' room?"

"Sure." Olivia set her purse on the desk, her eyes already searching the off limits monitor button on the board. "Take your time."

"Bless you." Beatrice removed her earpiece and scurried away.

Olivia fitted the earphone on and studied the lines. Hiltorn's extension lit up. She found the forbidden button and pressed it. His voice came through. "You get the trollop who bewitched your husband to pick the piece from the pawn and we're good to go."

Mrs. Baldwin replied with her sugar-laced voice. "Are you sure your ex-employee will comply?"

Hiltorn snorted. "She did everything I asked of her for five years. I'd say she's conditioned to obey."

Olivia's chin dropped. Their plan was further along than she suspected. She turned to the computer and punched in her login info. The blue circle spun and she doubted her login was valid, but the screen filled up with icons. Her high security clearance allowed her access to systems and she opened the switchboard logs. There she found the log for the monitor button and deleted the record. Beatrice rounded the corner, a grin on her face and toilet paper stuck on her heel, dragging on the shiny floor.

"Thank you for this." She skirted the desk just as Olivia logged off.

"You're welcome." Olivia removed the earpiece, her hands still shaky. For a moment she contemplated whether to tell the woman she should look into an early retirement, but decided it wasn't her place to meddle in everyone's lives.

She picked up her purse and left Intelcorp for good. Hiltorn's phone conversation bugged her. With her knowledge, she couldn't let an innocent man get shot and a naïve girl get arrested. If she changed the course of the events, would she get to see Tom again?

"Olivia," Jess's call reached her on her way to her car. "Olivia, wait up."

She halted and pivoted in her direction. Jess's bag and curls bounced with her strides and a big grin matched her smiling eyes. "You're right, quitting is liberating." She heaved. "And there's a line forming in front of Hiltorn's office."

CHAPTER 20

Wind blew hair across her face. Olivia snagged an annoying lock and shoved it behind her ear. The June breeze rippled Jess's shirt, sending her flaxen strands in all direction. She slid her arm through the strap of her purse, the smile on her lips confirming her decision to quit made her happy.

"Let's grab a drink. Getting freed from the Intelcorp calls for a celebration." She looped her arm with Olivia's.

Olivia's legs froze. Her assistant must've lost whatever brain cells she had. "Jess, you quit your job on my account?"

Jess frowned, flicking her hand as if she swatted a fly. "No, silly. I've been meaning to give my notice for a while, but I stayed because of you. Come on." She tugged her arm. "My car is closer. Do you want go to the bistro?"

An inner shudder shook Olivia's core at the thought of the greasy diner she'd met Jess for lunch in Tom's world. Olivia reached into her purse and pulled out her key. "I don't want to leave my car here. I'll meet you there."

Stepping backward, Jess raised her finger. "I'll get you your usual."

"Yes." Olivia called over her shoulder on her way to her car. Then halted. *Her usual?* Seemed she'd had coffee with Jess more than once. She shrugged. From now on, she would drink many coffees alone. Right now she craved company and her empty home was the last place she wanted to be.

A few minutes later, she joined Jess in the eclectic restaurant. The tall cup of steamy coffee waited on the table, but the memory of its abominable taste squeezed her throat. She hung her purse on the chair. "So what are you going to do now?"

Jess closed her compact mirror. "Something's going to come up, something always does. What about you?"

"I don't know." Olivia propped her chin on her knuckles. "For a while I've been toying with the idea of starting my own recruitment agency. Represent working mothers—it's a shame the way society shuns them. Putting families before their career is not a crime."

Jess snapped her glance from the purse on her lap. Olivia turned her head from side to side, scanning the few patrons immersed in their conversations, then frowned at her new friend. "Do you think it's a bad idea?"

"It's a wonderful plan." She leaned over the table. "It's time I start putting my license in commercial real estate to use. Let me look for the location."

Olivia pursed her lips. If she were to go ahead with this, she would need to hire the real estate agent anyhow. Could she trust Jess? "You know, as I remember, we weren't friends before today."

Jess tapped her spoon on the rim of her cup and set the plastic utensil on the table. "Funny you should mention it, but when you returned from Vancouver, you became…different. I don't know how to describe it. You're calmer. You don't bite heads off and even say please and thank you." She shrugged. "And we hit it off. Only thing was, you used up all your vacation and sick days. You don't remember me visiting you at home? You said you couldn't get enough sleep. I thought you might be pregnant."

Please and thank you, small yet powerful words once non-existent in her vocabulary. Tom had said them often and so expressing her gratitude had become her second nature.

"Pregnant?" Olivia scoffed and shook her head. She'd had two children, yet she had no idea what it would be like growing them in her belly. "Is that what pregnancy feels like?"

"Who knows?" Jess blew on the steam of her coffee. "The reports on that are confusing. Every woman seems to experience different things. All weird, though. You can't remember me visiting?"

"Vaguely," Olivia lied. She couldn't talk about her past three months when Jess remembered the things differently. Could this other woman Jess befriended be Olivia's double? Hadn't the angel said she'd been sent into future? Judging by her oldest child, some six years ahead, there were no alternate, only her. But could she exist simultaneously in two different time frames? Maybe she moved back and forth—that would explain her sleeping most of the time, and slacking at work.

Olivia sipped and pushed the cup away. Tom had spoiled her; no other coffee would do. "Our chat's been eye-opening. Well. I'm heading home. Lot's to do."

"Like what?" Jess's voice took on a curious tone. She squared her shoulders.

Olivia got on her feet and sighed. *Oh, just turn in an unregistered gun to the police, send an anonymous letter to the possible victim of Hiltorn's shooting and scour the Internet in search of her husband from the future or for anyone who may know him.* "The usual stuff."

Jess stood as well. "I should go, too. So will you give me the chance?"

What the heck, Jess had proved invaluable, putting up with Olivia's moods. She deserved the support. "Sure, knock yourself out."

"Goody." Jess clapped. "You won't regret this, I promise."

"I know I won't." Olivia smiled. If her mother found out she'd quit her job under obscene conditions, the stiff hag would drop dead. The hell with her, it was time for Olivia to shed the feeling of inadequacy that followed her through her life. Mother had done enough damage.

Olivia drew in a long breath. The bad premonition had kept her up at nights not long ago now sat right. The angel's voice hummed in her head. She was on a right track.

. . .

Olivia held the air in her cheeks and eyed the entrance of the police station. Her stomach lurched. Perhaps pawning the gun would be easier. At least there would be no hard questions asked. Or she could muster enough courage to not hang up before Detective Maloney picked up the line. He may know Tom. But to explain the possession of the gun, her life with Tom, and a high profile crime case that could happen in the near future without sounding crazy would be impossible.

She blew the air out of her mouth and strutted ahead. This was the right thing to do and something Tom would expect of her. Her bruises had faded enough to cover them with makeup, but her stomach twisted all the same. No doubt there'd be lots to explain and her beat up appearance could add to her list.

"Hi." She greeted a uniformed officer at the reception desk.

The tall man pressed a button on the phone and replaced the receiver then nodded. "Yes, ma'am. How can I help you?"

In an instant her voice abandoned her. Sweat laced her palms while her mouth turned dry. She wanted to run away, but then she would raise suspicion.

"I…I'm…turning this in." The box thudded when she placed the case on the reception desk in front of him.

The cop gave her a suspicious look, flipped the lid open, tilted the box and whistled. "What have we here?" He fixed her with a hard stare. "Are you licensed to carry this, lady?"

His stern tone sent prickles down her spine. She shook her head. "It was a gift of a sort."

"A gift?" He handled the gun and peered inside the firing mechanism. "Looks like it had never been fired." The metal clicked as he snapped the barrel back.

She swallowed against her dry throat. Her best course would be to say the least possible and not go into lengthy explanations. "No. I never used it."

"All right." He set the pistol down and planted his big hand over the receiver of a ringing telephone. "I need to see some ID."

Pulling out her driver's license from the wallet proved hard with shaking fingers. The cop handed her a clipboard with a form stuck on it and took her ID.

"I need you to fill this out. Answer every question." He slapped the pen on top of the papers.

She forced her fingers to hold the pen and write steadily, and by the time she flipped the form to its last page, her hands had relaxed. The cop plopped her ID in front of her. "You have no priors and your record is clean, so we'll let this slide. Thank you for turning the gun in."

Though the officer sounded accusatory, his tone carried a hint of warning. A load lifted off her shoulders. Tom would be proud of her. His words proved right. Handing in the weapon wasn't as painful as she thought. On her way to her car, she mailed the letter she'd written addressed to Baldwin. This was all she could do to prevent the crime. Fingers crossed, her efforts would pay off.

Her cell chimed. *Tom.* Her heart rejoiced, then shattered when she read Jess's name on the display. She swallowed the disappointment and answered the call. "Hey what's up?"

"I've found a perfect space. You won't be able to find a single flaw about this one," Jess reported. "It's smack downtown and close to everything you want, and the best part is, I've got lease papers ready. All you have to do is sign them."

Olivia couldn't help but smile at Jess's efforts. In the past weeks she'd shown her some six rental properties, all of which she'd found fault with. "I'm downtown already. Give me the address."

"Fifteen McCaul Street. Do you need directions?"

"I'm good, thanks. See you in a few minutes." Olivia ended the call with Jess still boasting about the place.

The phone chimed again before Olivia returned it to her purse. Unknown caller displayed. Tom?

"Owen," Hiltorn rasped in her ear, crushing her hopes. "Have I not instructed you to take the piece to the pawn shop?"

"Mr. Hiltorn, please refrain from calling me, and as for the gun, it's in good hands." She cut the call and his irked tone. Hopefully, this would rid her of him for good. Damn, blocking him had proved futile. He could call her from any phone. She would change her number if it weren't for a small chance of Tom's call.

Her possible office stood a two blocks south. Summer had officially started a couple of weeks ago, but today was the first day without rain. A walk would do her good. She'd spent weeks cooped up in the house, getting her business going and spending any spare moment searching for Tom. So far, the Internet turned up no results. Or his law firm frowned upon employees joining social media network sites and he had a profile under a pseudonym. Many employers, Hiltorn including, would resort to scare tactics to prevent workers from hanging on such pages and posting things about their place of employment.

Or the angel interfered. The entity hung around, she was certain. Each time Olivia felt she was on a right trail, the screen of her laptop would blank out or the Internet connection dropped. In the empty, silent house, unexpected whispers didn't escape her, even with music blaring through her headphones. She'd resisted the angel's urges to join Tom in the afterlife. Their life together waited for them here, on Earth.

Jess waited for her on the street in front of the building displaying a large for rent sign. "Don't you just love the front?"

Olivia chuckled at her raw enthusiasm. "Yes, looks great."

"Wait until you see inside." Jess pushed the glass door and ushered her in. "A spacious reception." She pointed at the long, black desk.

"I like it so far. Let see the rest." Olivia followed her down the open space area. Okay she wasn't crazy about taupe walls, which reminded her too much of Intelcorp's, but a fresh coat of paint would cover it.

Jess spun in the middle. "Plenty of space for at least three desks, and there's even a small boardroom over there. Or we can use it for copier and filing room."

We? Olivia eyed her with a hint of suspicion. Jess was once her right-hand person who had turned into a friend. What subtle hint was she dropping? "Do you want to continue to be my assistant? I can't pay you as much as you earned at Intelcorp but…"

Jess's shoulders lowered with her long exhale. She placed her hand to her chest. "I thought you'd never ask. Of course I would. There wouldn't be us without you and me."

Olivia pressed her lips tight, stiffening a whimper. Jess had proved resourceful and indispensable, and most of all a great listener. She would cherish her new companionship and not ruin it with her hasty actions. Maybe someday she'd tell her the whole story of Tom and the kids. "What are we waiting for? Let's sign the lease."

Jess bounced on her toes. "Let's do it over lunch. My treat."

"Sure." She looped her arm with Jess and followed her down the street to a small restaurant.

The cast iron patio chairs scraped the wood floor when they sat at the table under the bright colored sun umbrella. Warm weather coaxed people out and the hostess led a steady stream of customers to the tables around them.

Olivia savored the meal, but sadness settled over her at the thought of Tom's home cooking. Would she ever get to enjoy his dishes again? She pushed her empty plate and leaned back. "That was great. I haven't eaten a decent meal in weeks."

"Look at this big belly," a man's deep voice boomed behind her. A baby giggled at man's blow of a raspberry.

"Tom! Rosie!" Olivia whirled around. Her heart sunk. It wasn't her Tom or her baby girl.

Jess's mouth parted in confusion, her hand holding the forkful of lettuce froze above the plate. "Who are they? The names you called."

Olivia closed her eyes, trying to loosen a knot in her chest. "It's nothing."

Jess placed her hand over Olivia's. "Do you want to talk about it?"

"Drop it, Jess. It's really nothing." At her snippy tone, Jess plucked her hand away from Olivia's. "Look, I'm sorry. I'm just tired."

"I understand." Jess patted her lips with a napkin. "When you feel like talking, I'll listen."

"Thanks. I appreciate it. We'll be busy buying office furniture and equipment, so I'll head home now." Olivia reached for her purse. In truth she wanted to sit in front of her laptop and search for Tom. Jess's wrinkled forehead and chewing her lower lip stopped Olivia from getting up. "What did you do?"

Jess's face relaxed. "A friend of mine closed his business and I helped him out. All his furniture and equipment is barely used, and I'm sure you'll like it. He'll even deliver it and set it up for us at no charge."

Olivia let out a short chuckle. How could she argue with such a deal? Jess's enthusiasm was rubbing off on her, plus her friend's eagerness freed her time to turn up her search efforts. "Great. We're all set then."

"We should be ready to move in our new office by Monday." Jess flagged the waitress and asked for the check.

Olivia snatched the bill from the tray before the waitress could set it down. "Let me pay for the lunch. You earned it."

• • •

The house phone rang by the time Olivia stepped inside the foyer. Its shrill sound filled the silence where once her children's laughter greeted her. She picked up the receiver from its cradle on the corner stand.

222

"Is this Ms. Olivia Owen?" A man's baritone came through.

"Yes," she said eagerly, hoping the caller had news of Tom.

"It's Dr. Mason. You left a message with my secretary."

Olivia's insides relaxed. His secretary had assured her Dr. Mason never answered unsolicited calls. "Thank you for calling back, Dr. Mason. Do you maybe know Susan?"

"Hold that thought. Hey, babe, it's her." His voice drifted from the distance. Someone's quick steps drew closer and a female's voice thanked him "Oh my god," a woman shrieked into the phone. "Olivia, it's me, Susan. How on earth did you find Gregory?"

"Susan, so good to hear from you," Olivia gasped, her composure threatening to crumble. Perhaps not all her efforts from the future life had been in vain. "It's a long story."

"I've got all night." Susan laughed.

Her university friend had not changed, at least not from the inside. She was still a straight shooter so why beat around the bush? *Go for the meat, Olivia.* "Do you have two teenage boys?"

Susan sniffed after a short pause. "You seem to know a lot about me. Greg and I, we're doing it backwards. Seventeen years and two kids later, he finally proposed."

"Hey, congrats then." Jealousy pinched Olivia's stomach. Her happy times were snatched from her, and getting them back would require more than she may have in her to give.

Catching up with her lost friend took a couple of hours, but there was much to talk about. She contemplated if, how and when to ask her burning question. From Susan's chatting Olivia concluded her friend didn't remember their meeting in the future.

Susan's laughter ceased and her pause turned into a long silence. "I've been having weird dreams about you, but they are all weird when you think about it. I see snakes in every dream and I had to look into it. They mean a new beginning."

Olivia frowned. Interpreting dreams got to be Susan's new leisure pursuit. And knowing her, she got obsessed about it, just as with each new hobby she picked up in the past. But Olivia couldn't let her tongue loose and spill out her heartache, not yet. "I hope you're right. It's getting late. We'll talk again."

"You bet." Susan ended the call.

...

The first week passed by in a whirl of activities. The word got out and the recruitment process commenced.

"The reception duties take too much of my time." Jess complained. "Do you think we can afford to hire a receptionist?"

"Perhaps." Olivia picked up the receiver on her desk. "Owen's Recruitment, how may I help you?"

"Finally." The man's exhausted voice blared in her ear. "I need to speak with Ms. Owen, please."

"Speaking." Olivia leaned over her desk. They couldn't have an unsatisfied client already. Their screening process was grueling, but once they represented an employee, they were positive they made an excellent match with the employer.

"Ms. Owen, you're a hard person to find. My name is Dr. Wade. I'm calling in regards to your sister. She needs a surgery and, given her infirmity, we need her family's consent. It would also benefit your sister if someone is with her during this time. Is there a remote possibility you could come to Vancouver?"

Olivia turned to Jess typing away at her computer. Her assistant would be more than capable of running the business by herself for a week or two. There was no way she'd make Tadem to go through the surgery with no one by her side.

Olivia drew a long breath before speaking. "I'll be there, Dr. Wade."

"What was that?" Jess's habit of slowly tapping of her pencil on the paper vaguely irritated Olivia, echoing the steady onslaught of events she couldn't stop or even slow down. "Tadem needs me." She stared at the phone. "I have to go to be with her."

Jess stepped to her and placed her hand on Olivia's shoulder. "Go to your sister. You'll be only a phone call away."

"Thank you." The angel had said Tadem was severely ill. A foreboding squeezed Olivia's chest and refused to loosen no matter how deeply she breathed. "I'll leave on the first flight."

Deep in thoughts she couldn't snap out of, Olivia packed for the trip. Memories of her childhood spent with her fragile sister followed Olivia on her flight, and all the way to the hospital. When she first met Tom, he had believed she returned home from attending Tadem during her surgery. Could this be the beginning of the life she had shared with him and their children? Everything would be fine. Tadem would live to see her nephew and niece. But the self-assurance did nothing to ease her nerves.

The short doctor met her in the surgical ward. "Tadem's quite upset today. We need to get the tumors out or she'll face the harder procedure the longer we wait."

"I'll talk to her, doctor." Olivia set her small suitcase against the green wall of Tadem's room and approached the bed. Her sister looked every bit the same as when she'd seen her in her fantasy world. Grown and heavy. "Tadem, it's me, Olivia. Don't be afraid, the doctor knows what he's doing."

"My angel," Tadem slurred, drool rolling down the corner of her mouth. But it was the indifference in her stare that made Olivia shudder. Her sister looked at her as if she were another stranger.

Olivia regarded the nurse with a hard stare. "Is she drugged?"

"She needs to calm down before the surgery." The nurse tucked the blankets around Tadem's feet.

"My angel is gone. She left me. I need her back." Tadem grabbed her hand. "Please, good lady, can you find her? I don't want to go anywhere without her."

"She's been like this since last night." The nurse shook her head. "Yammering away about some angel."

"It's okay, Tadem." Olivia smoothed her sister's scraggly hair. How dare the nurse? Had she seen Tadem's angel, she'd shiver in her shoes. "Your angel will come back. I'm sure."

"Here are the forms Dr. Wade needs you to sign." The nurse shoved the clipboard toward Olivia. She stepped behind Tadem's bed and unlocked the brakes. "It's time we roll her into the OR."

Olivia held onto Tadem's hand until they reached the blue pivoting door displaying "Staff and patients only."

"A moment with my sister, please?"

The nurse stepped away.

"Tadem, honey, look at me." Olivia swallowed, tears burning her eyes. She had to be brave for her sister. "It'll be all right. You'll be out faster than you think. Okay?"

She kissed the top of her head. Tadem presented her with a grin. She appeared calmer—could be due to the drugs or her angel had returned.

The nurse grabbed onto the railing of the bed. "We have to go now."

Olivia couldn't let go of her sister's hand. The bed passed through the door, Tadem's fingers slipped out of her hold.

"Olivia," Tadem shouted, but the gurney rolled through and the pivoting panes flapped, shutting in front of Olivia's face.

Olivia clamped her lips between her teeth and stifled a cry. A distinct feeling this was the last time she would see her sister alive burned deep in her mind. Where in the world was their mother to give her consent for her daughter's surgery? They waited too long.

Hours ticked away. Olivia flipped through an old magazine in the waiting area. Her presentiment increased. At the throat clearing, she snapped her glance toward Dr. Wade standing a few feet in front of her.

Sadness in his eyes and his thinned lips told her the unimaginable had happened. Grief poured over her and a long wail escaped. She wrapped her arms around her abdomen and rocked back and forth.

Dr. Wade sat in the chair facing her. "She was worse off than what showed on her x-rays. Every growth we cut caused massive bleeding. Had she survived today, it would have meant more surgeries, treatments, chemotherapies. Not the kind of life anyone would like to live."

Olivia pressed her hand to her mouth, tears dripping over her fingers. She understood what the doctor was trying to convey yet she found little solace in his words. Another night of hard crying alone in the hotel room was all that remained for her.

Through her tears, she studied her face looking back at her from the dark glass of cab's window. Time seemed merciless and deepened the lines around her lips and eyes, despite her best efforts to buy youth in a jar.

Once alone, she sat on the bed in the chain hotel, reminiscing of her visit to this city at Christmas. How happy they'd all been. Now her son would never have a loving aunt with whom he shared his little secrets. She'd just have to tell him everything about Tadem one day and not let her pure spirit die.

"Angel? Are you here? If you can hear me, you staked your soul, so return Tom to me." Olivia waited for any sign from the entity.

After a few moments a soft melody sounded from the distance and lulled her into a trance. "Tadem's soul arrived in Heaven. She's happy now and whole. Tom's life is slipping away—only your love, if strong enough, will save him."

Olivia clutched the pillow to her chest. "My love is strong. Please, oh, please don't let his life fade."

"Sleep now." An invisible hand brushed her face and closed her eyes. The music grew fainter and so did Olivia's will to stay awake.

She woke to a hot summer day, yet she barely paid much attention to the heat. She was dressed in her black suit she'd never thought to wear for her sister's hastily arranged burial. A few flower arrangements decorated Tadem's plain grave. Olivia placed a single red rose on the casket and stepped back, nodding to the priest. She laced her fingers to stop them from clutching to the fabric of her skirt. Mother's assistant had sent the wreath of white chrysanthemum and a store bought card. No personal touch, no sorrow, only a few words of Mother's important business in Paris and an insincere regret for not being able to attend personally.

After the funeral, Olivia headed to Tadem's room in the residence where she'd spent most of her short life. Her few meager possessions packed in cardboard boxes waited by the door, ready to be dropped off at the Goodwill. The place was now ready for the next resident, just the way the world moved.

Olivia reached for a colorful notebook on top and flipped through the pages. The words Tom and Olivia inside hearts stood out. She lowered herself to the lumpy mattress and read Tadem's big, round letters. In a few simple words, Tadem had detailed Olivia's life with Tom and the children. Olivia devoured the story and burst into tears at the happy ending. Tadem must've written the events the way her angel told her. And knowing her sister, she would have pestered her angel to tell the story over and over.

CHAPTER 21

Seated in the Vancouver hotel's lobby, Olivia read Tadem's story again while waiting on the airport taxi. The pain of loss sliced through her chest as she made peace with the fact her sister was in a better place. Poor Tadem, her death could have been avoided. In her misery, Olivia had forgotten her sister—how could she be so selfish?

The woman sweeping the lobby came into Olivia's focus over the top of the pages and she lowered Tadem's notes to her lap. The cleaning lady stopped the mop and stared back at her. Prickles ran down Olivia's back when she recognized the maid's face. It was the Intelcorp employee she'd discharged from duties on her last firing tirade. Olivia stood and slowly approached her.

"I'm sorry, didn't mean to stare." The cleaning woman's stringy hair hanging from the flowery scarf shook when she snapped her head and returned to mopping the spilled drink.

"Nela, right?" Olivia extended her hand, but the woman shoved the cleaning utensil in her cart and hustled to polish the wood trim.

Olivia followed her. "I can't blame you if you don't want to talk me, but please hear me out. I don't work for the same company anymore."

Nela halted and spun on her heel, facing her. In the light of the sun beaming through the high window, her facial lines stood out. "What do you want?" she snapped with her usual hard accent. "Last time I saw you, you caused me nothing but grief."

Olivia took a step back. She couldn't right all the wrongs she'd caused, but if she could help one unfortunate soul, the guilt on her conscience would lessen. "I want to offer you a job."

Nela opened her mouth as if to bark at her again. She wobbled her head, her expression changed from sour to curious. "It's my last day here and I have no other job offers. I'm interested."

Nela's bitter tone and accusative eyes disappeared, and Olivia continued, "I need a receptionist. Would you consider relocating to Toronto? I could help a little with your moving expenses."

Nela shrugged, wriggled her nose and finally smiled. "Tempting. I'll consider."

Olivia handed her the business card. "Contact me when you make your decision, but don't wait too long."

Nela took the card in her dry and chapped hand. "Who am I kidding? I accept. There are a few things I need to do before I make the move."

"Take your time. My airport ride is here, I have to go." Olivia returned to her suitcase and waved to Nela from the door. Nela waved back.

Olivia spent most of her flight staring out the window. Easiness settled over her. Maybe being so high up put her closer to Tadem. The fluffy clouds reminded her of stories she told to her in those few rare moments they'd spent together. Her poor sister had lived a humble and short life. She deserved to be happy in Heaven.

Jess waited for her at the Toronto airport. "I'm so sorry, Olivia. Why you wouldn't let me come to Tadem's funeral? I'm sure it wasn't easy for you to do it all with no help."

"Your help was tremendous, Jess. You did what you could from here." Olivia scrolled through her emails and smiled at Nela's message. She opened the memo and then said, "Our receptionist will start on Monday."

• • •

With every good deed, Olivia pictured Tom's proud face. She could almost touch him. She would not let the angel take him away.

Not until she took her last breath. Why then did she stare at the computer screen unable to focus on her task at hand? Her thumb slid back and forth over Tom's smooth tie clip. Jess had caught her crying in the bathroom several times. Olivia had brushed her away, blaming a stubbed toe or headache. But for how long could she carry on this farce?

The door to her office opened and Susan stepped in, in her hands a cardboard tray filled with large coffee cups.

Nela locked the door and flipped the door sign to Closed. Her eagerness to please was overwhelming at times, but she settled into her routine fast.

The three women surrounded her desk. Olivia eyed them with suspicion. "What are you doing?"

"Olivia," Susan set the tray down. "Enough with this denial. We don't buy your 'I'm fine' excuse anymore."

"What are you talking about?" she scoffed, but her friends only regarded her with harder stares. No way could she slip out of their clutches now. They had planned this.

"We're worried. You talk to yourself." Jess took the seat across from her desk. "Cry when you think no one's watching, stare into the blank space."

"I do?" Olivia arched her eyebrow. Mocking the three ladies wouldn't work.

"It's for your own good, so speak up." Susan plopped on the chair next to Jess and pulled coffee cups out. "Think of this as a brainstorming session."

Olivia drew in a deep breath. *Brainstorming, right.* Perhaps she could tell them a thing or two, but not the whole story. Okay, how to start? She stared at the plain ceiling then lowered her gaze at the three pairs of wide eyes. "Could you see me as a wife and a mother?"

"Anything's possible." Susan tapped Olivia's hand, but Jess and Nela frowned and shrugged.

Olivia studied her friends' narrowing gazes. "What I'm about to tell you will sound crazy."

All three leaned over her desk as she pushed her story out of her mouth. She had planned not to disclose it all, but as she kept talking, the details just poured out. Except the part about the gun. Her friends didn't need to know how close she'd come to breaking the law.

Susan clamped her hanging mouth shut. "Are you sure you didn't dream this?"

"I'm positive. Don't you remember holding Rosie?" Olivia swung her glace at Jess. "You too bounced her on your knees."

Jess plucked the stir stick out of her mouth. "You must've dreamt that part. Last time I held the baby, I ended wearing my nephew's lunch." Her lips stretched in a mocking smile. "My sister forgot to tell me babies have to be burped first. Do you have any idea how much baby barf reeks?"

"I do." Olivia masked the pain slicing her chest with a short chortle. "And I'd give anything to smell it again."

Jess twirled the chewed up stir stick between her fingers. "I don't think things through, that's what you often say, so this may be nothing or it could be something."

"Spill it out," Susan demanded. "Because I draw a blank."

Jess angled her chair, facing the two women. "Well, this angel took Olivia to the future, right?"

"Right." Nela and Susan answered in unison.

"So now Olivia has to find Tom here to live her future."

"We already know that." Susan took a sip of her coffee and scowled. By now their untouched beverages had turned cold.

Jess raised her index finger. "We have to make sure Tom is real."

"He is. I'm sure." Olivia nodded. How else would she have his tie pin she'd given him in the future? Susan was right, this brainstorming proved helpful. "I don't know where else to look."

Jess's eyes lit up. "You said you remember this guy from the campus. What year did he graduate?"

Olivia's mind raced, counting years backward. "Nineteen ninety-five. Why?"

Jess's shoulders rose with her long inhale. "Do you think the university would keep yearbooks that far back?"

Olivia dropped her chin. Why couldn't she think of that? "You're a genius."

"Let me try something." Jess raced for her laptop. The keys on the keyboard clicked under her flying fingers. "Well hello, Mr. Tomislav Medar. He's so handsome."

Olivia flew to the Jess's desk. Tom's black-and-white picture glowed on the screen. His graduation robe covered his athletic frame, but the mop of his hair hung loose under the cap. Those must've been the last of his rebel days, before he had it cut and took the lawyer job. She brushed her hand over the photo. The university record and his photo enforced her belief that he is real. *Where are you, my love?*

"You said he is Croatian?" At Nela's voice she peeled her gaze away from his image.

"Yeah, his family moved back to some split town."

Nela sneered. "It's the town of Split. Exact same spelling, different meaning. The name comes from the Latin word *Spalato*, the palace. Italians kept the original name. The city was founded by the Roman Emperor Diocletian who built his retirement residence there."

"And some residence it is." Jess threw her remark over her shoulder, then faced the screen again. "Listen to this. The biggest Dalmatian seaport, and the pics are fabulous. Is the sea really this blue? Just look at the sun-bleached buildings rising straight from the water. I would love to see this place."

Susan sprung to her feet. "We should go. It'll be a great getaway and who knows, we may just find Tom."

"I can't go to Croatia," Nela shrieked. "I'll stay here and mind the business."

"Nela, we need a translator." Jess typed away on the keyboard her eyes glued to the screen. "Hey, hey. Look what I found." Jess licked her lips and grinned at the screen. "This guest house is up for rent. It's in the middle of downtown inside the palace. It accommodates four people and they have two weeks available as of now. What do you say? Shall I book this?"

"Yes." Susan jumped, clapping her hands. "Great find, Jess. We're going."

Nela lowered herself to the seat. Color drained from her bleak face. "You'll find many people who speak English. There are too many painful memories. I can't go."

"All right, Nela. We won't force you." Olivia rubbed her dry hand. Nela's face lit with a slight smile. "I hope you find him."

Olivia propped her head on her folded arms. Just by opening up, in the past hour she accomplished more than all her efforts in the past. This was all moving way too fast, but if travelling to Tom's country meant finding him, she'd cross the distance. He would do the same for her.

CHAPTER 22

The downpour washed the ancient city of Split, leaving the stone-paved, narrow roads glisten in the light of street lamps. Clivia leaned her head to the wood trim of window frame. Rain settled to steady rhythm, the drumming of the drops against the window seemed to mock her, confirming her fear. The trip to Croatia had not turned up Tom and she couldn't relax and enjoy this exotic country the way it was supposed to be relished. The love she harbored for Tom could be just a fantasy and she should let go of the illusion. But he made her a better person, added zest to her life she didn't know was missing, and the amazing love they shared, the way he'd kissed her, he'd given her the best days of her life…she closed her eyes at the thought. Could she keep waiting for him?

"Olivia." A soft hand squeezed her shoulder. She whirled and faced Jess's sorrowful expression. Wow, her friend had managed to get away from Nikola. Their gracious host stood no chance when Jess quickly wrapped him around her little finger.

Jess tapped her hand and gained her attention. "Sometimes you have to stop worrying, doubting and wondering. Things will work out, you'll see. Maybe not exactly how you want them to be, but how they supposed to be."

Olivia stared at her friend. Her words made sense. "When did you acquire such wisdom?"

"Just something I read on Facebook." Jess bit her lower lip and sighed. "Let's go pack. Even if I so don't want to leave."

Jess was right—she didn't want to leave with the first light tomorrow. Their trip had not produced desirable results, but Olivia would relive the impressions for the rest of her life. This land of olive trees, vineyards and lavender bushes growing among stones, the barren rocks of Biokovo Mountain raising straight from the azure waters of the Adriatic captured her heart. Just like Tom.

• • •

Gray clouds hovered above Toronto's skyscrapers and threatened to dump their load. Olivia paid the cabby, grabbed her luggage and scurried up the steps to her house. She scooped the newspapers thrown at the front door.

A young man in black hoodie approached across the lawn. "Miss, the mail got mixed up. This came to our address."

She took the envelope from his hand. "Thanks. You're Jason, right?"

He squirmed as if uncomfortable she talked to him. "Yeah, that's me."

Olivia pointed her chin at the young girl standing on the sidewalk. "Is that your girlfriend?"

He smiled. "Julie. She likes Madonna."

Olivia waved to the bleached haired girl in black fishnet stockings and cherry Doc Martens. The girl's many bracelets chimed when she waved back. Olivia returned her glance to Jason. "Tell her to pay special attention to the lyrics of 'Papa Don't Preach.'"

"All right, I will." He nodded and strutted toward Julie.

Olivia left her suitcase in the foyer and proceeded to toss the rolled up newsprint in the recycling bin. She halted her hand at the headline reading *Baldwin Escapes Death*, pulled the paper out of the clear, plastic bag and read.

Mr. Jim Hiltorn and his son Ike were arrested in the Baldwins' residence following a bizarre shooting incident. Mr. Baldwin was warned of his possible endangerment by two anonymous letters and turned the matter to the police. The details are not clear at this point, but police are investigating the involvement of Mrs. Baldwin ...

Olivia read the short article over and over. Two letters? She'd sent one. Could Tom have sent the other one?

"Your determination is powered by love." The angel's voice pierced the silence of the still house. "Tom is ready to be with you again."

Olivia darted her glance from side to side, but couldn't see anything. The house once again stood quiet. And her heart rejoiced at angel's words.

• • •

Tom yanked the glasses down and pinched his nose bridge. His eyes burned from staring at the Olivia's picture on the computer screen. The fantasy woman had helped him out of the darkness, but in this real world, she may not know who he was. Or not care about him. That would explain why all his efforts produced no results. No, it couldn't be. She promised. Something stood between them and tampered his search, not allowing his messages to go through.

A knock on his office door pulled him from his morose thoughts. Constable Sealy stood at the threshold. "Sorry to disturb you. I tried your number, but got voice mail."

If the cop paid him a special visit at this hour, he must have some important news. Tom gestured toward the chair. "Come in, Sealy. I suppose what you have cannot wait."

"This came across my desk an hour ago." The uniformed man stepped into his office and plopped a sheet in front of Tom. "The accident reported here is strikingly similar to yours from nine months ago, only that victim of road rage suffered minor injuries. The lady must've kept her wits to scribble the license plate of the pickup that rammed her into the ditch. We got them this time."

Tom picked up the paper and scanned over it. "The report dates back three months ago."

"Yes, the local department is slow to forward copies." The officer shrugged.

Tom scanned to the bottom of the form. His pulse quickened when his gaze fell on the familiar handwriting. He drew in a quivering breath. "Olivia."

"Yes, the young woman was fortunate." The cop got on his feet. "I shouldn't take up any more of your time."

"Thank you for notifying me of this." Tom stood too. The officer had made it his personal battle to investigate Tom's accident and so far his efforts turned fruitless.

"It's the least I could do." The man touched his cap brim and left.

Tom dialed Owen's Recruiting. To his surprise the phone rang. Until now he believed the business was a hoax. Each time he'd called he got a busy signal or a mechanical voice had told him the number wasn't in service. Emails he'd sent returned as undeliverable or were not replied to, and his attempts to find the address brought him to a few back alleys. For starters, the address on their website didn't correspond with the street numbers.

A woman's cheerful voice came through and gave him the details of the business hours and other available options of their automated answering service. He left a message under a different name, requesting to see Ms. Owen. He must be discreet and not come across like some pushover. After all she'd never seen him in reality. But would she remember what they shared? Would she want him? He would find out at tomorrow's lunch.

• • •

The rosemary basted lamb, the signature dish featured on the logo of the posh little French restaurant, drifted to Olivia from the pivoting kitchen doors.

The hostess greeted her with a grin. "Welcome to '*Le Clair de Lune*'. Do you 'ave *réservation?*"

"I'm meeting Mr. Jones. I believe the reservation is in his name."

"Mr. Jones is not 'ere yet, but I'll show you to *votre table.*" The young girl's long pony tail brushed the back of her white shirt as she led Olivia to the table.

Vexation stirred in her. First this Mr. Jones demanded the lunch meeting at the short notice and now he couldn't have enough decency to make it on time.

The hostess pulled a chair from the table and set the menu in front of her. "*Votre garçon* will be with you *dans un instant.*"

Olivia pasted a mocking grin. Part of her annoyance came from the hostess' fake French accent and mispronunciation. The old Olivia would tell the girl to drop her lilt.

Instead, she drew in a calming breath and focused on the menu.

"How's a man to concentrate here when such a beautiful girl is sitting at his table?"

Her back straightened. The menu slipped from her hands. Slowly, she stood and turned to the man whose smooth voice resembled Tom's. She reached out and placed her trembling hand on his. "Tom, is that really you?"

That wicked smile of his lit up his face. "It's me."

She gasped and grabbed onto the chair, scanning down his body. "You walk with a cane?"

He took her by her shaky elbow. "Why don't we have our lunch in my penthouse? It's in this building. I already had them deliver the food there, actually."

Holding onto her jittery hand, he led her out of the restaurant to the brass elevator door. He struggled to keep his lame leg from limping. Her heart fluttered with his soft smile, and she averted her glance at the tiled floor. "I almost had my receptionist cancel this lunch, but something told me to go."

His piney aftershave set her body on a tingle. How she wished for him to wrap her in his arms. The chime announced they arrived to the penthouse. He ushered her inside his condo. The round dining table set for two, stood by the ten foot window overlooking the city. "Do you want to eat right away?"

"I want to talk. And maybe kiss a little." She stepped to him.

He didn't seem to need further encouragement to take her in his arms and pull her close. "We can do more than a little."

"A lot then," she managed to say before his lips crushed on hers. At his gentle coaxing, her mouth opened and he plunged his tongue inside. She wrapped her arms around his neck. How she missed him, and now she was in his arms, ready for his love. She tightened her hold on him when he shifted to lean his cane against the wall. "Don't let go."

"I'm never letting you go, Ms. Owen." He pulled her down on the sofa and settled her on his lap. "After a bunch of drunken guys sent my car flying into a ditch on Blair Road, I've spent six months in deep coma. What we shared is not something I intend to let go of, ever."

She cupped his face in her palms. Wide-eyed she studied his face. "Same thing happened to me…on a snowy night, on the same road."

"I came out of coma the night we got torn apart." He undid the clip of her hair, setting the locks loose, then brushed his finger through. "Soft as I remembered." Holding her neck cradled in his palm, he traced her jawline. She gulped air at the stormy sea of passion that rocked her insides. "I wanted to run to you. But months of therapies followed. The psychologist ensured me the fantasy of you was a coping mechanism, but I knew better. I pushed my body hard and played along to get out of there and start searching. Something must've impeded my efforts. Everything I did produced no results."

A tear rolled out of her eye and down her cheek. Her crying was release of pent-up anxiety. Thankfully, he comforted her with a surrendering embrace. She drew in a long, quivering breath. "It was the angel. The entity tested us, wanted to see if our love remains no matter what gets thrown at us. There were moments I questioned my sanity, but I knew I would find you." She tilted her head at the staff propped against the wall. "Your accident explains the cane."

He slapped his thigh and grinned, then cupped her neck. "Good old leg will be fine when the pins come out. The main thing is we've passed the angel's test." His smile dropped and he stared at her for a moment, as if afraid he'd wake and find her gone. "I was a wreck. My body was giving up and the doctors wanted to disconnect me from the life support. Then you came and…I can't explain it other than I found a purpose to live."

His words set her mind on a whirlwind and fresh tears stung her eyes, but she pushed them away. "Did you truly experience a heart attack when we visited Tadem?"

"I went into cardiac arrest and was resuscitated." He wiped her tear that escaped and kissed her forehead. "I wept when I found out we lost Tadem. She was a special kind of angel."

Olivia nodded, her eyes fixated on his handsome face. She dug her fingers in his hair and drew him close. "I even traveled to Croatia to find you."

She pressed her cheek to his and tightened her arms around his shoulders. "I missed you, Tom."

"I missed you, too." He trailed his lips to her temple.

She pulled back. His eyes narrowed at her wondering gaze. "There're no surprises for us. We know we'll have a boy, Milo, and a girl, Rosie."

"Honey." He wrapped his arm around her waist. "We lived a fantasy. In real life we don't know anything for sure. We could end up with a set of triplets."

She loosened his tie and pulled the loop over his head. "Bring them on."

He grunted and slid his hand inside the pants pocket. "I hoped we could have a few practice runs before that, but first…" Pulling the velvet box out, he flipped the lid open, flashing three diamonds set in the white gold ring. "Forgive me if I'm too forward, but will you marry me?"

Her chin dropped, a few gasps puffed out of her mouth. There was a special spot in her heart reserved for him. His love made her whole and she would not survive without him. She brushed her lips on his and whispered, "In a heartbeat."

About the Author

Zrinka Jelic lives in Ontario, Canada, with her husband and two children. A member of the Romance Writers of America and its chapter Fantasy Futuristic & Paranormal, as well as Savvy Authors, she writes contemporary fiction—which leans toward the paranormal—and adds a pinch of history. Her characters come from all walks of life, and although she prefers red, romance comes in many colors. Given Jelic's love for her native Croatia and the Adriatic Sea, her characters usually find themselves dealing with a fair amount of sunshine, but that's about the only break they get. "Alas," Jelic says, with a grin. "Some rain must fall in everyone's life."

A Sneak Peek from Crimson Romance
(From *Of Consuming Fire* by Micah Persell)

Dr. Grace Tucker pulled herself deeper into the corner and tucked her arms tighter around her unshapely belly. As her hands and arms touched her large middle, it repulsed her nearly as much as it seemed to repulse the opposite sex. No, there was no disappearing a plus-sized woman, but her sloppy appearance got most people to look away quickly, which was as close as Grace was ever going to get to being blessedly invisible.

And, not for the first time, she desperately wished to be invisible.

Grace huddled in the main room of the top-secret government facility where the Trees stood. As always, she ignored them. She was never awed by the ancient trees. She'd taken one cursory glance at their branches that most described as majestic. Their fruit—covered in glittering diamonds for the Tree of Eternal Life, swirling black and white for the Tree of the Knowledge of Good and Evil—was interesting only in that it loosely related to her work. She didn't stand there and stare at them for hours as she was told was the expected behavior for new employees.

And yet right now, Grace wasn't the only one ignoring the Trees. The somber mood in the facility was nearly suffocating. Not one of the dozens of employees had spoken in hours. They moped from room to room, desk to desk, casting great, wide-eyed glances upon everyone they crossed. But that wasn't the reason Grace retreated to the corner.

They were *touching* one another.

Any person they came into reaching distance with. A hand on the shoulder. A hug. A squeeze of the arm or lingering pat on the back.

It was only a matter of time before one of them tried to touch *her*. And that simply was not going to work. End of story.

And, so, she was in the closest thing to a corner the domed room provided.

A young soldier in army fatigues walked by, and Grace went rigid, holding her breath until he passed.

He didn't once glance in her direction. Grace's breath flew from her frozen lungs even as her heart seized at the casual snub. She hugged herself tighter as she cursed her weak emotions. Without fail, every time her carefully cultivated armor of acerbic wit and slovenly appearance actually worked as she'd meant it to by keeping others away, her irrational side would come up bruised, as though it didn't know perfectly well the reasons human contact was not in Grace's cards.

She sighed almost silently, and forced herself to look cheerfully upon the fact that standing in the corner was working. She would make it through this. She *would*. It wouldn't be like all of the other times. There would be no scene. No gut-wrenching screams shooting from her body without her control. No hysterical sobs. No sedation. No awkward return to work. No inevitable summons to the boss. No starting over with the knowledge that this was her life—on repeat.

She closed her eyes. The sad truth was, this *was* her life. And right now, she was huddled in the corner, praying to be invisible, worrying with all of her strength that someone would touch her.

But her friend's impending death? Not even a blip on her emotional radar. Jericho Edwards was dying, and Grace was worried about herself.

Jericho was everyone's favorite, but for a reason Grace couldn't explain, he was *her* favorite as well. It had been thirteen long years since Grace considered a man as anything other than something to be avoided at all costs. Thirteen years since Grace had carefully erected a wall around her heart. And yet, somehow, Jericho found his way around that wall the tiniest bit.

It might have been the very obvious fact that Jericho would never, ever pose a threat to her. She'd known two seconds after being introduced to him that he was head over heels in love with someone: his Impulse mate, Dahlia. Jericho was nice to *everyone*, men and women alike. In fact, Grace had never met anyone so good.

And he'd taken one look at her—her frumpy clothes, excess body weight, bird's nest of red hair, black-rimmed glasses, and man-hating glare—and deemed her a friend, working tirelessly at cultivating a relationship with her when everyone else just avoided her.

And now, he was dying. Worse, his survival depended upon *Grace* and Grace's work.

Three months and a week or so ago, Jericho cut his finger on the sword—the artifact that Grace was commissioned to work on. It was a flesh wound that should have healed in seconds given that Jericho, Dahlia, Eli, and Abilene were all immortal after eating the fruit from the Tree of Eternal Life. But the simple wound hadn't healed. And things came to a head a few days ago when Jericho returned to the facility with his brand new wife, Dahlia. In the process of moving, Jericho managed to rip the tiny, unhealed wound wide open from the tip of his finger into his palm. It had been bleeding profusely ever since, and his body couldn't keep up.

And suddenly, Dr. Grace Tucker was very much in demand. She couldn't count the number of times she had to remind them "I'm not that kind of doctor." Their situation was so unique that her PhD in dead languages made her much more qualified to help Jericho than an MD would on its best day, but her work took more time than medication or surgery ever would.

She'd made her breakthrough this morning.

The ancient, dead language on the sword said *What the Tree gives, the Sword takes. What the Sword takes, the Tree gives.*

At least, she was ninety-nine percent sure that's what it said.

Grace gritted her teeth, closed her eyes, and reassured herself that she was never wrong when it came to her work. Never. She was wrong when it came to everything else, but her work was infallible.

That's why she was here. She was the single most prestigious language expert in the world. And it was going to change her life. That was the plan. She'd worked hard to make sure no one noticed her. The weight she'd gained, the fashion-backward wardrobe, the overt hostility—when she couldn't disappear into her surroundings, she kept people away with every weapon her extensive intelligence and vast vocabulary could come up with.

But Grace's secret dream *was* recognition. She just wanted it on her terms. She was going to make *the* discovery of all time with this sword. It was the work she'd been waiting for her entire career. And now it was here. And, as long as her translation was right, it was about to save one of only four immortal human beings on the planet.

Career. Made.

Everyone would know her name; everyone would know she was something. And the best part? She'd be absolutely untouchable in a way she could not dream of cultivating on her own. No one walked up to the winner of the Nobel Prize and gave them a hug. They got the recognition without all the messy social baggage associated with being members of the human race. They were members of a class considered above such things. And Grace couldn't wait to be admitted into their ranks.

Grace's eyes snapped open when she heard the sharp clack of men's shoes on the hard floor of the facility. Sergeant Collins was approaching.

Grace shrank back further into her corner, her shoulders bending in on themselves, but it was too late: he was looking right at her, and double damn, he'd noticed she was trying to turn into wallpaper if the arch of one of his salt and pepper eyebrows was any indication.

He stopped before her, and Grace couldn't prevent the hitch in her breathing. Reaching distance. The man was within reaching distance. She bit her bottom lip to avoid a whimper.

"Dr. Tucker?" Sergeant Collins asked in his smooth, Southern whisky drawl. He then looked her over once more. His eyes softened. He took a step back and crossed his arms behind him, effecting "at ease" posture.

Relief flooded through her so strongly it momentarily overshadowed the embarrassment she felt at having someone else recognize her reticence at human contact. But only momentarily. Damn it, why couldn't she be normal?

She straightened to her full height—a whole five feet five inches—and worked her hardest to look as un-crazy as possible. "What can I do for you, sir?" A lock of her frizzy, red hair fell over her glasses, blocking Sergeant Collins from sight. She shoved it out of the way, tucking it behind one of the pencils stuffed into her "style" of the day.

"Nothing more than you've done, ma'am," he said with polite distance. "I've come to report that your findings seem to be accurate."

Grace wanted to sag in relief, but was so wary of causing Sergeant Collins to think any less of her that she clenched her jaw and forced iron into her spine. No one would know how worried she'd been about her translation. She'd emit cool confidence all day long. Her "findings" included the recommendation that whatever damage the sword caused could be un-done by administering the fruit of the Tree of Eternal Life topically. They'd been forcing the fruit down Jericho's throat for days to no effect. It was a nuance of the language that had given Grace the idea to apply the fruit to the site of Jericho's wound.

"So, Jericho's recovering?" Grace forced herself to ask, alarmed a little at the obvious worry in her voice. She didn't care about him that much, did she?

A new voice sounded as it approached. "His skin is knitting together before our eyes." Dahlia Edward's brown eyes peeked around Collins's shoulder, warm for the first time ever that Grace witnessed.

Grace actually liked Dahlia a lot, and not just because Jericho did. Grace hadn't met many people who seemed to hate all others as much as Dahlia did. She was even more socially hostile than Grace. It was…refreshing.

"They think he'll wake up any moment now, and I want to be there when he does, but I had to come thank you first," Dahlia continued.

Grace felt her eyes widen. "Thanks" often involved touch of some kind. "That's not necessary," Grace muttered, crowding the corner again.

Dahlia rolled her eyes. "Relax, Red," she said with a laugh. "God, it's not like we're going to attack you with hugs or anything."

Grace didn't laugh. She didn't even notice when the two before her exchanged a worried look as her eyes glazed, and her mind turned over one of Dahlia's words.

Attack. Attack. Attack.

A loud snap erupted in front of her face.

Grace refocused to see Dahlia's fingers before her eyes as the woman snapped again, this time accompanied by a sharp, "Grace!"

Grace sucked in a breath.

"Is she…" Sergeant Collins trailed off as both women's heads snapped around to glare at him.

Grace opened her mouth to speak, but was cut off with Dahlia's curt, "She's fine, Collins, God." She then stood directly in front of Grace, blocking her from Collins's sight, giving her a chance to compose herself. "Nothing some lunch and a good night's sleep won't fix. We've run her ragged. Give her some *grace*." Dahlia snorted.

Collins threw Dahlia a wobbly smile. "I'll just…um…call Miss Esperanza then. Tell her Jericho's fine." His mouth moved like a caress over the name of Dahlia's former mother-in-law, his accent adding at least two syllables, and his eyes twinkling like a kid.

Dahlia looked at Grace and winked. "You do that, Collins."

He cast one more concerned look toward Grace's corner, not quite meeting her eyes, and backed off, hurrying away to his office.

As Dahlia watched him go, her hand fell to the small bump beneath her shirt. Grace was pretty sure she was the only person in the facility who had guessed that Jericho and Dahlia were expecting. There had been no announcement; there hadn't been time before Jericho fell gravely ill. But Dahlia made that little movement often when she thought no one was looking.

She turned to Grace now and arched a perfect eyebrow.

"I really am fine," Grace offered weakly.

Dahlia scoffed and muttered something in Spanish that Grace perfectly understood—dead languages weren't her only specialty. Grace bristled. "Look, I'll just get back to work." The news of Jericho's recovery was already spreading if the increased chatter in the room was any indication. She could re-join life now. She needed to get started on writing this up, though she knew publishing any of her top-secret findings was going to be an uphill battle. Possibly an impossible one.

Dahlia nodded once and began to turn away.

"Hey," Grace blurted. Dahlia turned back to her. "Um…when he wakes up. Tell Jericho…I'm glad he's okay." Grace was shocked to find out she meant it.

Dahlia's eyes roved Grace's face for a moment, but then she smiled. "You've got it, Red." She took two steps toward the medical wing, then stopped.

Grace watched the black waves cascading down Dahlia's back rustle as the stunning Latina tilted her head to the side.

"Do you hear that?" Dahlia asked.

Grace frowned. "Hear what?"

Just then, the lights flickered. A distant rumbling seemed to seep in through the walls of the facility.

All of the hopeful chatter in the room faded and then fizzled out as people began to look around curiously.

A huge clap of thunder rent through the building with such force that loose items throughout the main room clattered where they sat.

The lights went out completely.

Emergency lights along the walls illuminated, casting Dahlia's caramel skin in an unearthly glow as Grace stared at her in barely subdued panic. The others in the room began to mumble to each other, their voices rising in pitch. She felt her nails digging into the skin of her arms and realized she was hugging herself again.

A man in a lab coat raced into the main room, skidding around the door and barreling toward Dahlia as soon as he spotted her. "He's waking!" he yelled at Jericho's wife. "Come quickly."

Dahlia took a quick step toward him, but then stumbled. She threw out an arm to catch herself against the wall. "*Shit,*" Grace heard her mutter.

Dahlia spun around and pinned Grace with a wide-eyed look. "Earthquake," she told Grace in an odd, disbelieving tone. "Big one."

Dahlia lunged forward and grabbed Grace by the arm, hauling her quickly to a nearby desk and shoving herself and Grace in the small area beneath it.

Shooting pains emanated from the skin Dahlia's fingers touched. Grace hissed and tried to wrench her arm from Dahlia's grip as she spluttered, "What—how do you—"

"I can hear it coming," she said impatiently. "Take cover!" she bellowed to all the gawkers.

No sooner had the words left her mouth than the first wave hit the building. A sound, louder than the eardrum-cracking clap of thunder, ricocheted through the room like a freight train, and Grace watched with wide eyes as the floor began to ripple at the edge of the room and move toward them like oncoming ocean waves.

And, even though paralyzed with fear, all Grace could think of was the scorching pain of Dahlia's fingers where they still clutched her arm.

Screams began to echo as the men and women who worked at the facility realized what was happening. Feet thundered as everyone sought shelter.

But Grace scrambled away from Dahlia and out into the open as soon as the woman's grip on Grace's arm slackened.

Dahlia's arm snaked out and captured the back of Grace's jacket. "What the *hell*?"

"Don't *touch me*!" Grace shrieked so loudly that Dahlia drew back in shock.

A huge chunk of plaster fell from the ceiling to land right beside Grace. A cloud of white exploded from its impact and dusted both of them. Desks began to skitter across the floor.

"Do you want to die?" Dahlia yelled, blinking the white powder from her lashes.

Die or be touched? No contest. Grace didn't move.

The earthquake gained in intensity. The glass that made up the ceiling of the dome tinkled and Grace looked up as a crack spider-webbed from one end of the dome to the other.

"Okay," Dahlia said fast and low. "I won't touch you. Just get your ass under here right now!"

Grace dragged her eyes from the ceiling to look into the dim space beneath the desk. Dahlia pressed herself against the side, leaving more than enough room for Grace to fit without having to be against the other woman. And still she hesitated.

Across the dome, bookshelves began to fall like dominoes, each one hitting the ground with a resounding boom. The tinkling of the glass ceiling increased and one or two shards escaped and plummeted toward the ground.

With a deep breath for courage, Grace dove into the area beside Dahlia just as the ceiling gave way.

The glass chimed like clock-tower bells as it fell. It tinkled off of every surface and bounced from the floor in glittering arcs. Grace watched in horror as a huge shard caught one of the soldiers as he tried to dive under a desk a few feet away. His scream cut off as the glass sliced through his chest and pinned him to the floor right where Grace had been kneeling seconds before.

Grace huddled into the corner and buried her face against the wood of the desk so hard she thought her nose might break.

The waves of the ground moved as though alive beneath Grace, hitting her in the shins and knees again and again as she knelt and causing her stomach to lurch as though seasick. Beside her, she heard Dahlia begin to recite the rosary in Spanish in a low, breathless voice. As a backdrop, the glass on the floor clacked and pinged as the entire building shimmied with the rage of the earth.

And in the next heartbeat, everything stopped.

Grace's frantic breaths in the sudden absence of sound were excruciatingly loud, but the silence didn't last for long. Moans from the wounded began to fill the air.

She heard her boss, Eli Johnson, bellowing his past-due pregnant wife's name as he barreled through the dome from his office and toward the medical wing.

"Jericho," Dahlia breathed next to her. Then she scrambled from her hiding spot, sliding in the blood that slicked across the floor from the impaled man before gaining purchase and sprinting in Eli's wake.

Grace stared dumbfounded at the glassy eyes of the dead man in front of her before forcing herself to emerge from the desk.

Utter destruction waited for her. Her eyes skimmed over the demolished main room of the facility. Everything was…gone. Desks were smashed. Books were flung to every wall of the room. The glass on the floor glittered like diamonds among the pools of blood. It looked like after-pictures of a tornado.

But the trees stood resolute in the center of the room. Not one fruit had fallen from their branches. And on the desk beneath them, where Grace did her work, the sword glowed. The sword, usually covered with flickering green and gold flames, was now… *angry*. It was the only word she could use to describe what she was seeing. The green and gold flames had morphed into red and black. The metal, engraved with the words she had translated to say *what the tree gives, the sword takes; what the sword takes, the tree gives* was now pulsing with emotion. And coming off of the sword in waves was an otherworldly *heat*. The sword had always emitted a cool indifference. Now it was raging.

"Oh, God," Grace gasped. Her breathing sped up even more, and black began to edge in on her vision.

Something had angered this inanimate object. Fear, so familiar and yet, in this case, so different, choked Grace's throat. She had a gut feeling that in completing her job she betrayed a secret. The sword's secret.

Someone was coming. Coming for them. Coming for her.

She had one thought before losing consciousness: *What have I done?*

In the mood for more Crimson Romance?
Check out *Midnight Sun, Inc.*
by Debbie Vaughan
at *CrimsonRomance.com*.